NIGHT WATCH

ALSO BY STEPHEN KENDRICK

Holy Clues:
The Gospel According to Sherlock Holmes

NIGHT
WATCH

A Long-Lost Adventure in Which
Sherlock Holmes Meets Father Brown

STEPHEN KENDRICK

Pantheon Books, New York

W

Grateful acknowledgment is made to Polebridge Press for permission to reprint excerpts from *The Complete Gospels* edited by Robert J. Miller. Copyright © 1992, 1994 by Polebridge Press, Santa Rosa, California. All rights reserved. Reprinted by permission of Polebridge Press.

Library of Congress Cataloging-in-Publication Data

Kendrick, Stephen, 1954–
Night watch : a long-lost adventure in which Sherlock Holmes meets Father Brown / Stephen Kendrick.
p. cm.
ISBN 0-375-40367-1
1. Holmes, Sherlock (Fictitious character)—Fiction. 2. Brown, Father (Fictitious character)—Fiction. 3. Private investigators—England—London—Fiction. 4. Catholic Church—Clergy—Fiction. 5. London (England)—Fiction.
I. Title.
PS3611.E54 N54 2001   813'.54—dc21   2001031397

Book design by Johanna S. Roebas
Floor plan on pps. 122–123 by Matthew Songer

Printed in the United States of America
First Edition
2   4   6   8   9   7   5   3   1

This is the hour, O soul,
thy free flight into the wordless . . .
Thee fully forth emerging, silent, gazing,
Pondering the theme thou lovest best:
Night, sleep, death and the stars.

—Walt Whitman

Have you found the beginning, then, that
you are looking for the end? You see, the
end will be where the beginning is. Congratulations to the one who stands at the
beginning: that one will know the end and
will not taste death.

—The Gospel of Thomas

Watchman, what of the night?

—Isaiah 21:11

Contents

The Order of Canonical Hours

CONTENTS

Help and defend us through the night.
Danger and terror put to flight.
Never let evil have its way.
Preserve us for another day.

—Compline Hymn

NIGHT WATCH

Prologue

How I Came to Possess This Document, Including the Last
Will and Testament, Codicil, of John H. Watson, M.D.

When Dr. John Watson mentioned a battered old tin dispatch box kept for safekeeping in the vaults of the London bank of Cox and Company, he would never have dreamed that, nearly a hundred years later, this legendary repository of dozens of unrecorded cases by his friend Sherlock Holmes would be yielding book upon book, much like the bottomless prop of a stage magician.

This, at least, has been the claim of many writers who, since Arthur Conan Doyle's death, in 1927, have continued to add new cases to the Holmes saga. These stories, novels, plays, and screenplays (called pastiches) have ranged from stirringly authentic to painfully feeble. Unfortunately, these well-intentioned pretenders to the throne of Doyle have all ignored one important fact.

Cox and Company, Dr. Watson's safe and solid financial repository in Charing Cross along the Strand, like so much of the London of Holmes, was destroyed by German bombing during the Blitz. There will be no more authentic cases from the many unpublished cases of the world's greatest unofficial consulting detective.

Such was my belief when I recently wrote a book on the spiritual clues cunningly threaded throughout the Sherlock Holmes stories. I occasionally spoke to one of the Sherlock Holmes societies dotting the nation, people who dearly love these late Victorian detective tales. These Holmes societies are not literary fan clubs (like people with I'D RATHER BE READING JANE AUSTEN bumper stickers on their car), for to these small societies Holmes is a living entity, almost a cargo cult figure.

After one talk—at a dark, leather-and-polished-oak New York men's club, to certain prominent Holmesians whose elite status leads them to prefer not to have the name of the group revealed here—I was taken aside by the president, an English expatriate with the brusque manner of an army colonel.

"You mentioned that you travel to London each February. Here's the address of a lady I'd like you to contact when you next go. After hearing your talk tonight, I've decided she should chat with you." He handed me a stiff cream-colored address card. "When your book on Holmes and religion was published I sent it to her, and she asked me to take the measure of you." He paused, his brusque, husky voice lowering. "I think you'll be *quite* interested in her story."

He refused to say more, and other members were now starting to crowd around us, anxiously awaiting, I supposed, port and cigars. Only later, riding in my taxi along Madison Avenue to catch a train home to Hartford, did I hold up to the speeding flash of streetlights the slightly crumpled address card:

Mrs. Mary W. Alston
431 St. John's Terrace
St. John's Wood, London

On the back, in spidery ink, was scratched the phone number of the Pavilion, a private women's club along Pall Mall, with the notation "Call any weekday noon to arrange tea the following day."

The next February, arriving jetlagged at a drab little London bed-and-breakfast near Russell Square, I dutifully took out the card from my wallet. I wondered if an elaborate trick was being played on me. Wearily, I went ahead and confronted the British telephone service (it is said dialing phone numbers in the U.K. is complicated, which is not true, provided quantum mechanics doesn't daunt you) until at last I reached the club.

A reassuringly calm voice told me, "Mrs. Alston will be at the club tomorrow, sir. I'll ring her and arrange for tea. Would four o'clock be suitable?" I assured him it would, and I laid my body down.

The next day, walking in a cool rain along the long rows of exclusive private clubs that line Pall Mall, each a silent and inscrutable marbled-faced bastion of English tradition, I reached the Pavilion Club. Climbing the front steps and shaking out the umbrella I had just hastily bought at the Oxford Street Marks and Spencers, I surveyed the dignified Grecian front of honey Bath stone.

After announcing that I was here to meet a Mrs. Alston, I found myself being escorted through the silent halls of dark mahogany paneling and fine red Indian carpets. As we came to a small private dining room, a Romney portrait of a long-dead Georgian beauty gazed down in cool appraisal. The room was empty except for one small elderly woman, who sat comfortably before an elegantly set tea table. She looked up and smiled, extending her frail mottled hand.

"Please come and sit with me. We have much to talk about." She turned to my escort. "Thank you, Mr. Jennings. Would you bring tea in about ten minutes?"

I sat down and waited. This meeting was, after all, hers to guide. She leaned back in her lavender straight-backed chair and nodded to me in an amiable and gentle manner. Mrs. Alston's lively face was painfully thin, as if she had recently been ill, and yet her pearl gray hair was rich and lustrous.

"You're very kind to take time during your visit here for a stranger," she began. "I'm very happy to meet you at last. I've wanted to speak to you ever since I read your book last year about Mr. Holmes and matters of the spirit."

Thanking her for her kind invitation, I added, "I wrote it for my own enjoyment, and so every time I encounter someone who's read it, I somehow feel surprised, like they're in on a secret."

"As indeed we are. A reader is entering a wonderful conspiracy every time we open a book."

As we comfortably chatted, I was trying to understand exactly why I was here. Mrs. Alston appeared to be in her mid-eighties, her face finely lined and powdered. Her eyes, black and piercing, were kind in a steady yet mild gaze. She possessed the easeful classic British polish of manner, but somehow she was more direct than most English people I have known, for whom reaching the point of a conversation can be like the cautious circling of a plane before settling down through the clouds to a fogged-in airport runway. I thought she would be coming to her purpose directly, and I was not wrong, although in all else I was blind to the extreme.

"Reverend Kendrick, I resolved last year to talk to you personally. I'm going to share something with you that I rarely tell anyone. You will understand why when I relate my story." She sighed, and nodded to the waiter, who after pouring steaming water into our teapot, silently retreated. "You may think me an elderly eccentric, a dotty old thing, but I assure you that what I tell you is true.

"I am the daughter of Dr. John Watson and, in fact, am now the only living relative of my father's line."

For a moment I wondered if she was mad. "I'm sorry, I afraid I don't completely understand."

She gave a little chuckle. "I've always protected my privacy, and my husband, Ronald, now gone two years, was adamant we not be harassed by critics, biographers, lawyers, and Holmes fanatics. Only a few close friends know, and of course the people who look over the rights and royalties of my father's work."

"But—but what about Conan Doyle?"

"Oh, my father owed him everything, really. Father was trained as a doctor, not a professional writer, and so he and Conan Doyle, who was both, formed a fruitful partnership for decades. Honestly, haven't you wondered why Conan Doyle so denigrated Mr. Sherlock Holmes, when the detective so overwhelmed his other literary work? Imagine what he would have felt, having everyone around the world praise work he had only edited and polished to make more commercial. My father took many years to become a decent writer, but he was the first to admit he needed Doyle's style. Oh, but Father had the stories."

"Presuming everything you say is true, Mrs. Alston, I still don't understand why you'd wish to see me. There are many great authorities on the stories, and biographers aplenty who would die to talk to you, or for that matter even to know you're alive."

"That's always been the problem, and it's why I'm hesitant even to speak to you. But you're a minister, are you not? And this is my little confessional, this room. No, I don't think you would betray that trust if I asked you to maintain my secret, my privacy. In your book you treated my father as a whole man, a noble and good man, not a mere stolid and befuddled sidekick. I don't think you would betray him, either."

She had me there.

And God help me, I was starting to believe this woman, as astonishing and unlikely as this interview was. "No, I would not betray either of you. But I need to learn more; you can appreciate how startled I am, hearing this."

"Oh, I can well appreciate your shock. Through the years I've learned that to share my family history is to invite a mixture of 'Wonderful spoof, that' and 'You *are* daft . . .' So I don't tell many people. My friend in New York, the one you met, was an early confidant of my Ronny and me after we married and moved to the States. I loved thinking of myself as a classic war bride, though I was a little old for the role." She paused, savoring her memories, a soft smile playing about her lips. "I loved living in New York City all those years, but after Ronny died it made sense to move back home to London. So here I am, teetering between death and pleasant afternoons with friends, sipping tea."

"I've got so many thoughts going through my head . . . Such as, what about some of the odd little discrepancies in the stories, like exactly where Dr. Watson took his bullet in Afghanistan? Or how many wives he had? Or—"

She laughed, cutting me off. "My father was a precise doctor, and he used to laugh at how Doyle confused so many facts, such as the location of his Afghan wound in the stories. Besides, a man knows *where* he's been shot, especially when it's in his backside. Doyle was just so careless and quick with Father's notes! After a while Father stopped complaining, because Doyle did have such a great knack for bringing the tales to life.

"As to my mother, she was his second wife, Violet Duncaster, a nurse assistant in his practice, whom he married in 1903. I was named for Mary Morston, his first wife. Father died in 1928, when I was twenty." (This meant she was ninety-one, much older than I had realized.) "But frankly, I did not invite you here to clear up careless errors in the published tales. Such things tend to bore me, I'm afraid. No, I want to show you something."

Setting down her cup and saucer, she took from a side table an old legal document and a stack of typed pages that looked like an old ink-scrawled manuscript. "I want you to read this; it's part of Father's will."

Last Will and Testament, Codicil, of Dr. John H. Watson, M.D. Inscribed July 28, 1928

This is the last story I shall ever write about my friend Sherlock Holmes. One of the most difficult aspects of the medical profession is one's inability to evade portents of mortality. Increasing hammer blows of pectoral angina are growing impossible to ignore, and I feel fortunate to have finished this account of the closing months of Holmes's active career. This is the only manuscript I have not submitted to my friend and literary agent, Mr. Arthur Conan Doyle. As such, it may be rough and patchy, but I fancy that I learned more about writing from Doyle than I ever did about detection from Holmes.

A recent dream of mine prompted this last effort to record one of Holmes's remarkable cases. The state of my present health precludes uninterrupted sleep, so I find I am waking often during the night with the most vivid dreams of my life. Two weeks ago I dreamt, with astonishing clarity and preciseness, of the proud twin towers with their jagged battlements of St. Thomas's Anglican Church, then its altar, dark and haunted with a chill and stagnant air. Chest pain woke me, but not before the dream degenerated into a nightmarish tableau of the broken body of Paul Appel—the man whose church this once was—crumpled under the gold crucifix. I knew, as I fumbled in the darkness for my nitroglycerin tablets, that at last I must return to this remarkable and disturbing case, and the horror of that long night watch.

My instructions are to keep the manuscript separate from my archives and notes held at the Cox Bank; I am, instead, placing it with my family solicitors for publication seventy years following my death. The private nature of the account, the possibilities of numerous religious sensibilities being offended, and sensitive political ramifications make this case of Holmes's worthy of separate treatment.

"The game's afoot" was Holmes's summons to me through the years of our friendship, and I always responded—but despite the sensational tone of many of my accounts, these cases were no games but serious business, more deadly than readers have allowed. It is the greatest pride of my life that while I often trailed behind him, I never failed him in courage.

Dr. John H. Watson

I set down the yellowed document and looked at the thick stack of papers Mrs. Alston was nestling in her painfully thin lap. "And is that the manuscript referred to in the codicil?" I asked, my voice a little shaky. I felt like I had Kate Dickens in front of me, handing me the completed *Edwin Drood* manuscript that she had just happened to find under Dickens's bed in Gadshill.

"I have run away from my father's fame all my life. Now that I am facing my own death, I have decided to at last take seriously this account he wrote in the face of his own final illness. As you will see, the religious setting and the interfaith aspect of Father's manuscript make *you*—not some Holmesian expert—a person I think I can turn to. Read it, and see what you think.

It may need the same work that Doyle provided, although I think this is by far Father's best work even without the editing. There need to be historical notes added and some larger perspective offered—the world has changed so much since then."

We met many times over the next two weeks, and legal arrangements for publication were swiftly set in place. As we signed legal documents and went over the manuscript line by line, I felt that I got to know this kind and extraordinary woman quite well in that period, short as it was. We of course corresponded often in the crucial next six months, and Mary Alston was helpful in every aspect of preparing this book. My publisher and editor were startled at how quickly the project fell together, which was providential, for I was notified of her death only three days after receiving the galleys, and so I face the publication of *Night Watch* (a title I selected, with her approval) with a sense of fulfillment and sadness in equal measure.

So, after more than seventy-five years, this major case of Sherlock Holmes and Dr. Watson is at last published. The novel aspects of its character are many, but perhaps the most intriguing is the revelation here that on the verge of his retirement Holmes met and was assisted (and tested) by the young curate Father Brown, who later earned his own legendary status as a detective.

Above all, this manuscript offers an intriguing insight into one of the most perplexing aspects of Holmes's life. Many have wondered how a figure like Holmes, who is described in Watson's first story, *A Study in Scarlet,* as having "null" interest in religion and metaphysics, could become someone who at the close of the saga is depicted as happily retiring in his late fifties to a Sussex farm to tend bees and, in Watson's words, indulge his interest in "philosophy."

Quite a shift in twenty-five years. *Night Watch* is the first

Watsonian indication, subtle though it be, about how such a re-markable philosophical and spiritual transformation took place.

I suspect that it will take some time for this and other aspects of what can only be called sensational revelations contained in *Night Watch* to be absorbed and for its status to be confirmed as an authentic addition to the Holmes canon. Perhaps it may never be, but Mary Alston's wishes have been realized.

To that end, I dedicate this book to the woman who made its publication possible:

To Mary Watson Alston
1908–1999
Born and died, London, England

One

NONE

Oxford to Baker Street, 3 P.M.

Snow descended on London, swirling in on brisk winds, catching the pale yellow glare of the streetlights as it laid its ghostly white upon our familiar haunts. I stood at our window overlooking deserted Baker Street, marveling on the rare London snow and savoring the strange quiet.

Christmas morning had come and gone, and Holmes was clearly relieved the dreaded festival was almost over. We had just this afternoon returned from Oxford, where Holmes had tried, and singularly failed, to hide away in the Bodleian Library, studying the ancient, musty musical manuscripts he so loved. Instead, we had been dragged into the tinseled maw of a perplexing domestic drama in the home of Holmes's old tutor, now master of St. Mark's. Hailing a hansom cab at Euston Station upon our return to London from Oxford, we hastened straight back to our rooms, thoroughly exhausted.

After a brief rest, a shave, and a light repast of strong coffee, eggs, and kippers, provided by Mrs. Hudson, we were now sharing a convivial silence on this winter's approaching night. In the inner reflection upon the window glass, I could see Holmes as he placidly sat pasting newspaper crime articles into his vast alphabetized volumes, his lean face partially obscured with pipe smoke.

Against the storm, the warmth and light of our apartment seemed a stay against the chaos of city life, whose dirty, coal-smudged tracks, mud, and grime were being sheeted by the innocence of white. From the distance, I heard the faint tinkling of horses' bells as hansoms traversed the oddly muffled streets.

"Yes, Watson, indeed the rose is the most beautiful of the flowers."

"Good God, Holmes, you have been playing this trick upon me for a good many years, and still leave me dumbfounded." I turned to face my old companion. "How in heaven's name could you read this in my manner, for I surely betrayed no sign of such a thought?"

He leaned back and sucked in upon his brier-wood pipe, eyeing me merrily. "I have indeed been reading the Book of Watson for some time, the purity of my observations augmented by close familiarity. I saw you set down that book by your chair, page faceup, as you rose, and it opened naturally to a poem most precious to you."

"Yes, Lodge's 'When I Admire the Rose,' but surely—"

"Ah, follow the mind under suggestion. You passed our mantel, where you set our few Christmas postcards, two of which are adorned with roses blooming in winter, one of the glories of our clime. Then, as you stood at the window you absently placed your hands in your pockets, and as you did I could see, reflected in the glass, a look of melancholy cross your face. You were, I believe, touching the rosary that you carry in your pocket, given to you by your late wife, Mary." He paused. "I believe that was the trail of your thoughts. It seemed natural to bring these mental fragments together, the term 'rosary' coming from the rose garden," said Holmes, setting aside his glue pot and heavy book. He went to the mantel to poke at his pipe, adding a little shag tobacco.

I sat down in my chair across from him. "Yes, Holmes, that was precisely the gathering of my emotions. You know I am not a religious man; I carry her rosary not out of any feeling of faith but because she held it once."

"A twelfth-century Persian poet said, 'Mystery glows in the rose bed, the secret is hidden in the rose.' " He leaned back in his old velvet chair dreamily, his eyes half closed, as if he were listening to a piece of favorite music at the Royal Hall. "Think of how much of our lives, Watson, we have pursued such secrets, sub rosa."

I had a little secret of my own from him.

I wondered if this was to be the last Christmas season we would share in our old comfortable digs. My proposal of marriage to a remarkable young woman, a lovely nurse in training I met on rounds at St. Bart's, had been recently accepted. Since she was with her parents in Essex for the holidays, I had more or less invited myself along on Holmes's recent college expedition. Though impatient to be married again after so many years, I also harbored a certain nostalgia for these years of bachelor conviviality that were to end in the autumn. I dreaded informing Holmes about my approaching marriage; I knew he would greet this news with his typical asperity and a sharp comment or two. Oh, our long friendship would go on, but subtly changed, more distant, haphazard.

"You know, Watson, it might amuse your readers to someday record our little Oxford adventure." He shrugged, and added with a sardonic touch, "The incident illustrates the lesson I have tried to impart to you through the years: that close observation of minute details, not grand theorizing, is the key to revelation."

As he languidly waved his match out, he gave me an amused look signaling both permission for me to write up the case and, at the same time, a bemused dismissal of my literary efforts.

"It really *was* a remarkable red ruby sapphire, Holmes, was it not?"

"Yes, it was. You owe it to your readers, Watson, to fully describe it, especially after having confused them years ago with your Yuletide tale of the famed blue carbuncle—only that blue gems of that variety do not exist."

Ignoring his jocund jibe at a literary license I had taken years ago to obscure the facts of a case, I instead nodded a restrained thanks. I do indeed owe it to readers to describe our little encounter with the Scintilla Stone, because it offers a glimpse into the religious feelings of Holmes, an icy reserve rarely revealed.

In our rented Oxford rooms, I had been happily reading the holiday issue of the *Illustrated London News* when Holmes unexpectedly reappeared, rousing me with a bag thrown upon his bed and a resigned request: "Come, Watson, the past has claimed us. Gather our things, for we are due shortly at the master's house of St. Mark's College." His old tutor, the Reverend Dr. Sydney Rosewater, unexpectedly encountered in the Bodleian quad at dusk, was insisting we join his family's celebration. The detective had known in an instant that the quiet evening he had envisioned after his long day in Duke Humphrey's library was doomed.

It was a short walk from our hotel to St. Mark's, our footsteps resounding along glistening stone walls. Into the bustle of Broad Street, we were greeted with a small brass band playing "Good King Wenceslas" in front of the great stoic stone heads of the emperors.

"You seldom talk about your college days, Holmes."

"My two years here were not stellar, Watson. In fact, when

that bull pup bit my ankle on the way to chapel, I took it as a divine sign to be on my way to London."

"I suspect that dog interrupted your last attendance at any religious service."

"Well, with my then certain heady scientific sensibility, I determined that the compulsory chapels of my youth contained truths too fantastic for me. I am not a scoffer at religion as my brother, Mycroft, is, but I determined then that I would give my sole allegiance to facts, not faith. Yet strangely, I find I am mellowing towards religion in recent years."

Hoping to keep this rare colloquy from the private Holmes flowing, as he almost never referred to his past, I inquired, "How so, Holmes? I can't remember when either of us expressed the slightest interest in religion."

"Ah, well, the faith of crucifixes, stained glass, vestments, and all the paraphernalia of English faith—true, that realm of faith has no appeal to me. But oddly enough, my year in Tibet and my exposure to Buddhism opened my eyes. The monks taught me to still my mind, and surprisingly, I found the rudimentary meditative techniques they gave me congenial to my austere temperament. And suddenly, the religious trappings of a foreign faith made me a trifle more open to religion as a kind of visual poetry, a universal language. Still, I sincerely dread Rosewater's invitation."

He would have been far happier if he had known that instead of sentimental piety, his old teacher would soon be giving him the present of the kind of mental puzzle he so delighted in. Soon the imposing white walls of his old college loomed before us, covered in trailing bands of ivy laced with frost. With a sigh, Holmes strode through the imposing Gothic gate. The master's house, beyond the chapel, was lit with a benevolent yellow glow. Our knock was answered by a suave young man in formal wear, balding and lean.

"Holmes, is it? Come in. My brother said he had snagged you to join our rituals." He extended his hand and took our bags. "I'm Jeffrey Rosewater, up from London; your territory, Mr. Holmes. And you must be Dr. Watson."

Five children ran by us in a laughing rush in the entryway. Jeffrey Rosewater rolled his eyes indulgently. The dapper man, trim black mustache giving him a military look, dabbed at his shining forehead with a handkerchief. "Sydney insists all of us must return to Oxford, the Rosewater homestead, in honor of our deceased parents."

A pretty chestnut-haired young girl, eleven or so, danced back and embraced Jeffrey, crying, "Oh Father, come help us glue our Christmas crackers! Bring us those exploding snaps you brought us from Paris!"

We were then spied by the master, who joined us in the foyer. "Welcome, welcome," cried Rosewater, small and rotund in a quaint, Pickwickian fashion. He ordered his brother to take our bags. As Jeffrey Rosewater obeyed, standing four inches over his older brother, he was sleek and fastidious compared to the slightly disheveled master. It was clear the master easily and effortlessly dominated his younger brother. It occurred to me that no one knew better than Holmes what it was like to have an impressive older brother who held tenaciously to long dominance.

The little girl interrupted us, saying that they needed to complete their Christmas crackers. This new custom of beginning a perfectly proper meal by yanking open explosive paper rolls and then putting on colored paper crowns clearly filled Holmes with despair, but I found I was enjoying being here.

Master Rosewater leaned near Holmes to whisper, "Lovely little girl, Elizabeth. Her mother died eight years ago, and she's not taken on Jeffrey's airs yet, thank goodness. He does the best he can, though he leaves her alone too much with all his travel."

"Of course," said Holmes. "I've been trying to place where I've read his name; he's the *Daily Telegraph's* Russian correspondent. I have seen his articles from Moscow and St. Petersburg many times."

The master sniffed. "He could have been a fine scholar; even better in Greek than I am, truth be told." He shook his head wearily. "I'm glad our father, the bishop, is not alive to see a Rosewater descended all the way down to reporter."

When the master was called away, Holmes whispered to me, "Jeffrey Rosewater's name is familiar because he recently incensed my brother, Mycroft, with a recent article. Apparently, young Jeffrey revealed the name in print of a notorious Russian agent."

"Journalists are noisy, interfering creatures without a shred of patriotism," I hotly exclaimed. "Typical. No wonder the master regrets his brother's lower trade."

"Yes. Quite like a certain doctor I know who regularly writes for popular journals," Holmes mischievously replied, happily taking a glass of proffered sherry from a college servant. He raised his glass, glinting golden. "Cheers, Watson."

Ruefully, I clicked his offered glass. "Touché, Holmes. Merry Christmas."

Soon we were surrounded by the swirling colors and smells of a typically domestic English Christmas Eve, with the master's house warmed by a great fireplace. As we sat to dinner, Master Rosewater raised a glass of bubbling champagne. "To our guests, the warmth of our home and our hearth this Christmas Eve."

At the table that night was Rosewater's sister, Abigail, a plump and profuse conversationalist, regaling us with the mercantile exploits of her husband, Humphrey, a steely-eyed Birmingham coal merchant, who sat calmly across from us. Next to her was the college chaplain, Augustus Simon, gaunt, nervous, and hardly able to repress his excited anticipation of ringing the great college bells in the St. Mark's tower at midnight.

I heard Holmes quietly speaking to Sydney Rosewater. "If I may indulge your forbearance, Master, we should embark for London early in the morning."

"Nonsense, Holmes, it will be Christmas morning; and besides, you can go nowhere until you see the college's acquisition, the Scintilla Stone adorning the Glastonbury Gospel. Eight hundred years old, and truly a remarkable treasure. In fact, it will go on display at the British Museum next month with other illuminated manuscripts."

"I do not doubt its power to draw attention, Master," snapped the chaplain, "simply that this kind of attention will be more for the decoration and fine jewels than for its intrinsic ecclesiastical importance."

"Nonsense, Simon," sputtered Rosewater, his holiday affability pricked. "Through the great generosity of my brother-in-law, Mr. Thompkins, the college has scored a bibliographic coup."

"Then, Master, I must see this wonder for myself," interjected Holmes; and so within minutes we were walking out into the cool drizzle to the dark library. The master enthused over the Glastonbury Gospel. "Near as we can guess, it is nearly a thousand years old, veneered gold with intricate repoussé metalwork and cloisonné enamel portraits of the disciples. But that is not what makes the gospel unique—it's the remarkable star ruby at the heart of the design. That is why it is called the Scintilla Stone; so fiery and warm is its red glow. You know, Sherlock, the Greeks felt that there was a divine spark, a scintilla, at the heart of all of us."

Rosewater flicked on the electric fixtures. Holmes saw the master pause, a sudden look of horror on his round face. Immediately Holmes saw the source of his shock. Glass was shattered everywhere. Weaving as if he were about to crumble to the floor, Rosewater breathed, "Oh no, oh no." He leaned up from the case, gazing at Holmes, his pallor parchment white. "The ruby is gone."

Holmes brushed by him and quickly surveyed the damage. The ornate gospel was still magnificent, but small scrapes of a blunt tool revealed all too clearly what had happened at the center of the ornamental metalwork. The dark lead setting where the ruby had previously nestled yawned open like a cavity.

"Step back, please, Master, and let me inspect the setting before there is any more disruption to the scene."

Dazed, Rosewater asked, "Who would do such a thing?"

"That is what I intend to find out." But it was quickly apparent that, unfortunately, there were few useful physical clues present. A simple pocketknife could have pried loose the ruby. Dusting for fingerprints, Holmes spoke. "You must be absolutely honest, even ruthless, Master, if we are to recover this precious stone quickly. We must quickly establish who was present when and where during the late afternoon in your house. I presume the culprit is nervously wondering what to do next, now that I am on the scene. I am forced to conclude, unless you yourself are the culprit, that a member of your family or a close colleague has stolen the Scintilla Stone."

The old man mutely shook his head.

"Quickly, Master. Face up to this reality and help—or this precious gospel will be forever mutilated. Now, who among them might have wrenched the stone from the metalwork? Your chaplain, Simon? He made a negative comment at dinner. Did he have access to the gospel this afternoon?"

"Yes, yes, of course he did," muttered the master. "He has the key to the library, but that means nothing, because I stupidly left the library unlocked when I left, thinking nothing of it. Holmes, anyone could have done it, anyone."

And that is exactly what he is so afraid of, I thought. Someone in his family has betrayed him. This ruby might as well have been ripped from his own chest.

I interjected, "Chaplain Simon, would he be capable of such a thing?"

"No, I don't believe so. Yes, it is true he resisted the college buying the gospel, but he was always an honorable opponent. Yes, he is a little pedantic, but I've never met a more moral man."

"How did you purchase the gospel? At dinner, you make some reference to your brother-in-law, Thompkins."

The master explained they had been considerably short of the asking price when Lord Derby's heirs secretly sought to sell the Glastonbury Gospel last year. Rosewater had gone to Humphrey and asked him to back the bid. He generously offered over five thousand pounds, and they narrowly won. Then, six months ago, his brother-in-law came to him without Abigail's knowledge, shaken and nervous. He asked if the gift could be rescinded; he was unexpectedly on the verge of financial collapse. But it was too late.

"He is a good man, Mr. Holmes. He would not shame his family by an act so blatant and despicable."

"There is no chance his anger at his now mistaken, and perhaps foolhardy, generosity might have compelled him to take back the gem? It is, after all, one of the most desired stones in the world. In his trading world, no doubt he has connections to sell it and keep the transaction covert," replied Holmes.

"What you say is true, but no, I cannot imagine it."

"Then your brother . . ."

"Ah, the nerve is struck. Yes, I can imagine that, though such an admission is ashes on my tongue."

"I'm afraid I have to ask to inspect your house, your guests' things—their luggage, coats, even their toiletries," replied Holmes. He was grim and resolute, even when the master's brother protested. Calmly, Holmes spoke to the young man as we began the search. "I will be searching everyone, Mr. Rosewater, even the children when they awake. The master himself remains under suspicion, for your information. I am not here to be liked, but to find something stolen."

The hours of painfully awkward inspections revealed little, as did all the first questioning of the master's household. Even the Christmas cake was probed for the missing ruby. Holmes instructed me to shake the glowing ornaments on the tree, and to the master's horror, to inspect all the morning's gifts, especially the children's stockings. Five hours later, none of our questioning or the ransacking of the house had availed. At two in the morning Holmes at last allowed the adults to go to bed. "I'm sorry, Master. I will try again in the morning with more precise questioning."

Master Rosewater bid Holmes a despondent good night.

Christmas morning dawned dull and rainy, matching the mood of the household. With the coming of the ashen dawn light, Holmes prowled the vicinity of the library. Just as he was ready to return to the master's house, he spied a glint of silver under an evergreen bush on the far side of the quad from the library. We knelt down to inspect a sterling silver knife emblazoned with an ornate R, matching the silverware we had used the night before. The sharp edge of the knife was scoured with minute scratches, and there was a decided bend to the tip.

Getting up from the muddy ground, Holmes saw the Rosewater family, preceded by Chaplain Simon, preparing to go to chapel for the Christmas service. Thompkins reminded Holmes that the service was about to begin.

"Surely you have enough information to catch this scoundrel, Mr. Holmes. Your exertions last night should surely have convinced you none of us have anything to do with this . . . this impropriety. I don't know what we can tell you besides what we told you last night."

Despite everyone's resistance, Holmes persisted in asking them once again about their actions the previous evening. Mr. Thompkins repeated he had been resting in the front bedroom before dressing for dinner. Holmes turned to the resentful Abigail, who pursed her lips in disapproval at this upstart guest who was now acting as their persistent and graceless nemesis. She repeated she was with the children most of the afternoon, except for a nap near teatime. I saw a sudden eager light in Holmes's tired eyes.

"I thought you were to help the children make Christmas crackers for our meal today."

"Oh, Jeffrey surprised me when he came into the children's playroom and shooed me away. Having brought the chemical paper snaps from Paris, he knew best how to supervise the children stuffing in the treats."

"So he was with them the hour before dinner?"

"Yes," she said in exasperation. "Mr. Holmes, we are expected at the service. May we please go?" A pensive Holmes nodded.

At last the time of the Christmas feast arrived, the college boar's head ready. A worried Master Rosewater came to Holmes. "Any progress, my dear Holmes?"

"Events must still play out, Master, but I have hopes of securing the stone within the hour." We were seated at our places, and the master blessed the meal. Then "Amen," and the adults reached for their napkins, and the children for their Christmas crackers, ready at last for their explosion. Holmes looked up and stared hard at Jeffrey Rosewater. The man's lean saturnine face was a mask of placidity.

"I was just wondering, Jeffrey, if I could change places with your daughter, Elizabeth." Holmes then rose quickly and circled to the end of the table where Rosewater's daughter sat, circled by her laughing cousins. "May I, my dear?"

"Are you sure you want to sit with us children?" She spoke with a giggle.

"Absolutely, Elizabeth. Adult conversation has wearied me." Everyone at the table stared at Holmes's strange behavior. Holmes sat and said, "Shall we?" He took his bright gold paper Christmas cracker from her dinner place, raised it, and prepared to yank it open. The others at the great table proceeded to pull open their explosive Christmas favors, and soon the table was full of laughing and the loud pops of the crackers exploding.

Then, unnoticed by everyone but the watchful master, Jeffrey Rosewater silently mouthed the word "No." Holmes lowered his cracker unopened and motioned for Jeffrey to join him away from the table.

On the train home from Oxford, Holmes related to me the pitiable conversation. Standing in front of the blazing fireplace, Jeffrey simply said, "Thank you, Mr. Holmes, for not pulling that open."

Holding out one end of the cracker, Holmes asked, "Will you now?"

Reluctantly, the young man took one end of the bright cracker and pulled. It ripped open with a sudden pop, and falling down into Holmes's outstretched hand came a printed motto, a rolled blue paper crown, and instead of the child's toy, a glowing red ruby. Holmes lifted it up and gazed at the stone, fire glow blazing from the core of the great gem.

"The master was correct; there really is a star reflected in the ruby," said Holmes, impressed.

"Indeed there is," said Reverend Rosewater, joining them at the fireplace. "This is as I dreaded. Why, Jeffrey?"

His brother raised his head, his face flushed. "Do you think I

27

would have not returned it to you?" he said, his voice shredded of all pride. "All I needed was one great story, one only I could be in a position to write. 'Oxford Treasure Stolen'—imagine the fuss and sensation! The great and glorious Scintilla Stone missing, and after a suitable time, I would have secretly mailed it back to the college. I could not bear," Jeffrey Rosewater bitterly added, "the indignity of crawling back to you, with the ghost of the dear bishop frowning down upon me, the failure you and he always declared me to be. At least at the *Telegraph* I had the freedom to roam the world, far away from Oxford."

The master was shocked, regret and not anger in his anguished expression. "Oh, Jeffrey, have I somehow shamed you?"

"I have shamed myself, Sydney. Imagine me opening the door yesterday afternoon, with that jewel burning in my pocket, all ready to write the article of the year. As usual, brother, you effortlessly place me in the shade, having just invited the world's most famous consulting detective for our little Christmas soiree! I realized at that moment that what I had conceived more as a resentful prank upon you would be, in the hands of Mr. Holmes, something a great deal more." He turned back to Holmes, who had been silent all the while. "How did you guess?"

"After searching everywhere, I knew the location of the stone would not be easy to ascertain. No one had been expecting me, and I realized my entry into the home unexpectedly raised the stakes. The thief would have to very quickly hide the stone. Within minutes of my arrival, you took yourself off to the children's room. You thought to yourself that dropping the stone into your daughter's Christmas cracker would tide you over for a little while; she would think it only a glass trinket like the other toys in the children's cracker. It was not a perfect hiding place, but certainly it worked; at least until I talked to your sister this morning. When I found the knife this morning, I realized that my suspicion that someone in your house, Master, had pried out the gem was on point. The children were working near the kitchen, you were there with them, and there was a pile of small prizes to place within each cylinder. You thought it was a better than even chance that you would leave this afternoon with Elizabeth holding the jewel in her child's purse."

"The only thing I could not have borne would have been the ignominy of being exposed before her. Thank God, Mr. Holmes, you spared me that."

The master shook Holmes's hand. "Thank you, Sherlock. Here it ends."

"No, Sydney," said Jeffrey. "Something begins here. There is much I have to atone for. I do not excuse myself for my selfish and absolutely reckless behavior. But there has been something false and rotten between us for a long time."

All this Holmes told me as the train rocked homeward. I asked, "How could any gentleman mar a treasure like that magnificent gospel?"

He said nothing at first, brooding on the pallid green fields smudged by the shifting shadows of gray snow clouds sweeping past our windows. Then he turned to me. "Watson, yesterday you asked me about religion. I am not devout, true, but I do believe that to forgive a man is saving something more precious than any ruby. That belief will have to do, I'm afraid."

Many people through the years have asked how I could abide trailing behind such a man as Sherlock Holmes, arrogant, self-absorbed, distrustful of women, curt, and sarcastic to the extreme. But they never sat with him as I did that afternoon of Christmas, and sensed his great heart. Then I had an inspiration, whimsical as it was.

"By the way, Holmes, your Christmas gift." I tossed him

an unopened Christmas cracker from the master's table, and laughing, he tucked it into his greatcoat. Each lost in our own thoughts, we did not speak again until we arrived at Euston Station.

The insistent jingle of our downstairs bell rang out, interrupting our affable conversation by the fire. Holmes leapt up, his manner transformed in an instant. He seemed instinctually to know when there was a client at the step. He paced to the door, his sharp jaw set, all focused anticipation. Mystery was more beautiful to Holmes than any rose.

Coming up the darkened stairs to 221-B, shivering in a snow-flecked black overcoat, came Scotland Yard inspector Lestrade, breathing heavily. He had come up these seventeen stairs many times, but we were all getting a little older. Snow frosted his old bowler hat. He came up alone.

"Ah, Lestrade," Holmes said with warmth and even a touch of concern. "What brings you out in this snowy twilight?"

Snatching off his oily old hat, exposing thinning hair swept back from his narrow, pale forehead, Lestrade stood just outside our doorway. "Mr. Holmes, the best of the season to you, and of course to the good doctor . . ." He nodded at me in his meek, almost supplicating fashion.

"Come, take off your coat, Lestrade, and tell us about the murder that has brought you to us," said Holmes.

"Why, how could you have heard . . . ," sputtered Lestrade.

"Come, Mr. Lestrade," I offered quickly, "for once you and I do not have to impart to Holmes any special knowledge. Why else would you approach us on this dreadful evening?"

Lestrade's manner was indeed grim, his long face bowed down, a worried twist to his thin lips. I could not tell whether it was sweat or snow melting upon his white brow. "Mr. Holmes, I have been placed in charge of a most odd murder investigation," he began, his eyes shifting uncomfortably. "In fact, the case is so sensitive the prime minister has demanded the Metropolitan Police consult with you, but only under a special condition."

"Yes?" asked Holmes evenly, almost nonchalantly.

"That Mr. Mycroft Holmes, your brother, must oversee every detail."

"I'm familiar with the name, Lestrade," interjected Holmes with a sudden dour expression. I knew him well enough to know he did not relish the idea of working under the eye of his older brother. "If Mycroft is involved, then this case is sensitive beyond measure, and has some import concerning His Majesty's empire. Mycroft is not wheeled out of his customary shadows unless his superiors feel a desperate plight. All right, Lestrade, tell me all that you know."

Holmes motioned for Lestrade to sit opposite us, and I stepped forward to take his coat and hat, which I set near our fire to dry. The policeman sat stiffly, still not at his usual ease with us. Some punishing responsibility was pressing in on him.

"The prime minister, under the direct urging of the archbishop of Canterbury, asked us to consult with you immediately, while the scene is still fresh and undisturbed. Indeed, it seems the government sees you as having powers nearly superhuman."

The close of the year 1902 was a time of transition, with Edward VII, our new king, ascending the throne at virtually the same time as the new prime minister was taking the reins. You could feel the old certainties of Queen Victoria's long ascendancy slipping away, and London was now a place beginning to literally hum with electric tension. Electric lighting was going up everywhere, the Underground was being expanded and converted from steam power, and motorcars starting to appear alongside the familiar horse carriages and hansom cabs. With all this dizzying change about us, we were all having to get used to this new frantic pace of life.

"It is wonderful to be admired, and it certainly brings in business, but I crave details. What is the nature of this crisis?"

"Mr. Holmes, a priest's body was found early this evening at St. Thomas's Church, Kensington. He was savagely mutilated." He let this shocking statement sink in, and then went on. "But first, before we go to St. Thomas's, we are to meet with Mr. Mycroft Holmes at his club, which luckily is well on the way to the murder site. Apparently, at the club we will be given some sensitive information from a churchman who was in attendance at a secret convocation of religious leaders. Apparently, this high-ranking cleric knows quite a lot about these holy men's background, and will tell us why they were meeting so secretly. Sounds all a bit odd, sir, but then, I'm no religious man. The cleric we're supposed to talk to is an assistant to the archbishop."

"Curiouser and curiouser. This case has tendrils already in many directions—political, foreign, ecclesiastical." He gave a quick brittle laugh. "It must no doubt pain Mycroft to have to turn to me for assistance. He refers to me only when practical forensic experience comes to the fore, for Mycroft is certainly able to solve sensitive puzzles well on his own. Then let us waste no time. Give me the details."

"May I remain?" I interjected.

"Oh, yes, Doctor. Mr. Mycroft Holmes expressly asked if you could join us tonight; your medical assistance could well be useful. As I understand things, this evening, at about four o'clock, this horribly mutilated body was discovered in the crypt of St. Thomas's Church." Lestrade consulted a dog-eared little notebook. "The body was immediately identified as the

Reverend Paul Appel, the rector. The church was already being guarded by four policemen, and no one entered or left during the day or early evening. In addition, the snow on surrounding sidewalks reveals no footprints of any kind. I trust my men's observation."

"Which indicates the murderer remains in the church," mused Holmes. "But why would the Foreign Office authorize such unusual security in such an unlikely place as a church? For surely Mycroft was the one who ordered it—or you would not be here now."

"The circumstances, as you surmised, were quite unusual. Inside the church were seven men representing different faiths, all there under secret invitation of the archbishop of Canterbury. That is all I know at present, but we are expected at the Diogenes Club as soon as possible to be told more. All I can tell you, Mr. Holmes, is that my policemen, posted outside only, heard and saw nothing."

"And now we find the host priest dead, and the assurance that his killer is one of the representatives of a major religion," said Holmes as he leaped up from his chair and began heading for his dressing room to take off his old lounging coat. He turned back to us, his dire words in singular contrast to his eyes, which glittered with the old excitement of the chase. "I don't need to tell you, gentlemen, what a nightmare this presents. It is not just the embarrassment to His Majesty's government, to the archbishop of Canterbury, and the Church of England—but as well the possibly severe ramifications for our entire foreign policy. We have no time to waste, and I pray that the suspects, no matter how august or venerated, are under extremely close scrutiny now."

"Oh, yes, Mr. Holmes," said Lestrade, the thorough professional. "They are all in their rooms, and a guard is posted over the scene of the murder. It is a most distressing sight, it is, with the poor father's body in tatters, mutilated. To see such a thing in a church is unthinkable, sir."

Hoisting on his greatcoat and a top hat, Holmes answered mildly, "Only if you have never noticed the figure on the cross in front, Lestrade."

Two

VESPERS

Baker Street to Pall Mall, 5 P.M.

I have seen much of death in my days.

From my days as a naive young soldier facing my first battle, in Maiwand, Afghanistan, to the very close of my medical career, as a field surgeon behind the nightmarish trenches of France, I have seen the worst that violence can do. Under swaying lamps and upon hastily erected operating tables, it seemed all of Europe's mangled sons lay draped and shattered under our knives and saws. I have also seen, in my less dramatic London practice, all the ravages of time upon the body, and physical dissolution in all its creative and final varieties. As an associate of Holmes, across twenty-five years and hundreds of cases (though few, thankfully, were involving murder), I was exposed to violence in quite spectacular and bizarre forms. Nothing much could surprise or shock me. I had seen it all.

Yet the remains of the Reverend Paul Appel, flung like a bloodied doll upon the cold stones of the undercroft of St. Thomas's Anglican Church, his skin flayed and his extremities savagely cut in jagged gouges, remain to this day the most singularly shocking and offensive sight of my long exposure to death's many masks. I will always remember how Lestrade's stark and pitiless white lamplight upon that sight brought back to me so strongly the quality of a field hospital after the maelstrom of battle. But even after witnessing the chaos of the Somme, I have never seen a battlefield wounding as strange and appalling as that human clay.

The church was softly lit from the lights of the Royal Court Theatre across the way, when our cab pulled up to the curb. The playgoers were unaware of the drama within the imposing Gothic Revival church across the square. We gazed up at St. Thomas's, somber and impressed at the west front, marked with two imposing towers and the flowing tracery of a great stained-glass window between them. Even in the darkness, St. Thomas's glowed, with a façade of banded brick and fine white marble, with each elegant wide pointed window marked beneath with an unusual spiked metal railing. Even Holmes, whose taste in buildings ran more to the starkness of medieval Norman, seemed struck by the flowing, inventive beauty of this new church.

Yet for a time, none of us moved, our will paralyzed. Then Holmes's resolve stirred and he flung open the cab's side door, the cold wind shocking us all into action. Standing in the brisk snow for a moment, Holmes took off his top hat before the wind could whip it away. He uttered, sighing, "And now, let us go see what we have come to see."

"At least it will be warm in there, sir," said Lestrade encouragingly. The police detective turned and motioned to the frozen blue-clad policemen standing guard, and the great four-quartered red church doors, under the shadow of a Tudor arched gateway, swung open. We followed in, stamping our feet and shaking off our hats and coats. The nave spread far before us, spacious and broad, softly lit by numerous brass sanctuary lamps, each within ruby glass. The long sanctuary before us was dark, except for the golden glow of recessed light fixtures for the high altar, all blinding white cloth, and the gold Latin cross of the crucified Christ suspended above it. The church was surprisingly warm, so we left behind our greatcoats and followed Lestrade down the south aisle.

"All right. Lestrade, we are now in your hands," said Holmes.

"The way to the crypt is by the Lady Chapel," he said. "You go down on the left side and come up on the far side of the chancel. Down these stairs, sir. My man there has lighted the area with extra lamps."

Though St. Thomas's was a relatively new church, it had already acquired the smell I associated with churches: the musty odor of old hymnals, incense, and undisturbed dust, particularly as we went down to the bare stone undercroft, marked by great squat columns with arched memorial tomb placements. Such is the power of Gothic that a church less than twenty years old could seem so dank and haunted, a chill grip upon the susceptible soul.

Lestrade motioned for the guard to back away, and took his lamp. "His body is tucked in there, in the third alcove." I thought of how far Holmes and I had come from that restful Baker Street fire of only hours ago, and how much more we needed to learn about the strange circumstances that had brought together these ecclesiastics from all over the world.

There was the strong iron smell of blood.

Holmes had been aghast when we were first instructed to go the Diogenes Club to meet his brother, Mycroft. His every instinct was to be inside that church, prowling its corridors and staring down the holy suspects.

"Politicians," I heard him mutter on our frozen cab ride as we sped through the emptied streets of the city. "Watson, I fear we'll have to operate under the bidding of both the archbishop of Canterbury and the prime minister, doing things the polite, the political, way. And time slips by."

"The archbishop of Canterbury isn't a politician," I said.

Holmes just looked at me, then chuckled, his frustration interrupted. "I think you'd better reexamine your assumptions, Watson. Next we'll be talking about the reality of Father Christmas." Snow still whirled and whipped past our hansom windows, coating the old Christmas decorations along the closed shops of Regent Street, reviving somewhat their now tattered magic.

Beyond the lights of Piccadilly Circus, merrily ablaze even in this storm, we soon entered the more austere and subdued land of the clubs of Pall Mall. Entering the imposing doorway into the foyer of the Diogenes Club, once again I thought how it must be one of the queerest locales of London, this reclusive social club for those who found the necessity of being social unbearable. Once you were through the entrance foyer, the club was as quiet as the proverbial tomb, the rule of silence enforced here as rigorously as in any monastery. Mycroft and other powerful figures in government and commerce seemed to find this place, where they were not obligated to converse, a needed respite and a sanctuary.

Personally, I found the club to be a splendid idea, as it collected and concentrated together the oddest and most eccentric individuals in the capital. In fact, I wondered for many years if my friend Holmes was a secret member, making use of the opulent facilities to think quietly (which meant to smoke) without me, to sample an infinitely wider menu than our good Mrs. Hudson could provide, and to hide out from his more aggressive enemies. But the prospect of spying his brother so often, even if Mycroft was tucked behind a *Times*, was no doubt an impediment to Sherlock Holmes adding his own oddities to this group.

The three of us were ushered to the guest room, the only place where we could talk freely. Standing by the fire, rocking impatiently from toe to heel, Mycroft stood alone, an abstracted scowl upon his great beefy face. Holmes walked over and shook his hand in a dry, laconic fashion, as if they were business acquaintances, not family; and not for the first time I reflected that there could not surely exist two less sentimental brothers in this world. It could be years between their meetings, although they lived less than two miles apart in the center of this vast metropolis.

Then Holmes motioned for Lestrade and for me to stand beside him. Mycroft, his heavy-lidded eyes giving us a greeting with the warmth of a cobra, surveyed the three of us and shook our hands as well, his palm soft and talcum powder polished. "Thank you for coming so quickly. The archbishop's representative has just called and is on his way."

"We should be on our way to St. Thomas's, and have him meet us there. There is no time to waste," cut in Holmes, anxiously. He could not abide government protocol under the best of circumstances, whereas such niceties and complexities were the very slippery medium in which his brother Mycroft swam.

Mycroft invited us to sink down into the club's large red leather chairs, the ultimate in comfort for men who seemed to hate returning to their homes. "Patience, my boy." He tightly smiled. "How are you, Sherlock? And you, Dr. Watson? You are, I trust, recovering well from that nasty wound from the Garribeb fellow?"

"How—how did you hear about that?" I stuttered. "I've not yet published that account."

"We're both fine, Mycroft," answered Holmes for us, "if a

little tired out from a holiday jaunt to Oxford." Bemused, he then turned to me. "Watson, you know how my brother prides himself on knowing everyone and everything. You included, as my Boswell." My naiveté never ceased to amuse him, as if any member of the Holmes family would by natural order know all that happened in our world. With a mischievous twist to his lips, he now directed his biting mood to his brother. "But you, how are you recovering from your recent Russian blowup? I ask because Watson and I are just returning from quite a run-in with your nemesis in the press, Jeffrey Rosewater of the *Telegraph*."

"I hope you clapped the fellow in jail," Mycroft hotly responded. "The inky fool's near-treasonable recent article allowed a damnable spy to go free, and don't you smile about it, Sherlock. After a year's hard work, I almost had a dangerous Russian conniver named Medved finally cornered—until that little *Telegraph* column by your Rosewater alerted him to go to ground. I suspect it will be some time before I track him down again."

"Terribly sorry, Mycroft," muttered Holmes, his mood shifting to being somewhat sympathetic, and then he offered an amusingly brief description of our college Christmas, to Mycroft's evident discomfort over Holmes's charitable treatment of Jeffrey Rosewater. If the brothers' roles had been reversed, I suspect Mycroft would have happily wrung the arrogant young Rosewater's neck before the master's Christmas-festooned mantelpiece.

"I trust this holiday mood of yours, of 'forgive and let live,' is fully satisfied, brother," Mycroft moaned, and then he turned to Inspector Lestrade and asked, "Are you confident that things are secure at the church?"

Mycroft's voice, unlike my friend's even tone, was like the

rattle of gravel in the throat and yet pitched oddly high. Portly, calm, and confident in his manner, Mycroft was as squat and secure as the Bank of England. The sleek, lithe form of his brother seemed impossibly related to this expansive bulk of Mycroft, but there was no disguising their sibling relationship: the same piercing dark eyes, the sharp and pointed nose, and the keen, alert expression of fierce and unrelenting intelligence.

Lestrade hesitantly nodded. Facing not one but two Holmeses would be intimidating to any man, especially the meek inspector. "I believe so, sir. Two men are guarding the undercroft, where the body was discovered. Each of the participants of the conference is confined to his room, and guards are placed on the front and rear entrances to the church."

"Good. There are a few background considerations, brother, that I need to appraise you of before you go sniffing about the church," huffed Mycroft. "We cannot go barging into the crime scene without some consideration of the archbishop's sensitivities. That is just the way it is. That being said, yes, Sherlock, I entirely agree time is of the essence. In fact, I would say the government desperately needs this murder solved within twenty-four hours. You are," he said, glaring at his brother, "the only man who can solve this quickly; no disrespect to the forces of the Metropolitan Police."

Lestrade sputtered, "None taken, sir. I would have hied myself to Baker Street whatever your wishes, sir, to be equally frank."

I smiled, remembering a quite different relationship between Holmes and Lestrade and the other inspectors of Scotland Yard twenty years ago, when suspicion, resentment, and (on Holmes's part) aloof ridicule ruled. Hundreds of cases later, Lestrade had now adopted more of a reverential attitude to the consulting detective, and Holmes in turn had softened toward

Lestrade, praising his industry, thoroughness, doggedness (leaving unsaid his fatal lack of imagination). They had now formed an oddly effective partnership and, for someone as reticent as Holmes, a comradeship nearly hearty.

Glancing at Holmes, I could see that, struggle though he might to conceal it, he was deeply affected by his brother's admission of need. "Then, Mycroft, let me have details. I need facts."

We all sat down, and Mycroft poured us each a small port. It was incongruous to sit in a Pall Mall club sipping fortified wine, speaking of a bloody death, but none of us demurred. On this cold night, we needed it. As I raised the deep red port with its velvet warmth to the tongue, I reflected how much it clearly pained Mycroft to ask his younger brother for this aid. Though both men were in their late fifties, there was still an ancient and instinctive rivalry between them.

Beneath the turnstile of politicians who came and went, Mycroft Holmes remained, quiet and invisible and essential to the government. These public men who ruled our vast empire had long ago learned to bow to his wisdom and long experience (even as Scotland Yard gave deference to my friend in his own special sphere of crime detection). Mycroft kept in his expansive skull all the movements and pulsations of a vast and growing empire, and with hidden-hand diplomacy could trace the danger zones and the points of opportunity, from the sweltering jewel of India to the cooler mountain passes of Nepal that lead to the mysterious and vital frozen plateaus of Tibet; from the far Pacific possessions of New Zealand and Australia to the scalding and far-flung cities of Jerusalem and Khartoum and Pretoria; from the wheat prairies of Canada down to the Falkland Islands, off Argentina, to the escalating trinity of dangers: the Russian probes south for a seaport and access to the Raj, the growing duel of Germany for dreadnought equality upon the seas, and most pressing, the fractious and rebellious Boers in the Transvaal of South Africa . . . and on and on. It took a great deal of covert diplomacy and smooth intrigue to keep a third of the world colored pink on the schoolroom maps.

Still, it was not astonishing that the prime minister had instructed Mycroft to turn to Sherlock Holmes. The successful resolution of a case I have previously published as "The Illustrious Client" had placed Holmes very much before the eyes of a very grateful British government; and although Holmes never admitted it to me, his trip to the virtually inaccessible capital of Tibet, Lhasa, during the three years he was in hiding after his murderous confrontation with Professor James Moriarty at the Reichenbach Falls had the fingerprints of Mycroft's doing all over it. I may have been his Boswell, but Holmes kept plenty of secrets from me.

Yet I am certain Holmes was careful never to become a paid agent of the government. His sentiments as a patriot could be appealed to, however, and the chance to prove himself to his brother never failed to arouse his competitive instincts. While love of country was strong in him, his own code of an English gentleman's behavior proscribed his being the pawn of any government, even his own.

"As I believe Lestrade told you, this evening at about four o'clock the badly battered body of an Anglican priest named Paul Appel was discovered and immediately identified. Scotland Yard was called in to take control of the scene, and there things stand until we arrive. No one has been allowed to enter or leave. The church was being watched by four policemen, and no one has entered or left, as I said. Lestrade tells me, in addition, that the snow on the surrounding walkways, and even the windowsills, reveals no footprints of any kind."

"Tell me about Appel."

"The man we are waiting for, one of the archbishop's principle canons, will be able to tell us more when he arrives, but I understand that Mr. Appel was parish rector of the church, St. Thomas's in Kensington."

"I read about the place the other day in the *Times*," I interjected. "It's a new building, apparently quite gorgeous, wildly expensive. It is a short walk from Sloane Square."

"I didn't know you were certain where even Westminster Abbey was, Watson," Holmes said dryly. "The only churches you seem to enter, you tend to leave as a married man."

As he quickly turned away back to the inspector, I realized Holmes *did* know that I was planning to marry, that there was no secret of mine to keep. But there was no time for me to reflect on what he felt about my imminent defection from Baker Street.

"But I believe you told me that the church was under guard already . . ."

"Indeed, twenty-four hours a day, for the previous three days," answered Lestrade dutifully.

"But why would the Foreign Office authorize such unusual security in a church? For surely you, Mycroft, ordered it—or you would not be sitting here now."

Mycroft leaned back and lit his own pipe. "Well, as you surmised, the circumstances were quite unusual. Inside that church for the last three days have been eight men representing different faiths, in private discussion as to the possibility of a major World's Parliament of Religions to be held in London next year, hoping to follow on the amazing success of the 1893 parliament at the Chicago world's fair. These religious leaders are all there under the secret invitation of the archbishop of Canterbury. Now, normally, such sensitive talks would take place at Lambeth

Palace, but it was thought that these religious fellows' comings and goings would quickly invite speculation, and luckily, St. Thomas's is easily closed off, near Victoria Station, and is quite spacious and comfortable for visitors."

"Why the secrecy?" I asked.

"As it was presented to me by the archbishop, these talks were to be kept under tight seclusion because several of the clergy represent faiths that publicly oppose such discussion. Highly embarrassing, you see. If you ask me, it's all a lot of nonsense. You'd think in this scientific age we'd be past all this superstition."

"One man's superstition is another's truth, or at any rate, sustaining tradition," I offered. "How can you effectively do your work without taking account of the role religion plays in all the countries we rule?"

Mycroft rolled his eyes, a logical man in our new Darwinian age. "I deal with African headhunter tribes, Dr. Watson, but I don't subscribe to quaint little rites such as cannibalism and I don't think such customs represent the future. I include in this the custom of ours called Communion, by the way. At any rate, the archbishop himself is unsure about the wisdom of hosting such an event. I suppose it is all right to be talking with a Hindu, but the Anglicans know that too visible discussions with the Church of Rome would leave the faithful nervous about such a merger."

"Such speculation is all very fascinating, Mycroft," replied Holmes a little testily, "but tell me exactly *why* they were here. There is a murder to solve."

"They were in London for three reasons, brother. One, the international scope of Anglicanism; two, the fact that London is the center of the world's greatest empire, making such a gathering of the world's religious leaders promising, but oh so perilous; and lastly, the previous prime minister, who was in favor of the idea, felt that securing a shroud of secrecy in the capital was easiest here."

Sherlock set his port down without taking a sip. "That shroud image is now all too apt."

Mycroft sighed in genuine despair. "And now we find the host priest dead, and the assurance that the killer is one of the leaders of one of the great faiths. Inside that church tonight is a potential successor to the pope, Cardinal Cappellari; one of India's most famous poets and a sainted political rabble-rouser; and the most venerated rabbi of Europe—not to mention a Buddhist monk and a Russian Orthodox priest answering to the patriarch of Constantinople. What an unbelievable disaster! I don't need to tell you what an acute embarrassment this will be to His Majesty's government."

"That's just if we somehow catch the killer," Holmes added. "The situation's infinitely worse if we do not. So it sounds as if we must catch this demented fellow and, in the bargain, silence the murder itself. This *will* be difficult, Mycroft."

His older brother, who had been sinking into the red plush of his favored chair, leaned up from his previously languid repose. Mycroft removed his pipe from his glistening thin lips to thrust it at Holmes in exasperation. "Let me handle the public revelation of this sordid matter and the stain it leaves behind. You must find the man, that is all."

"That is enough," Holmes replied mildly.

"What I can't begin to absorb is the outrageous nature of Appel's death," I cried out suddenly, a little put out with all the talk of embarrassment and relations with the public. "Does it not freeze your blood to think of that body lying in the dark of a church?"

Holmes looked at me curiously after my outburst. "Such brutality is ever present in this old bruised world, Watson. You of all people know that, as a physician. What makes this murder more horrid than another?"

"Why, the fact he *was* a priest, and the setting a place of sanctity, of holiness ..."

"Have you not learned anything in the years of our association, Watson? What better mask for the baser passions than holiness? Where can political machinations function more fiercely and ferociously than in a place where all is supposed to be mildness and light? Trust me, the realm of faith is an ample setting for sin."

"It sounds as if Mr. Holmes knows church life quite intimately," spoke a new voice from behind us, a weary, low-pitched voice with an Oxford drawl. "Is this personal experience, or just learned from Gothic tales by lady novelists?"

Shocked, we wheeled around, not having heard anyone enter our small drawing room. We hastily rose to greet this new member of our team, and Mycroft, amused by the stranger's jibe addressed to his brother, made the introductions.

"Gentlemen, Canon Hugh McCain, assistant to the archbishop. He will be representing the interests of Lambeth Palace."

"Representing the *church*, Mr. Holmes," said the clergyman to Mycroft, in a clipped and precise retort.

"Yes, of course," Mycroft hastily agreed.

There was something about the austere clergyman that was coldly impressive, a stillness that commanded attention and a little care. McCain's smooth and cultured voice was both soft and intimate and yet suited to the most public of pulpits. His hair, still flecked with snow, was fully gray, like oiled pewter, yet his skin was smooth and pale. He seemed young for a prestigious position such as assistant to the archbishop of Canterbury.

Sherlock Holmes acknowledged the cleric with a small bow,

McCain's chilly sarcastic remark still hovering about the room. "You have the advantage of me, sir. My experience in the realm of piety is indeed small, but believe me, I am very well acquainted with the church in all its human guises and forms—the institution, that is, which is prey to the same temptations as any other."

"And even greater temptations. But then, Mr. Holmes, even you, famed for your logical mind, would also agree that perhaps its resources are greater still. Still," the clergyman added, with a decided shake of his head, "forgive the manner by which I entered. I feel off balance tonight, very much in shock. It is an awful tragedy that brings us all out on such a night—Christmas Day, of all times of the year! But the archbishop thanks you, as do I, and if there is anything I can do to assist your efforts to resolve this horror, believe me, I will do it."

Mycroft turned to Sherlock. "You see, Canon McCain has been at this closed conclave the past three days, and was even there this morning. You led the worship service there this morning, is that right?"

He stiffened. "Yes, I preached, but left at noon. All this is so shocking, so depressing—unthinkable. I revere each one of these leaders in the church." He shook his head, grieved, his hard eyes worried, downcast. "It is impossible for me to imagine how Mr. Appel could be so savagely murdered . . ." His voice trailed off, and suddenly McCain looked pale, almost in a state of shock.

I took his arm in a firm, hopefully reassuring way. "If I've learned one thing in twenty years with Mr. Holmes, it is that no mystery is ever impenetrable." The Anglican priest looked at me with a sadness that, despite his earlier mocking tone toward my friend, wrung my heart. He looked as if a family member had just died.

"Come, Canon McCain, let us talk in the cab on the way," said Holmes gently. "Your help over the next hours will be invaluable. Anything, anything at all that you can think of will help us find the man who murdered your colleague. And find him we must, because I am afraid Appel may be only the first to die tonight."

The Marble Arch was a gray shadow obscured by snow as we headed down Park Lane, the deep violet darkness of Hyde Park on our right. McCain was talking in a spiritless monotone, staring out the fogged glass of our hansom cab.

"For the last three days I have been with these men every moment, and I only left today in order to report to the archbishop about our progress. Gone just hours, and this . . . abomination." The Anglican priest looked at all of us crowded into the black confines of the cab. Our breaths hung, frozen wisps. His thin face was delicate, his skin in the pale fleeting lamplight pallid, deathly white. His manner was abstracted, as if he were with us only as a signal of light.

"What did you last see as you left St. Thomas's this morning?" Holmes struck a match, the flare illuminating our space for an instant; then the red glow and the comforting smell of his shag tobacco.

"They asked me to celebrate Holy Communion, which I did. Despite the intensely private nature of the talks, we could not fail to offer a public service on Christmas morning. The police were unobtrusive in segregating the public from the participants, who all sat in a well-guarded section. Mr. Appel, as the parish priest of St. Thomas, assisted me."

Holmes asked, "Did you know Mr. Appel well?"

McCain shook his head. "Only as an assistant to the archbishop would be expected to know the parish priests of the major pulpits of this city. That is a large number, as you know. We were not close, no; in fact, Mr. Holmes, I often found myself resisting opportunities to know him better. There was something about him I instinctively distrusted. That sounds dreadful, I know, to say even as we . . . well, as we go to the church."

To view the poor man's body, I finished for him in my cold thoughts. Our unspoken goal.

Holmes quickly replied, "If you do not wish to be present at the murder site, Canon, I very much understand."

"No. I will go with you. This is my duty, and the archbishop is depending on me. Also, you must understand I feel some intense personal obligation here. I am the man who gathered together these men, who wrote the letters of invitation, who met each of them as they arrived in London. I must see this through." His stoic expression could not conceal his apprehension. The clergyman's thin lips were pressed firm, his mouth set like a gash.

"Of course, it was his church," McCain continued, going back to Holmes's earlier question about the morning's service. "But as the archbishop's representative, I presided. The others at the gathering only witnessed Holy Communion, of course—my purpose was mainly to offer a message to hold up their morale. Religious talks like this are difficult, and despite all the goodwill in the world, misunderstandings and frustrations are frequent."

"Enough to spark a death?" I asked.

"I know where you are headed, Dr. Watson, and I will tell you gentlemen all I know and all I saw, but no, nothing in those three days of unusual spiritual cooperation gave me any sense of unease or worry. I left after the service today with the feeling that we were very near a breakthrough, a rough consensus that included even the Vatican representative, Cardinal Cappellari. No, I thought these men were getting along well."

"May we return to Mr. Appel?"

The archbishop's man looked back out the window, as if there was something in the blowing winds beyond the icy glass that could sweep him far from us, his escorts to a death. He was clearly struggling to maintain his composure. "As I said, I did not know him well. No, no more than I would know any other parish minister in London." The elegant minister glanced sideways at Mycroft Holmes, who was tightly wedged next to him. "When you reached me at my offices at Lambeth Palace, Mr. Holmes, you asked that I bring along Appel's official file, which I have done. I took the time to study it, and I can tell you a little now."

"I would appreciate it," muttered Sherlock Holmes, his sharp chin buried deep into his scarf. As was his style, he closed his eyes to concentrate.

"He was a well-regarded priest, a sound administrator, and his accession to a prime post such as St. Thomas's augured well for his future. He was only thirty-seven years old. The archbishop early felt he displayed unusual skills from the pulpit, and so he was groomed for this plum of a church, which he was appointed to six years ago."

"Tell me something of his history. Perhaps there is an fingerprint from the past, something trailing the man."

"I do not know much, Mr. Holmes, but apparently he was the child of Anglican missionaries, a Reverend Silas and Elizabeth Appel. After some time spent in northern India, Appel was orphaned in China quite young, and was brought home to live with kindly relatives in Mayfair. He was then, I believe, twelve. After they provided a generous public school education, he then received a degree from Magdalen College, Oxford, in 1890. He had an unusual interest in Chinese literature and world religions, and his divine reading was heavily influenced, I'm sorry to say, by German skepticism. He was a curate in training at a small parish in Kent for two years, then he assumed his first parish duties at St. Justin's in Tooting Bec. His slightly irregular academic interests never impeded his high standing with either the archbishop or with his parish."

"Explain, please."

"Well, he has published numerous articles on subjects ranging from Chinese pottery to Himalayan religious ritual. Still, we Anglican ministers are renowned for our at times rather esoteric interests, and as I said, his ministry at St. Thomas's was exemplary."

I spoke up. "Those interests you mentioned—considering the facts of his childhood, being orphaned and all in China, the tragedy of losing his parents, all this would surely help explain his unusual concern with the East."

As McCain nodded, Mycroft Holmes interjected, "Watson's correct, of course. His special interests, and the unusual aspects of his church, made him the perfect host for the archbishop's meeting."

"Quite," answered the priest archly.

Holmes, a cat frozen waiting for prey, suddenly pounced. "And his theology? You sounded slightly aghast at his liberalism." There was an edge of excitement in his voice, but I knew my friend well enough to know that this intensity was not born of any interest in theology, but rather, his interest in the dark corners of the heart, where superficial religious differences could fester and erupt in violence.

McCain grimaced, as if tasting something bitter upon the tongue. "Appel's views were, barely, in the range of the acceptable. Anglicanism is famed for its latitude in ranges of liturgy, from low church to high, but our openness in theology is even greater. We give our priests an unspoken freedom in many matters, and many of our laypeople would be shocked to know how liberal our clergy can be in the quiet of their rectories. All we ask is that these private views not interfere with their pastoral duties, performance of the sacraments, and their public proclamation of the historic tenets of the faith. Now, I did not know Appel at all well, but I was well aware of how closely he skated to the edge of the permissible. A certain passion, nearly evangelical, infused his preaching at St. Thomas's, and his growing congregation responded—his pulpit manner was brilliant, moving. He was sufficiently orthodox when he needed to be, though secretly Pelagian in theology."

"Pelagian?" I asked, thoroughly confused.

"I'm sorry, Dr. Watson. One of our worst faults as clergy is speaking in an impenetrable code. Pelagius was an early heretic who opposed Augustine, and thus the correct formation of the Christian creed. He believed human effort could justify ourselves to God, and that we did not suffer from original sin."

Holmes muttered, "In my field, very little sin is original." He shifted in his narrow space next to me and absently added, "Besides, you're being a little hard on the little monk Pelagius, who was, after all, British."

"Let's leave off all this rarefied theological banter," said Mycroft, entering the conversation with his usual skeptical exasperation. "Next we'll be concluding this Appel was a secret apostate because he served a church named after St. Thomas, the great doubter!"

Holmes interjected, "Actually, Mycroft, I was more thinking the association of Thomas as the apostle who traveled east to India might end up being far more suggestive. You scoff, Mycroft, but odd cases like this, steeped in the aura of religiosity, often turn on such fertile associations. The religious mind is richly metaphorical, and I would not be surprised that our murderer has followed just such a train of private connections, and that something of this nature will profoundly affect our investigation. But let us satisfy my brother and refocus on forensics. Tell me again, Lestrade, of the security arrangements."

"Gladly, sir. A plainclothes policeman had been guarding the front door, and three uniformed men have been patrolling the only other exits, a rear entry into a back alley and an entrance to the attached parish house. We are somewhat helped by the snow, Mr. Holmes, because my men report no footprints, no signs of entry or exit. Also, we have checked all windows, and snow lies undisturbed along all ledges and leaded panes."

"As it is pitch black, I will take your word for that, Lestrade. The answers, then, lie within St. Thomas's itself. Where are the guests staying, and are there any servants with access?"

Mycroft interrupted the policeman. "Sherlock, the reason St. Thomas's was chosen for this secret conclave is an oddity of the church—you see, since it was built only fifteen years ago, it has many amenities an old Wren London church doesn't have. It boasts an attached parish house with eight guest rooms, thus the selection. It is clean, has electricity, and in short, isn't a cold wreck. As to your other question, Appel dismissed his clerical assistant two weeks ago, and thus only his two table servants— his khidmatgars—and a female cook have been present for the proceedings. They are dark; Indian, I suspect. They hardly know any English."

"Are those private bedrooms being observed now? I don't want the murder scene disturbed or violated any further."

"Absolutely, Mr. Holmes," insisted Lestrade. We swung past Apsley House, and Wellington's statue towered over a silent and subdued London. Heading down Knightsbury, we turned into Belgravia with its rows of elegant white stucco houses and its charming maze of small closes and mews. It was nearly seven o'clock.

Holmes was oblivious to the beauty of the scene as we turned into Sloane Street and another commercial area. "Can you think of any reason that a parish rector would be killed with such violence?"

Canon McCain shrugged. "None at all."

"Tell me a bit more about the man."

"He was a vicar in his late thirties, not married, and as I said, had been rector at St. Thomas's for six years. There was never a whisper of scandal about his ministry; and anticipating your next question, Mr. Holmes, Appel was apparently normal in his, ah, romantic inclinations. He was engaged to marry three years ago, but the young woman broke off the engagement and attained a missionary post in India. Frankly, I can think of nothing that would answer the question of why this kind of violence was visited on his body."

"When was the body found?"

Lestrade answered Holmes's question in a laconic tone. "This evening at four o'clock."

"By whom?"

"By a young curate named Paul Brown, the translator for the Vatican representative. As I understood today's schedule, everyone at the conclave joined for tea at two, and then all dispersed to their private rooms for study and meditation. No one seems to have seen Appel after that."

"Well, we will question them closely on that score. Now, Canon McCain, I must see and assess each of them freshly, without the diversion of anyone else's projection or opinions. But what I *would* like you to do for me is to write down a brief biography, the traditions they represent, so that I can quickly know them."

"I anticipated you would need such a list, and so before I left my office at Lambeth, I wrote brief paragraphs concerning each of the leaders. I do not wish to sway you, Mr. Holmes, but I will

say this: these men are an impressive gathering, and each brilliant in his own way. Do not make the mistake of thinking their
devotion to their faith makes them anything less than subtle
contestants. You will need to be as subtle and agile as they are."

The minister handed a folded page to Holmes, who took it
with a rueful acknowledgment.

"I assure you I will not make the mistake of underestimating
any of these men. They would not be here in London without
being—how do the scriptures put it?—as cunning as serpents."

"I believe our Lord added, 'and as harmless as doves.'
Matthew 10:16."

"Well, we shall see about that," Holmes said, quickly glancing over McCain's short listing of the conclave's participants.
"You did your work quite well, Canon. The fellows certainly
run the theological gamut, from Hindu to Moslem, from a
Buddhist monk from Japan to an eminent German rabbi. This,
gentlemen, eclipses anything a novelist could invent!"

He was then silent, absorbing the pages quickly, the bright
glare from a theater's light illuminating his severe mien. The
list McCain had carefully written out in his Lambeth office read
simply:

Guests of the Archbishop of Canterbury
St. Thomas's Parish Church, Kensington, London

Representing the Roman Catholic Church:
*His Eminence Luigi Cardinal Cappellari, leading figure
in the Vatican Curia and close adviser to Pope Leo XIII.
Sympathetic to the Modernist movement, and thus a
target to counter, conservative forces. A possible candidate
to be successor to the pope, though a history of chronic
lung disease and his age, 67, will work against him. A*

straightforward-seeming gentleman, not at all the usual political fox that rises in church hierarchies. Born of quite poor parents, he retains a simple manner from his Naples childhood, but he would not be here unless he had the explicit trust of the bishop of Rome, and all that that entails.

(Due to the cardinal's somewhat limited English, Cardinal Vaughan, the archbishop of Westminster, has appointed a young curate, Father Paul Brown, a Norfolk man in his twenties, to act as his translator and to assist his walking.)

Representing the Eastern Orthodox Churches:

His Holiness Archbishop Aleksandr Demetrius, of the Russian Orthodox Church, St. Petersburg, representing the patriarch of Constantinople. Close ties to the Greek and the Syrian churches, and has traveled extensively abroad, particularly in America. Presents himself as a gruff peasant sort, though he is quietly sophisticated enough to let others state their positions around him, and then he reacts with the swoop of a hawk. An intimidating man, he is surprisingly sensitive to imagined slights and slurs, particularly to the Orthodox tradition. Emotional, temperamental, sentimental, he fills a room with bravado and, occasionally, charm.

Representing the Buddhist faith:

Kozan, zenji, of Yawata, Japan. Teaching master of the Rinzai Zen sect. Respected representative of Mahayana Buddhism. Author of book translated into English, The Christ and Buddha. *A marvelous diplomat for his faith, he is personable, direct, nearly jovial in manner. A man whose engaging and seemingly carefree manner masks*

*an incisive mind; someone whose charismatic manner is
palpable.*

Representing the Jewish religion:
   *Rabbi Leonard Mandleberg, chief rabbi of German syn-
agogues, Berlin.* Graduate and former professor of Leipzig
University; *author of* Isaiah and the Universal God *and*
The Covenant and the Jews. *Ties to Russian and Polish
Jewry and with London synagogues. A quiet, scholarly
gentleman with a mournful and distracted demeanor, he is
perhaps the most impressive of the representatives, steady,
kind, mentally agile, with an endless supply of stories and
parables, and ready to act as peacemaker and conciliator.*

Representing the Hindu tradition:
   *General Secretary Krishnan Viswarath, of the Brahmo-
Samaj, elite caste and reform movement within Hinduism.
Associated with the University of Calcutta. Famed Indian
poet and political figure, author of* India and the Colonial
Experience *and* The Nine Million Faces of God. *Impressive,
charismatic, with a tendency to angry retorts and romantic self-promotion, he has more than earned a controver-
sial reputation; yet reasonable and able to listen to others,
even when he is offended (which is often).*

Representing the Islamic faith:
   *Ali al-Khaledis, imam and mufti (legal adviser) to the
ruling Jerusalem pasha and member of the Jerusalem
Municipal Council. Offered special disposition from the
caliph, the sultan of Turkey in Constantinople, to meet
with us. Al-Khaledis is an astute politician, but also has
deep ties to the hidden brotherhood of Sufi mystics, an*

unusual combination. Smooth, political, cheerful, he is practiced in dealing with other faiths and shows little Islamic rigidity. The most engaging and personable of the representatives, and the one most adept at masking real thoughts and feelings.

> *Also present, representing the Anglican Church: host rector the Rev. Paul Appel and*
> > *the Rev. Hugh McCain (yours truly).*
> > *Dec. 25, 1902,*
> > *Lambeth Palace,*
> > *the offices of the archbishop, London.*

The detective absently tapped the canon's paper into his open palm. I could see that he was already memorizing the information, absorbing it into his brain's great and greedy maw. "Ah, I see we are almost to the church. Both you and Mycroft, I am sure, will add a great deal more, as the night goes on, upon each of our suspects."

"Brother," interrupted Mycroft hotly, "please do not use a word such as 'suspect.' These religious men must be treated as venerated guests not only of the Church of England but of the king himself. These are not the usual sort of ruffians you track."

"The sort of murderer I deal with, Mycroft, is seldom common. Lestrade and Gregson can track those sort without help from me, but this, this elegant little problem betrays a high sensibility as well as savagery. I admit, my religious sensitivities are not strong, but," and Holmes turned, his eyes glittering, "I will treat each of these men fairly. I can treat a common man as a king, and a nobleman as a pauper—depending on their telling me the truth. I know one thing, Mycroft: one of them is a man capable of murder."

With that mild retort, we pulled to a halt. I was the first out, and I assisted the rotund Mycroft Holmes out onto the slippery pavement. There were now at least three inches of snow on the ground.

As Holmes alighted, Mycroft pointed to the huge church towering above us, aglow from the strange luminance of the snow. "What is truth, brother? Mind Pilate's question tonight."

My friend did not reply as he stared up at the magnificent church.

Holmes knelt by the grotesque sight of Appel's twisted form. McCain and Mycroft Holmes hung back, so that Appel's corpse was barely visible, yet even so, I heard the canon's muffled gagging, then his awful retching in the far corner of the next alcove.

"Let him be, Watson. Help me here." Holmes motioned me forward to his side, and we gratefully accepted gloves, which Lestrade had anticipated we would need. They were quickly soaked through. Then Holmes gently, but with a methodical manner, swept back the white sheet covering the upper half of Appel's body. The body was still clothed, barely, in black priest's garb, and was horribly torn and shredded.

"Look, Watson. His arms and legs are literally in tatters, slashed and pitted."

"Filleted with a knife, I'd say."

I'm certain we sounded cold-blooded to the others, standing off from us, but as a doctor and a former soldier, I was able to focus on my task. At least the chill of the stone had kept the smell down. Holmes had already entered the realm of deduction, where this form was less a person than a mass of clues, a puzzle to engage his teeming brain.

And a mass it was, only just preserving the quality of a human being as opposed to a butcher's prey.

Whoever did this, I thought as I hesitantly reached out to touch the pitiable body, was nothing less than a madman. To be posing as a man of God made the connection even more shocking, if that was possible, as I surveyed this wreck of a human being.

I felt the skin, which was still pliable, and I extended a tattered arm, some white of bone exposed. "No rigor mortis, Holmes. I'd say he was alive three to four hours ago, as we have had indicated. But I've never seen anything like this."

Appel's face was a ghastly mask of a madman's carving, and his dry and now blackened tongue extruded from purple lips, his slate gray eyes glazed in the shock of death. The killer had, bizarrely, tied Appel's legs into an odd position, with his narrow knees drawn up and secured. It seemed obscene to have the bright police lamps trained on so vulnerable a sight, upon this body just barely still identifiable as a man.

"Watson—do you observe the clothes? The priest's collar?"

I looked beyond the horror of the manifold gouges and tatters of meat to concentrate on what Holmes had seen. At last I saw, though I did not comprehend. "Why, his clothes are on backwards!"

Three

COMPLINE

Sloane Square, St. Thomas's, 8 P.M.

Holmes paced impatiently back and forth, into darkness and back into the blinding glare of the police lamps. "Cover up the man." He motioned to Lestrade. "I've seen what I need to see." He wheeled to me and said in a husky whisper, "Watson, take Mycroft and Canon McCain upstairs to the church. This is no place for them. Have them wait for me there."

He paused, and turned to Lestrade, who was finishing draping the body of Appel. "Who did you say discovered the rector here?"

"A young Roman Catholic, a curate named Brown. He's assisting Cardinal Cappellari."

"Bring him down here, please. I want to observe his return down here and then ask him some questions. And Watson, take the body up with you and return as quickly as you can."

"Certainly, Holmes."

Mycroft seemed anxious to go upstairs, and was as pale and balefully affected as Canon McCain. Two burly policemen gently placed the inert body, one blackened arm extended out from the sheet, upon a canvas stretcher.

We stumbled up the dark back stairs from the crypt of St. Thomas's, the swaying lamplight ahead of us making every step treacherous. We were then led to the parlor of the church house attached to the great sanctuary, easily reached from the rear stairs of the undercroft. Mycroft, after consulting with Mc-Cain, decided that the priest's body should be placed in the only bedroom that was without a visiting clergyman. Each of the faith representatives was now sequestered in his small chamber, and none (excepting, of course, Brown) knew why they were being confined to their rooms.

Gently, we laid the stretcher down, and when left alone with the body, I set out to compose the priest's figure in as dignified way as I could. The eyes could not be closed, for the lids had been cut away in jagged frenzy. Long vertical strips of skin from the face had also been cut away, exposed meat with all of the effect of torn velvet, vermilion.

The effect of the brutally exposed and staring eyes was unnerving, so I hastily recovered the body with the sheet just as soon as I could fold Appel's tattered arms over his chest. His priest's black garb, so strangely and perversely reversed, was thick and now shone with dark caked blood. I turned off the small desk light, and the snow moon lay a milk white light across the still form.

Quickly, with a shiver, I hastened to rejoin the others, returning as I had come, back through a church parlor room, decorated as if Queen Victoria were arriving for tea momentarily, and then down the dark stairs to the undercroft.

"Was there anything we missed, Mr. Holmes?" Lestrade was asking. "We scoured the stone all along the crypt and found nothing, except this, a white bead rosary." He handed it to Holmes. "It appeared to have been dropped, then perhaps kicked into a dark corner."

Holmes gave it a cursory look and placed it in his jacket pocket. "No, I'm certain you saw what was there to see. What remains is to make sense of *what* we saw. The disposition of the body is terribly strange, but in that strangeness may lie the solution."

Lestrade sighed, his narrow face pinched with perplexity. (It was an expression I'm afraid I must have exhibited all too often through my long association with Holmes.) "You and I, sir, have seen many an odd sight through the years," said the inspector, "but I don't understand how a body could have been treated that way. What could possibly lead a man to do something like this? I am totally lost, Mr. Holmes. My mind can't absorb such brutality, and I have seen my share of murder victims, including those of our friend Jack's."

Holmes laughed bitterly. "You have made my point, Lestrade. We never caught the Ripper because he was too random, impulsive, and totally haphazard. I came up short with the Whitechapel murders. Still, despite that singular failure, I think I have done pretty well in this tawdry trade for the last twenty-five years. Lestrade, I'm beginning to think that our relative success comes because you and I have long operated in a society of social order and limits. I sense something shifting now, something desperate and disorienting." Holmes paused, thinking hard. I had never heard him like this. Then Holmes added, his calm tone belaying the horrifying vision he was conveying, "Now what I fear is a world developing where killers have become unintelligible, people who kill just to kill, thus producing common and featureless crimes."

My friend paused again, then added emphatically: "Not *this* one, though. I know one thing here: the odder the murder, the easier it will be to solve. The more bizarre the incident, the more the mind of the killer is fully on display. The more complex the murder, the more we have to snag him with." He was suddenly abstracted, his eyes closed in far concentration. At last he seemed to rouse himself, and he relit his pipe. He held the aromatic shag under his nose, as if to overcome the lingering smells of death.

"Now, something about that body in the vault is tugging at me, something I know I have encountered somewhere before. Something in the bizarre aspects of the presentation. But I can't grip it now, Lestrade. Perhaps more information as the night goes on will help me." The last was said in a soft, almost pensive manner.

"We can't keep these men locked in their chambers all night, Holmes," I interjected. "They don't even know why they have, in effect, been incarcerated for four hours. Mycroft wants them told soon."

"Then by all means, let's have them all brought to the church parlor in, let's say, thirty minutes. Would that satisfy my brother?" His gray eyes glittered in anticipation. The shattered corpse of the priest had turned my urbane and usually calmly logical companion into an angry, avenging angel. Rarely had I seen the nervous tic of his twitching eyes and the clinched jaws of eager vengeance. He wanted whoever this man was badly, and I suspected it was all he could do to order his mind to proceed with his usual care and precision. Then he clapped his hands.

"Lestrade, where's the young priest?"

"Here he comes, Mr. Holmes. Collins is bringing him down."

Suddenly, shuffling in an awkward gait, a small, rotund young man in his early twenties rounded the stone stairs. His long simple black cassock fell to his scuffed brown shoes. His spectacles, balanced halfway down his soft bulbous nose, glittered in the sharp light. This was a singularly unimpressive young man, whose blank gray eyes had a flat, glassy quality. He stared about him as if seeing the undercroft for the first time. He pressed the bridge of his sliding glasses up and looked at us passively.

"Yes," he uttered in a strong Norfolk accent. "The policeman informed me you wanted me here."

"You are the curate Brown?"

"Yes."

"Mr. Brown, my name is Sherlock Holmes, and I've been told you are the translator and assistant to the Roman Catholic representative, Cardinal Cappellari. Is that correct?"

"Aye." The young priest idly bit one of his nails carefully, unnervingly calm in this fraught setting.

"And what possessed you to go to the church undercroft around four, Mr. Brown?"

The little priest seemed unperturbed by the dangerous question. "I needed to take a walk, and I knew that, with the snow pelting down, it was too unpleasant to go out for a stroll along Sloane Street. The police at the door would probably not have let me out, anyway. Besides, I did not want to leave the cardinal for long. So after praying in the sanctuary, I walked down to the vault from the gospel side. The long bays of arcades are perfect for stretching your legs, and this wasn't the first time I had gone there to be alone, to think as I walked."

Holmes folded his arms and leaned forward, his sharp and angular face etched harshly in the lamplight, a singular contrast to the placid soft features of the diminutive priest. "You may have already told what happened to the police, but please repeat it for me. Try to remember any details you can; I assure you anything, everything you can summon up is crucial."

"Well, as I came down, I heard soft cutting noises, and I wondered if the cook was down there storing away game or poultry to season. I reached to the bottom of the stone steps, here, and I distinctly heard whispering and then hasty footsteps, and then, as I came around the corner, the sound went up the other side, there"—he pointed fifteen feet farther down the vault to the other stairs—"back up the sanctuary. If I had it to do over again, I would have retreated back up the steps I had just descended, so I could have spied the killer emerging from across the crossing of the chancel. But I went forward, and then, to my shock, stumbled upon the pitiable remains of Appel. There was just enough light to see the horrible sight. I knew, of course, he was dead, so I did not touch him at all.

"I remember running up the steps and outside the church to find a policeman. You know, of course, we had had four policemen guarding us, and I remember being slightly amused at the oddity of such a thing; but believe me, Mr. Holmes, at that moment no sight looked more welcoming than a London bobby. Within ten minutes, the authorities were informed and descending upon us."

"Did you say anything about the death of Appel or the manner in which he died to anyone other than that policeman?"

Father Brown shook his head. "No, not a word. The cardinal himself still does not know our host minister is even dead. I did not want to be the one to inform him of such a thing."

Nodding, Holmes seemed relieved that the others upstairs were still in ignorance. Except one.

"That was very wise of you, and I appreciate your circumspection in this terrible matter. Canon McCain and I will inform everyone momentarily of this dreadful death. Now, did you see more than one figure running away, up the far steps?"

Brown shook his head, placing the tip of his tongue over his thin upper lip in a pensive manner. "The echoes down here in the crypt are such that it was impossible to tell. All I saw were retreating shadows, and then, of course, I stumbled upon . . ."

"Yes," said Holmes. "It would be difficult to notice—indeed, almost inhuman—much else with such a shocking sight before you. Still, you must try to remember. Have you *any* idea who might have done this act?"

"No. It seems totally inexplicable." The curate bore a look of abstracted reverie. "Odd that at this morning's service Paul read Genesis 4—the very first murder."

"A strange coincidence, to be sure," I said.

Brown stared at me, then shook his head. "There will be no coincidences in any of this, I am sure. You are Dr. Watson, are you not?"

I nodded.

"I never dreamed I would suddenly find myself enmeshed in one of your tales. While I have often dreamed of standing in the detective's place, of solving mysteries with a godlike omnipotence, now I wonder. Often as not, I do manage to guess the conclusion, but you, sir, have fooled me more than most. But after tonight, I'm afraid I won't enjoy the game any longer."

Replied Holmes laconically, "Despite my friend's light style, they never were games, Mr. Brown. I sense you know the importance of your cooperation in this inquiry."

The priest nodded.

"I noticed a moment ago you used Appel's first name, the same as yours—Paul," Holmes added.

"I should inform you," added Brown hastily, "I knew him, though only slightly, before arriving here at St. Thomas's three days ago with the cardinal. We encountered each other several times at the Westminster Library; and on at least three occasions over tea at a local café, Appel and I had animated discussions about faith and true religion. He seemed to enjoy sparring conversation whenever we encountered each other. I think my views amused him, though his filled me more with dread than entertainment."

"Concerning?"

"Ultimately, the state of his soul. Appel, in his pursuit of the exotic and the novel in religion, seemed to feel any and all faiths were equal paths to God. I argued that God had forged a path to us, and that we were otherwise lost. That otherwise, *he* was lost. He posed as the kind of Christian who would pass muster with agnostics such as Mr. H. G. Wells. But my views are immaterial here."

"Oh, Father Brown, you are wrong. You were the one who found the body, and the one who called in the police. That is a strong position for a possible murderer to be in. You could have had personal animus toward the Anglican priest, and without the cardinal's knowledge done this horrible deed. The cardinal could have instructed you to use your acquaintance with Appel to lure him to the undercroft. I say all of this not to be offensive, but to indicate what a range of possibilities lies before us, and the investigation is young."

Brown answered blandly, "No offense taken. You may well decide that what I am about to say means nothing whatsoever to your investigation, but the Roman Catholic Church would not countenance murder under any circumstances. As an individual, or in league with the cardinal, I could not commit murder—it is a mortal sin. Further, to kill someone like Appel, with his heretical views, would be tantamount to condemning both parties, the murderer and his victim (in this case, under peril of his soul), to damnation."

"Perhaps," ventured Holmes, "some heretical views are vile enough that such a sacrifice is possible. It would not be the first time in religious history for such a death."

"As dangerous as his views were, they are far too common in this world to consider special," replied Brown laconically. "I had nothing to do with his murder."

With the curate ushered back to his room, Holmes and I walked upstairs, and for the first time my friend viewed the large and comfortable parish house attached to the church. From the Lady Chapel, on the right side of the sanctuary, there were two sets of heavy oak-paneled doors that led to a large parlor and waiting room, beyond which were the pastor's dining room, personal quarters, and kitchen. From the parlor, as well, was access to a great square of small retreat rooms off long corridors that faced a small garden for meditation. We found Mycroft and Canon McCain seated in the small kitchen area.

The Anglican priest sat ignoring Mycroft, his eyes hooded and disturbed. There was an aura about him of a deep isolation, of a resilient reserve that made his elegance and polish seem more of a defense than mere smooth social bearing. His deep-set eyes glittered with moisture, and he was obviously fighting hard to regain his composure. He rhythmically stroked his trim sandy mustache in fierce, harsh motions.

Mycroft, however, was obviously feeling somewhat recovered, and he rose as we came into the kitchen. He was a man who normally sat in his small Whitehall room in the Foreign Office, moving British emissaries and other covert agents like markers on a game board, blandly unaware of the real consequences of his decisions or their life-and-death realities. There was no such separation possible now, though he had his younger brother now to handle the distasteful work, the sticky spilled blood upon the ground.

"What have you learned, Sherlock?" he inquired.

Holmes filled in his brother, briefly describing the laconic conversation we had just had with the youthful Roman Catholic priest. "Chiefly, what I've learned is that nothing with this case is going to come easy. The young Brown fellow, who found the body, was not very helpful. Now my need is to observe closely these holy gentlemen, face-to-face, as we inform them of Appel's murder." He paused, and inquired of the pale and abstracted McCain, "Will you be able to tell them what has transpired this afternoon? Mycroft and I can inform them if you prefer."

Taking a long puff upon his cigarette, McCain visibly struggled to right himself. He squared his shoulders and concentrated his focus, his gray eyes darting to take us in. "Yes, Mr. Holmes. As I told you, it is my duty, is it not? I will find the words somehow. I make my way through life using words . . ." With harsh and merciless resolve, he turned and added, "Though I trust you and your brother will then indicate to them how the investigation will proceed. That we cannot leave this place without finding the man who did this."

Holmes answered, "We will tell them only those things which will help us uncover the killer, and that is all. The less they know of our plans, the easier it will be to observe the mistakes of the guilty. Let's see how these good men react to the news."

"Steady on, Sherlock," muttered Mycroft. "Mind my injunctions."

"I'll keep your suggestions in mind, brother," the detective replied, smoothing back his graying hair along his temples, as if he had a headache. I remembered he had not slept in Oxford the night before. Holmes's skin was pale, his eyes smudged with weariness.

Shaken by the horror we had just witnessed, we sat in the kitchen for a time in oppressive silence. There were just enough chairs for us all to sit. McCain lay down his silver cigarette case before him and smoothly extracted another smoke, his long delicate fingers shaking. Finally, Holmes spoke again.

"Gentlemen, let us try to move past the shock we all feel. There is so much to be done, and done quickly before more violence occurs, which I feel is possible, even likely. Now, Inspector Lestrade, I want you to start assembling our guests in the large parlor adjacent to us here. I also want to know what telegrams have been sent from here in the last three days. If we have to pay the message boys for the letters sent, do it, no matter how expensive the information. There is only one phone, in the parlor. We have to find out if any calls were made, and to whom.

"Now, I have to ask you, Canon McCain, to tell us something more about this secret conclave. What exactly were these clergymen doing here? I confess, their purpose here in London is still murky to me."

The priest laid out a file. McCain was still struggling to regain the calm assurance he had possessed outside the church half an hour ago. The bodies he normally encountered were no doubt clean and nicely outfitted for fine ritual words before the grave. Still, talking of church politics seemed to steady him, place him back in a world he knew so competently.

"Mr. Holmes, how much do you know about the World's Parliament of Religions, the great Chicago gathering of nine years ago?"

"Almost nothing, so please enlighten us."

The thin and graceful priest eased a colorful print from his collection of papers and showed it to us. "This magnificent collection of columned buildings is not ancient Greece or the center of Rome at its height. This was the famed White City of the 1893 Columbian Exposition. The Chicago gathering featured all the newest inventions and innovations, featuring art, literature, technology, politics—but then the founders had an inspiration. No one had ever thought of inviting representatives of the world's major religions together before. To everyone's surprise, the resulting World's Parliament of Religions was a great success. The Jews and the Roman Catholics were delighted to stand as equals to the Protestant denominations, but the real surprise was the astonishing impact that the Eastern representatives had.

"The Buddhist and Hindu figures, especially, held their own in public speeches, even shaming the arrogance of our own spiritual traditions, especially our missionaries. For the first time, they appeared not as benighted figures ready for conversion but as articulate and extremely sophisticated representatives of their Eastern faiths.

"The only problem with the parliament was that two crucial figures were missing. The sultan of Turkey refused any Muslim participation, and the other major holdout was, I am pained to say, my superior, the archbishop of Canterbury himself. He wrote to the organizers that Christianity, being the one true religion, could not stand with other religions without giving the impression of equality and parity. It was a terrible mistake."

I sputtered, "It's terrible to think our English church appeared to the world so standoffish!"

"Indeed, Mr. Watson. It was not our finest hour. Over the last ten years, the singular success of the parliament has made the archbishop rethink his position, and the role that Anglicanism ought to play in this new century. Many people said the World's Parliament was one of the great events of the last century. Now the archbishop wonders if an event greater, even more important, could be sparked by a new gathering at the *start* of our new century.

"At the first parliament of religions, you see, all that happened was a succession of papers and speeches from the delegates. In his prayers, the archbishop now wonders if it is at last time for religious people to stop fighting one another; that the real battle of the coming century will be people of all faiths striving against a growing tide of irreligion."

He stopped. The shattering of the archbishop's hopes were now only too evident. Violence had not waited even three days to force itself into the dream of this meeting.

Holmes set down the picture of the magnificent White City.

"Within a month of the Columbian Exposition's closing, all these magnificent buildings along the shores of Lake Michigan went up in smoke and fire. We thought we could do better," continued McCain. "Perhaps our faiths are not yet strong enough to withstand the intense heat of hatred. But I thought they could."

Mycroft said, "Canon, I want you to convey to the archbishop that the prime minister is completely behind this effort, and that I am authorized to use the full powers of His Majesty's government to ensure that scandal does not destroy this meeting. That is why my brother is here. He and the Metropolitan Police are working as a united force, and the government has full confidence in them."

The brothers soberly nodded to each other. My experience of these odd siblings told me that as the night went on, they would move past their prickly sparring and settle into a more comfortable mode of cooperation. Indeed, the longer they were in each other's company, the more the complementary strengths of their great intellects seemed to merge. The track of their equally great egos would also begin to converge, and Holmes times two would be impossible for the guilty to escape (or so I prayed this might be, this night). It was too horrible to contemplate McCain's despairing words proving true.

The elegant priest turned to the massive Mycroft and asked, "So, I implore you to help us tonight. There is so much more here at stake than simply Appel's death."

But it was Sherlock Holmes who answered the priest. "Perhaps. Perhaps there is *less* here at stake than you imagine. Perhaps some small and simple reason why one man has killed another. I would move heaven and earth to solve one man's murder, just as I would to preserve the whole world, simply because I believe these two efforts to be at last the same. And so would my brother.

"But that is the last of my rhetorical splendor tonight, Canon McCain, for my duties are now infinitely more prosaic. I do not have the gift of ecclesiastical eloquence. I have facts to collect. Which means, as we near eight o'clock, that we must confront the archbishop's guests. And I think I hear them gathering."

Holmes rose and turned to me. "Watson, it is blasted cold in this house. Could you put on some tea for us? Perhaps we should bring up that cook, and the two khidmatgars. They will need to be questioned, as well."

"Certainly, Holmes."

I set some water on to boil and went in search of Lestrade. But first, as I did, I was somewhat taken aback by the splendor of the priest's parlor, hardly what I would have expected from the plain chapel style of my Methodist upbringing. This room was in the Victorian high style, all golden oak furniture with opulent red-velvet button-tufted upholstery. The room was bustling with interesting and intensely colorful personal items, lacquered Chinese boxes, pale green vases upon the mantel (reflected back in the great gold-framed mirror), Japanese fans, and a huge wooden Oriental birdcage, sans bird, next to a candelabraed upright piano. An ornate tea service adorned the center cloth-draped parlor table, which was surrounded by large comfortable armchairs with plush pillows. The room was warm, comfortable, and vivid in tones of red and dark wood wainscoting. I wondered what the dowagers of the congregation thought of their bachelor priest's opulence and quite lush tastes. This was a room decorated by a willful and powerful man, not someone whose living space was ordained by a contingent of cautious church ladies.

Seven dignified and quietly bewildered men were warily seating themselves in this parlor of the parish house, escorted by three expressionless bobbies. Inspector Lestrade, looking dour, stood guard over them in the doorway leading back into the church.

"Ah, Lestrade, Mr. Holmes would also like you to bring up the two servants as soon as he confronts them with the facts of the murder."

"Certainly, Doctor, but Mr. Holmes won't get much out of them. They seem a little"—he placed his finger against his temple—"slow. But I'll have them brought up."

The assembled religious leaders sat silently. There was a sense of oppressive quiet in this room, not meditative but absolutely electric in tension. I was fascinated to have my first look at them.

They were an impressive lot, sitting solemn, reserved. Some were whispering quietly to one another, and there was a air among them of subtle confusion, shared mystification. I was also fascinated by their varied and exotic vestments, formal in colorful yet stately dignity. McCain was the only clergyman present wearing typical London evening wear, though his black Anglican shirt and stiff white clerical collar clearly marked him as a priest. I had no trouble identifying the representatives of the various religious traditions from their clerical finery: the white robe with a translucent black covering for the Buddhist, Kozan; the bright and imposing scarlet of the tall and heron-thin form of Cardinal Cappellari; the ink black robes of the rabbi and the Russian Orthodox priest (marked by the oddly jagged-shaped black hat that framed his broad face, with his great gray-black beard seeming to square the boxlike effect); and the smooth and exotic elegance (a match for the good Canon McCain's effortless grace) of the Hindu, Viswarath. Then there was the cool white Arabic robe of the little round man al-Khaledis, a little splash of innocence in the gloom.

Holmes entered the room with his brother and McCain, and the three of them sat themselves, forming a full circle. I stood back in the kitchen doorway, staying out of the way and waiting for the kettle to sing.

McCain grimly rose, and the priest began to speak to us in his smooth pastoral manner, grave, measured, suave, and somehow reassuring. He carried authority effortlessly, and I saw how the archbishop of Canterbury could confidently rely on him to represent the church's interests with other nations. In an odd way, he functioned as the Anglican Church's Mycroft Holmes.

How would he begin to tell his fellow clerics of the strange and appalling night ahead of us all? But he had not become the archbishop's man by being inarticulate.

He began, "Gentlemen, it was just this morning that we gathered together in this beautiful church's sanctuary to worship God, though we are of such differing faiths. But before we can be representatives of our religions, we are first each human, and all mortal before the same God. Tonight, it has fallen to me to tell you grave news. Our host, Paul Appel, was, tragically and inexplicably, found dead early this evening. He appears to have been murdered."

As he paused, his head lowered, there was an audible gasp from the circle of clergymen, the shaking of heads, and shocked disbelief. I saw Holmes watching them with the attention of a bird of prey floating above carrion.

"The archbishop of Canterbury," continued Canon McCain,

"has personally asked me to represent him in this terrible circumstance, and we apologize to all of you, as our honored guests, for any inconvenience or distress the investigation will entail. The British government has asked the famed detective Mr. Sherlock Holmes to join us this night, and I know that he will wish to speak to each of you personally. I trust that each of us will cooperate in any way he can, and tell Mr. Holmes and Inspector Lestrade any detail, any fact, that can shed light on Paul Appel's death. Mr. Holmes, if you would tell us how we can help you."

Sherlock Holmes stayed seated. He puffed insistently on his pipe, continuing to look at each of the men. His manner was calm, unhurried. Finally, he spoke quietly: "Gentlemen, in the crypt of this church is more than a simple scene of a crime, but a staggering sin against the tenets of all religion.

"A priest lies dead, a man known to each of you, and I will not disguise from you the peculiar and horrific nature of the killing. His legs and arms are mangled, his clothes shredded back and turned backward. His face is unmarked, and there is not much blood, leading me to conclude he died before the killer began"— he paused, searching for some delicate word—"to cut the flesh."

I looked at the assembled religious men, and they were pale, now absolutely still in disbelief and shock. The stout Buddhist monk, Kozan, closed his eyes and appeared to sink into meditation, his flowing robes a bright night bloom. The other exception was the nearly cadaverous Roman Catholic cardinal in his blood red cassock, who crossed himself.

The only man without a look of horror upon his face was the priest Brown, who sat next to Cardinal Cappellari; his round face was vacant, even bland. He was a soft Christmas pudding of a man. It was as if the young translator were listening to Holmes recite the Nicene Creed instead of describing a grisly murder. I resolved to watch this young cleric carefully, as he turned and whispered into the cardinal's ear.

A powerful-looking man in black with a towering Russian Orthodox priest's hat shook his great head like a dog shuddering off water. Archbishop Demetrius was plainly indignant, his long, flowing gray beard shaking. "No, this is not possible. Someone steal into this church. Perhaps English police here have murdered Appel."

"Under police supervision, the small public congregation left at midday, and no one has entered or left this church today, except for Canon McCain, who left after the Communion service, at about noon," replied Holmes flatly to the emotion of the Russian Orthodox priest. "He was at Lambeth Palace in his offices during the murder, and the archbishop of Canterbury himself verified this to my brother. The implications of these facts are clear." Judging by the sullen, shocked expressions of the gathered suspects (for that is what they now were, despite Mycroft's unease), it was indeed perfectly clear what an ordeal they were all facing. "I will, as the night goes on, summon each of you by turn to be questioned. It is likely to be a long night. Are there any questions?"

The Russian priest sat muttering. He shook his head and, brooding, touched the great golden cross upon his great chest in a sullen slow caress. "Yes. May we contact our embassies tonight? After all, we are in effect being accused of this horrible deed. I to our chief Russian diplomat, and these gentlemen to the Japanese embassy, the Turkish embassy, the German embassy, the Vatican . . ."

It was a reasonable request, but I saw the look of instant horror sweep across Mycroft's face. This investigation would quickly founder if diplomats and religious representatives swarmed over St. Thomas's, obscuring and delaying our every effort.

"Archbishop Demetrius," said Mycroft carefully but insistently, "we *shall* contact your representatives tomorrow. But for now, we shall all stay here, restricted to the church. We vow to protect each of you, and I can assure each of you that my brother is England's foremost private investigator." As Mycroft uttered this, without a trace of false pride or puffery, it occurred to me that this, to one of these men, was no assurance at all. "I think," he continued reasonably, "that this is what we all want at present, for this matter to remain completely private. Think for a moment about the damage to your respective faiths. You do not want this shame to be visited on what you each love the most."

"You speak of our shame," replied the Russian. "I will speak instead of what is the truth. I believe each of these men is innocent, but for now, I will trust you gentlemen. But tomorrow, at dawn, the church doors must open and we have opportunity to seek counsel."

Unhappily, Mycroft, after a swift glance at Canon McCain, nodded his reluctant agreement. The archbishop of Canterbury, after all, had no more leverage than I to hold these men, and Inspector Lestrade's hands were tied with diplomatic and religious pressures. So now the clock was ticking. With dawn, our vested blackbirds would fly, and there was little Sherlock Holmes could do about that, except solve this crime before then.

The rabbi spoke hesitantly, his hands shaking in a tremor, though his voice was firm, a deep, rumbling bass, guttural in a thick German accent. "Mr. Holmes, we have spent three days together, and apart from a brief moment of disagreement, there has been a remarkably amiable spirit among us. I find it incredible that you look at us as suspects in this terrible crime."

Holmes did not reply directly. "Rabbi Mandleberg, there will be, I suspect, layer upon layer of truth to be unveiled tonight. I am prepared to be surprised in all things."

The urbane Hindu, Viswarath, a tall bearded man in a long, shining, blue-black tunic of satin, broke in. He turned to address his fellow clergy, not us, the intruders. "Gentlemen, I am certain none of us have anything to fear. If we were in my country of India, I would hold some apprehension as to English justice, but under the watchful eye of Mr. Mycroft Holmes, I am quite certain we shall be treated fairly. Unlike some administrators of the empire, I do not doubt Mr. Holmes's honesty and goodwill, even to a man of color. For now, let us concentrate our minds in helping you, Mr. Holmes, find this killer. Mr. Appel's death is barbaric."

"I thank you, Mr. Viswarath," Mycroft said, acknowledging the compliment, which came couched in a dare to do justice to them. "You are each under the government's protection and good faith. As I have explained to the police and to my skilled brother, you are each the esteemed guest not only of the archbishop but of the king himself."

The Japanese Buddhist, Kozan, a bald little man, bowed to us and spoke—in a hesitant, soft voice—words that instantly cut through this consoling exchange. "Guests we may be, but we go nowhere until the man who killed my friend is found. Yes? Most of you only met Paul Appel this week, but I have known him for five years as a friend. He has been to Japan two times to talk with my monks. What other Englishman would do this? I think we should think less of our own guilt and think kindly of him now. I do not pray as you do, sirs, but we must here hold silence for his crossing over."

"Yes, thank you, Mr. Kozan, for reminding us of what is truly most important at this moment," McCain hastily replied, perhaps a little abashed he had not first thought to offer a prayer for his fellow Anglican priest. "Gentlemen, please, let us pray for the soul of Paul Appel."

He stood, his tall angular frame towering over us. He raised his left hand in a gesture of benediction. "May God tenderly hold him in his everlasting arms. May our brother Paul safely cross over to the glories of heaven. May his good works earn him eternal salvation. We ask this in your holy name, the God who is God of us all, Father and Sustainer. Amen."

The curate Brown raised his head and in a meek voice added the slightly shocking coda, "And Father, we also pray for the soul of one in mortal danger this night, the one who is in shadow to us, but not from you. For Lord, this man is in shadow now from himself."

The amens were a little anemic to Paul Brown's prayer upon the state of a killer's soul.

Just then the tea whistle blew, so I retreated into the kitchen to take the kettle off the boil. As hesitant conversation commenced in the next room, I let the tea leaves brew as I warmed my hands at the stove. My thigh hurt from the bullet grazing I had suffered some months ago in assisting Holmes, but I did not yet feel tired.

Looking out the window to the alley beyond, I felt sorry for the poor policeman standing in the cold. I could see it was Collins, one of the fellows who had helped me carry the body upstairs from the crypt. There was a strange blue-white cast to the snow still pelting down, giving the back alley a glow like that of the shine of a full moon, though no moon was visible. Holmes appeared by my side, now oddly buoyant, as he sometimes was when his mental skills were being fully tested and engaged. His recent weariness in the kitchen was gone. He had broken the ice and stared down the gathered suspects. The hunt was well begun.

"For now, I will let Mycroft handle the good men in there and all their questions. In the next few hours I am going to test each of them. It should prove interesting, one on one. Clergymen, as McCain earlier implied, can be quite adept at twisting and turning words to their advantage."

I took a sip of tea, and as I did, spat it out immediately. The tea water was odd, tasting of rancid butter and other flavors I could not identify.

"Watson, what is the matter?"

"This tea—it tastes so strange."

Holmes poured out a small sip into his china cup and gently rolled it, sniffing. He sipped it and smiled. "Butter, salt, soda—just the way they brew it in the high Himalayas. An acquired taste, to be sure, Watson. Quite odd."

Just then Lestrade walked into the kitchen and said, "Mr. Holmes, here are the servants, as you requested, for questioning. Where do you want all the clergymen now?"

"When Mycroft is done smoothing their shock, don't you think we should escort them each back to his room? Keep them isolated from one another—no private conversations among them, please."

"I would start the interrogations with Cardinal Cappellari and that small priest, Father Brown," I ventured. "His reaction to your questions earlier was strangely muted, and of course, he was the one who discovered Appel's body."

"The only one down in that vault we know of, Watson. There is nothing saying someone else wasn't down there before or even during his entrance. All right, we'll start with them." He then turned his attention to Lestrade, who stood with the khidmatgars, two small Indian gentlemen in black servant gear.

"Fine, Mr. Holmes. These are Appel's servants, by the name Malik and Harruad Losse."

The two brothers shuffled their feet behind the investigator, keeping their heads down, their hands held behind them. Looking at their submissive stance, I wondered what a dreadful world we lived in, that people such as these felt compelled to display such subservience before whites. I fiercely believed in the moral rightness of our empire, but at the same time I was ashamed that so often we seemed to degrade, not uphold, such men. Better to end our dominion if all we were creating was lesser, not better, men.

The expressionless faces of the Losse brothers had the burnish of dark copper, their faces broad and their black hair closely shaven. They wore the simple and inexpensive servant gear of their class, only with tattered and scuffed buff leather sandals instead of shoes. Their bodies appeared wiry and hard muscled, though so thin that one would have guessed they were almost emaciated, with suspenders clipped to their baggy and low-hanging brown-tweed trousers. Beneath their rolled-up shirtsleeves their lean arm muscles were like knotted rope.

Holmes asked gently, "You are brothers, yes?"

They nodded, and did not speak.

Lestrade continued, "They have papers saying they were born in Mongolia, and were hired by Appel five years ago."

"How is their English?"

"Passable, sir."

"All right, then. Malik and Harruad, I intend to find out who killed your master, and I will need your help. I need you to tell me everything you saw this afternoon. Now, when did you last see Mr. Appel alive?"

Malik, the older brother, who appeared to be about thirty, hesitantly began. "Mister, we clean up church and sweep the aisles. Mr. Appel then paid us for the week. He leave for his meeting, and we go to our rooms."

Lestrade then explained that their rooms, along with the

cook's, lay down a narrow corridor just beyond the kitchen. There was a system of bells that summoned them when needed, and Appel could ring from his bedroom, the dining room, the parlor, and even the pastor's robing room, off the nave, in the church itself.

"Did either of you leave the premises this afternoon?"

"No sir. We stay, in case needed by Mr. Appel."

"How did you happen to come to work for him?"

"Our father was house servant for his uncle, may his name be blessed, Mr. Horace Appel, government man in Delhi," said Malik.

At this information, Holmes cocked an eyebrow toward Mycroft. His brother nodded and added a confirmation.

"I knew Horace well, Sherlock. He was an administrator for the Imports Division of the Colonial Office, stationed for years in Delhi. He died about six years ago."

"Thank you, Mycroft. Very good, then, sirs," said Holmes to the waiting men, whose shining ebony eyes glittered nervously with both anticipation and desperation—in what percentages I could not read, but these men lived in a world where any and all questions from strangers were dangerous. "How did Appel happen to hire you five years ago?"

"We arrived in England by ship with money we saved, and took a letter to Mr. Appel. He happy to see us, sir, and took us in. He say we bring good memories, childhood in India, back to him."

"He treated you both well?"

"Very, very good, sir." I will never forget the attitude of respect—indeed, a look verging on devotion, seconded by his meeker brother—that accompanied Malik Losse's sturdy words: "He was *holy* man, sir. We follow him with great love. Yes, he was good to us, Mr. Holmes."

"Not many servants would use a word such as 'holy' to describe their master," I observed. "What made Mr. Appel someone you so respected?"

Harruad answered this time. "When we come here, he asked us what tradition we follow. We tell him of the Buddha, the Holy One. He listened well to us. He did not make us Christians." With a touch of pride and relief, he haltingly described how he and his brother had been allowed to build a small altar to the Buddha in their bedroom, and how Appel often visited them there, just to sit with them or ask questions. I imagined that little sacred area and the strangely lit scene, their sputtering butter lamp shining upon a small golden Buddha, all hidden away and huddled inside this magnificent edifice to the Christian God. I could not help but admire Appel and what an unusual minister he must have been.

"He did not try to, to . . . ," and Harruad paused, unsure of the word.

"Convert you?" I offered.

With a sudden great smile of tea-stained teeth, Harruad nodded. "Yes, yes sir. He say he much to learn. We pray he pass over well." The brothers both gave a slight bow, their thin hands together in blessing.

Holmes quickly asked the questions no doubt they had already answered from Lestrade. Had they heard anything, seen anything? Any noises, any sign of violence? Had they ever seen anything or anyone that threatened Appel? To which they shook their heads no, no, no. In their reticence, they seemed to withdraw within themselves. They bowed again, and stepped back, and I could see the younger brother choking back a sob. Their grief was so fresh, so real, that it occurred to me in contrast how stiff, how correct, had been the emotional reaction to this man's death by the clergy, with the noble and affecting exception of Kozan.

The detective looked at the Losse brothers for a few moments, with a gentle and mildly surprised gaze. Then, "Very good. No doubt I'll speak to you both again before the night is through. For now, I want you both to return to your room and *stay there*. Do not leave that place, please. Lestrade, please have one of your men go through their room now, and I will inspect it myself as soon as I can."

Lestrade motioned for one of his men to take the attendants back to their room. As soon as the two khidmatgars were out of our hearing, I asked, after Holmes's mild, almost desultory questioning, "Holmes, for goodness' sake, why couldn't the two of them be the killers?"

He shrugged. "Well, for one, they had years of opportunity to kill Appel, at their leisure and without observation." Wearily, he added, "Why wait until the church is full of international visitors? No, it makes no sense. Still, those two know more than they are willing to say, of that I am certain. And their living quarters will need minute inspection as well. Keep them under close supervision, Inspector; they could run at any time, and they may be silent witnesses to much we need to know. And the other servant, Lestrade, a woman . . . ?"

"Yes, a cook. She has a young baby, and their room is back here, down that hallway, behind the food pantry. I thought we should go to her now, before her little boy is asleep."

We walked down the dark corridor about fifteen feet. Lestrade lightly knocked, and after a moment the oak door softly opened a bit. I could see only a sliver of a small young woman, her face in shadow.

She whispered, "A moment, sirs." Then a slim young woman, attractive with raven black hair and smooth walnut skin, dressed in simple white cotton and a stained apron, slipped out of the small room. Unlike the utterly submissive Losse brothers, she did not look down, but rather stared at us with a direct gaze, calm and clear. I found her eyes to be almost disconcerting in their dark drenched beauty, but as Holmes reminded me over and over, I am readily susceptible to female beauty.

"Holmes, this is the priest's cook, a young woman emigrated from northern India. Appel hired her when her husband died here in London three years ago," said Inspector Lestrade. "Her name is Mrs. Senet Desta. Holmes, she knows about Appel's death already."

"Good evening, sirs." She spoke in a lightly accented voice, so soft I had to strain to hear her. "I hope you are well." Her quiet accent brought back to me long-forgotten but delightful memories from my brief posting in India, and a young soldier's amorous adventuring. Then had come my transfer to the plains of Afghanistan, that little taste of hell, and I had never been tempted to ever return to Asia.

"I have been better, Mrs. Desta. How are you and your child doing?" Holmes, who proudly claimed to be totally unaffected by female charms, was at the same time gentle and solicitous with female clients and those he encountered in his work. They seemed to be drawn to his quiet dignity and respectful manner. The hauteur and dismissive comments he privately exhibited toward women seemed to me to be an immature pose, hardly suited to a man of his intelligence. Yet, oddly, women seemed to respond to him as if the public and gentlemanly manner were, in fact, his true sentiment. I dearly hoped it was, but I could never be sure.

"Yes sir," Mrs. Desta whispered. "It is good to know the policemen are here tonight. I worry about my little boy."

"What is his name, and how old is he?"

"His name is Shunapal, and he is just a year." Her stoic façade cracked, and she let out a keening cry, restrained but the more heartrending for her attempt to rein in her grief.

Holmes asked the same questions of her that he had asked the Losse brothers, and received back the same blank look of innocence and firm denials.

"Mrs. Desta, what did you see or hear in the late afternoon?"

"Nothing, Mr. Holmes. I was in the kitchen, preparing the evening meal, barley soup and bread, a sweet pudding. Mr. Appel ordered me to keep meals simple, nothing rich or fancy. A policeman burst in as I was ladling out the soup, and he swept Shunapal and me into our rooms. Later, he let me take trays with dinner to each doorway for our guests, but he stood with me so that I saw and spoke to no one."

"Did you have a good working relationship with Mr. Appel? Did he treat you and your son well?"

"We all respect Master Appel, Mr. Holmes. No one would ever want to hurt him. No one." Senet Desta paused, gazing at us with a beseeching gaze. "Are you certain we are safe, tonight?"

Holmes turned to Lestrade. "Could one of the men outside guard this hallway? I would like Mrs. Desta to feel secure tonight, yet I need her here for more questions later."

Nodding, Lestrade assured the young cook that she and her child would be well protected.

"Then good night, sirs. May I rise at six to begin breakfast? Mr. Appel would not have wanted you gentlemen to be hungry."

"That would be appreciated, Mrs. Desta. Thank you; I trust Shunapal will not be awakened tonight, though I cannot rule out speaking to you again tonight."

As my friend was speaking, a lithe little boy squeezed out of the door and clung to his mother's dress. Mrs. Desta looked down at him, her expression affectionate and fearful all at once. Gently she brushed back his shining black hair, and the child delightedly reached out for her face with a puny fist. He looked younger than a year, small and thin and evidently energetic, with his mother's large and luminous dark eyes. Then the small child turned and stared at Holmes, his face suddenly and oddly still, studying my friend.

Then Holmes, to my astonishment, leaned down and smiled broadly to the child, holding out his hand. Holmes and little children, much less babies, did not normally mix, excepting his network of informants and messengers he proudly called his Irregulars. These toughened street rats he treated with gruff directness and startlingly generous coinage. Sentimental he was not, but something in the tiny boy touched him. Gently he inspected the bandages wrapped upon the child's forehead and ears.

Clinging to Mrs. Desta's black dress with a grip that was fearful, Shunapal suddenly laughed and slapped at the detective's hand.

"We will be watching you and your child carefully," said Holmes, and he offered a slight bow, as if to a diminutive little Buddha.

As we reentered the kitchen area, Holmes mused, "Quite an impressive young woman. Her English is quite remarkable."

I remembered her slight bow to us as she retreated back into the dark of her quarters, and the lingering of a scent, an intoxicating vanilla musk. Holmes was not caught in reverie, however.

"Still, I am disquieted," he continued, "by Mrs. Desta's lack of forthrightness. I'm certain that she, as well as the Losse brothers, knows something crucial to this business." He smiled tightly and waved them away for the moment. "Now let's start again with that tea. The church isn't getting any warmer." He robustly called out, "Mycroft, will you and Canon McCain join me for the questioning? Midnight beckons."

So the night of questioning the clergymen began.

Looking back upon Holmes's interrogations through that long night, they were indeed a frustrating experience, as McCain had warned us they would be. I will spare the reader the endless succession of repetitious questions from Holmes that each in turn so deftly fielded, for the case would later turn on quite different measures.

Yet I include some flavor of these interactions because I was fascinated by the power of their distinctive personalities, and also to convey something of their agile skills, and a little subtle deviousness. To this day I have never met individuals who awed me quite as these men did. And I was not particularly prepared to be impressed by them at all, with my own lack of interest in organized religion; in fact, "wary" and "slightly cynical" would properly convey my mood.

Were they so intriguing to me because they were, to my now staid Church of England soul (lapsed though it was), so exotic, so very unusual? I think not.

In fact, despite their differing accents and all the varied vestments they so proudly exhibited, what impressed me was interesting qualities they appeared to share. Each was a leader of his faith for a reason; they were all highly intelligent, and also, as we saw, oh so clever. Most possessed a sly humor and, despite the desperate circumstances in which they found themselves, could be witty and engaging, even Demetrius with his dark moodiness.

I even saw that, somewhat to his surprise, Holmes found himself enjoying the intense questioning of these men, the probing and prodding and seeking the essential mistake, the crucial opening into the heart of this baffling case. I even found myself, in the first two hours of these interviews, briefly forgetting at times that one of these charming and sophisticated men was a killer.

Canon McCain explained to us, as we waited for the first questioning, that Cardinal Luigi Cappellari was only unofficially representing Pope Leo XIII. "He holds himself fairly aloof from our discussions, yet we are delighted he is here at all. Cardinal Vaughan personally appointed the young priest Paul Brown to act as a translator to our Italian visitor, but do not be fooled, Cappellari knows and understands more than he pretends. He is a brilliant politician, a knight of the Curia around the aging pope. He could well become the next pontiff."

"I appreciate your forthrightness, Mr. McCain. Please bring them both in, Lestrade."

The two Roman Catholic priests were seated down before us, the senior man haggard and thin, the cardinal's eyes sad and almost bruised with gray. Under his black and scarlet cardinal's biretta, his hair was curled long and stark white. Before Holmes could begin, Cardinal Cappellari began to speak in a cascade of rapid Neapolitan-accented Italian.

"His Eminence wishes first to pay his respects for the services you have quietly offered to our Holy Father over the last twenty years," Brown translated in his flat Norfolk accent.

"Yes, I have managed to restrain Dr. Watson from publishing those sensitive cases. The Vatican does not like scandal, and neither do I. Please relate to His Holiness that I continue to be at his service when needed."

"These particular cases might have caused great consternation among the faithful," conceded the prelate, and his relief was palpable. Indeed, the public had almost no understanding how many cases Holmes had secretly handled in Rome, none of which I assisted him with. I stayed close to my London medical

practice, and Holmes's many Continental cases were mostly beyond my purview.

"Mr. Holmes, you have shown yourself a patron of the
truth," continued the elderly cardinal. His bright brown eyes
glittered, and for a moment we saw the engaged and eager per-
sonality that had made him invaluable to the pope. "We want to
do what we can tonight to assist you. The man who committed
this killing must be held accountable."

Brown, as before, betrayed no fear, or even evident interest,
as he deftly translated his superior's rapid Italian. Brown's voice
was meek, almost a whisper. His placid eyes were a fishy gray,
and he stared at us with an odd turtlelike gaze, appearing not to
need to blink. He was an unsettling young man, and he gave me
the shivers.

As opposed to the curate's slumped relaxation, Cardinal Cappellari sat stiffly in a formal and, it appeared, painfully rigid
pose. His red robes trembled slightly as he haltingly breathed in
and out. This man was never going to assume the papacy, I
thought. As a doctor, I gave him three more years of life, and
even those delicately poised on the edge. Yet I also sensed in him
still a residue of wiry peasant strength. Could he have killed
Appel? Perhaps he was not as delicate as he appeared.

"Ask His Eminence why he consented to attend such an unlikely council."

After a brief consultation, young Brown answered for the
cardinal. "He says he was instructed to. The pope is not adverse
to certain accommodations to Modernism, so quiet and veiled
discussions with other faiths such as this are possible—but we
make no promises, no commitments. The American Catholic
church had numerous representatives at the Chicago World's
Parliament of Religions, including Cardinal Gibbons of Balti-
more, but the reaction to the cardinal's presence there was not
uniformly positive."

"Tell me a little more about your impressions of Mr. Appel, both before this gathering and during it."

"He says our host was a man of great sophistication and, seemingly, profound erudition. The cardinal says he enjoyed his conversation and his ability to keep difficult conversations at a mild, engaging level. He is profoundly heartsick at the murder of a man who opened his church and his hospitality to all of us." Indeed, the cardinal's long expressive face was drawn and sorrowful, a harrowing El Greco countenance. I saw a tremble in his great peasant hands, great blue knotted veins under thin sallow skin chapped from the winter air. He and Holmes talked generally for ten minutes or so, as we learned something of the old man and why he found himself in the strange position of being hidden away in an Anglican church over Christmas, so far from his accustomed Vatican apartments.

"Where were you late this afternoon, from two-thirty to four o'clock?" Holmes asked, more to the translator, Brown, than to the elderly cardinal.

"The cardinal and I were together, in the double room directly off the kitchen. He was engaged in paperwork, and I was reading—that is, until I chose to take that walk."

The detective turned to Cappellari. "Is this so, Your Eminence?"

The old man nodded wearily, exhausted. Holmes asked several more informational questions, then mercifully ended the interview.

"Please thank the cardinal for his patience and his understanding."

"He says he hopes you catch the animal who did this act."

The old man rose and bowed, a gallant and gentle man. He rose and unfolded like an exotic crane, and actually towered over the six-foot Holmes, even with his stooped shoulders. Holmes shook the cardinal's hand.

"Good night, Mr. Sherlock Holmes, and we are happy to help if you need us again," the red-robed prelate said haltingly in English.

"I will call on you when you are needed," said Holmes.

As the two priests left the kitchen, Holmes looked at his brother, who had been seated with McCain. Neither had said a word during the questioning. As soon as Lestrade had closed the door behind them, he asked Mycroft, "What think you, brother?"

"Cappellari is a dead man, and Brown is a nonentity. No murderer there, Sherlock. The cardinal looked incapable, as you noted, of such a thing—it looks as if he could hardly attack his steak at dinner with knife and fork."

"Yes," said Holmes cautiously, "you may be right about the good cardinal. What about his health, Watson? Would he have the strength to literally shred a human body like that?"

"Yes, I think so. The cardinal is plainly quite ill, but we are strangely capable of unlikely acts of strength and stamina if motivated enough. Who knows? I would not rule him out."

Holmes considered this, then turned back to his brother. "But you are quite wrong about the young man, Mycroft. Father Brown bears watching, and listening to. Watson loves to write down my most complex cases, but he ignores all the stunningly mundane times the criminal is simply the first one to 'find' the body. Killers are not, as a rule, very bright or original. No, the fellow first kneeling by the corpse is all too often the killer. While I am not sanguine about this being true tonight, still, believe me, we should pay close attention to the little priest. He might be the slyest one of them all."

There were so many questions Holmes needed answers to that I hardly knew where he must turn first. But he snapped, "Watson, I need you to help me inspect Appel's office. I'll get to his personal rooms and bedchamber as soon as I can, but I noted something strange when inspecting his body."

"Everything about his corpse was strange, even fiendishly macabre, Holmes."

"True enough, Watson, but I'm not talking about the bizarre aspects of his body, the clothes, the flaying of the limbs . . . No, I am talking about something easily overlooked because it is rather prosaic. Did you notice what was missing?"

"I'm sorry, I don't follow you, Holmes."

"On the body there were no papers, no appointment book, or anything at all helpful to a parish minister's duties in his pockets, not even a church key. I have to conclude the killer took away everything personal from his body. But perhaps in his office we will find a wall calendar, or notes upon a desk pad, or bits in a wastepaper basket. Surprising how often a case turns on refuse and scraps."

As we were shown to the small, orderly oak-paneled study, Holmes muttered, "The answers to this case are still in the church, I am convinced. Besides, it always pays to closely examine the texture of a man's life, his calendar, his habits, whatever I can find that helps me understand him. This was no random killing—something in Appel's life somehow attracted this violence."

"Holmes, years ago I used to think solving a killing was simply finding the criminal; now, I think we are really unveiling the one murdered, uncovering everything. We have to first solve the man who is dead."

"Aptly put, Watson. Which is why this trade of mine can be such a grisly business, an autopsy in more ways than one. We will have to pry our way into this man's secrets, his cast of mind."

Along the hallway leading to the pastor's office there was a placid parade of paintings of previous Kensington ministers, and at the last place, instead of a painting, there was a large recent studio photograph of Paul Appel. We both gazed at his formal portrait, the dead priest staring back at us in his stiff priestly pose, this formal face somehow a mask. Appel's aristocratically handsome face was narrow, unruffled, and a touch arrogant. He was smooth shaven, and his receding hair glowed white under the photographer's lamps. I guessed his hair must have been a sandy hue (probably beginning to gray at the temples); it was parted in the middle, thin at the crown, giving his forehead a noble prominence. I stared at the portrait for quite a long time, wondering how this estimable Anglican priest had ended up on the stone floor below us, a tattered carcass.

"His eyes are cold, set far apart, which gives him an abstracted, distant look," said Holmes. "The narrow and patrician nose and the thin structure of his face make him appear delicate, precise, certainly a little intellectually haughty."

Holmes was right, there was nothing of warmth in the portrait, and the sense I received of the man was of someone who loved ideas perhaps more than people. In short, a cerebral soul, and certainly a forceful presence.

There was a strange glittering anger flitting in those hooded eyes, a look I had seen in other charismatic men who found success early in life. In an odd way, McCain's earlier cautious, even slightly disdainful description of his fellow Anglican signaled that perhaps here would have been a portrait of McCain's future rival within the church.

Yet something beyond even this in this portrait left me uneasy. I found myself extremely glad I had never had to deal with this man in life.

The priest's office was immaculate and supremely ordered,

not a paper or book out of place. It was the opposite of the ornate and elaborate splendor of the sitting room, a private enclave where work was supreme.

"You must love this orderly space, Watson, as much as you have complained over the years of the clutter of my collecting." Holmes sat himself in Appel's desk chair and leaned back, his hands together, rubbing absently along his sharp chin, trying to sense something of the murdered priest here in this sanctum and retreat. I readily agreed; Holmes truly was a pack rat. Yet beyond the preciseness, there was an odd sterility about Appel's study, something austere that fit my reading of the visage we had just contemplated. The only note of softness in this place was a photo of a lovely young woman, held in a small ornate silver frame that sat on the fireplace mantel. I wondered who she was. Holmes looked for a moment at the beautiful young woman's picture.

"Did Appel have any siblings?" I asked.

Holmes, now riffling through a desk drawer, answered, "I think not; didn't Canon McCain say Appel was an only child? I think his parents' photo is here on the desk, proper Victorian missionaries. Where would the Chinese heathen be without them? No, Watson, I think that woman's picture might be Appel's lost fiancée."

Gazing at her portrait, momentarily mesmerized by her warmth and graceful manner, I rather gracelessly added, "The more fool he for losing her."

"Come, Watson, cast your mind on something other than the opposite sex. The lass is likely far, far away from this case, and I sense something important for us lies in this room."

For the next twenty minutes, Holmes methodically went through every paper on the desk, in the drawers, and any personal object that Appel kept close at hand in his study. I was no more successful prowling about the rest of the office and quickly looking through his files, mostly old sermon manuscripts and notes from church meetings. I knew Holmes would want to go through all this again himself, but I applied myself to the task, though the reams of religious rhetoric were numbing to my sensibility.

Dispirited, I went to the fireplace and took a poker to stir the ashes. Only a few dimming embers were still glowing. Holmes saw and joined me, kneeling down to begin to sift through the blackened dust.

"Capital idea, Watson. I suspect this office is as picked clean as the poor fellow's pockets, which means whoever came here might well have wanted to burn something crucial."

After a precise and minute inspection sifting through the hot ashes, he at last grunted and rose. Delicately, he held aloft what he had found, a charred metal wire.

"The binding of a wall calendar, Watson. Someone *has* been here before us. The pockets emptied below in the crypt, a calendar burned here. I only pray they did not have the time to completely rifle through his files."

Encouraged, he knelt back down and I joined him, both of us careful not to burn ourselves. We found many small bits of torn paper, most charred and now unreadable. We tried to read the nearly burned remnants as best we could, and almost all of them were either unreadable or inconsequential. At last, curled under the rear leg of the Hessian fire iron, I spied a larger bit of unburned paper, and I delicately extracted it. A tightly curled comma of a tag end of a December calendar page, it was just a grayed slip. Holding it up, I could just make out, in a barely legible pencil notation, the phrase *Victoria, NUMBLND, 22.*

Carefully scrutinizing it, Holmes was delighted. "Excellent, Watson, though we don't know what the phrase means. I would think it refers to Victoria Station. Well, it will come clear. Everything else here seems to have been efficiently burned and destroyed." He brushed off his gray soiled knees and proceeded even more methodically to inspect Appel's office. Together we inspected every inch of the study, and though it took some time Holmes eventually found, by plunging his hands deep into the folds of a rose plush velvet couch, a small black book.

"Watson, I've found something," he cried delightedly. "Our unknown visitor perhaps missed something crucial. Perhaps Appel was interrupted and simply shoved it down. It seems to be Appel's daily appointment diary." He immediately started thumbing through it. "Perhaps our Rosetta Stone?"

"Or perhaps," I suggested with a smile, "the little calendar slipped out of his pocket as he sipped a sherry after service this morning. Clergy have been known to nap at a moment's notice."

"Not this high-strung one, Watson," Holmes grunted, grateful that we had found anything personal at all. But his high hopes were quickly chastened. He hastily read through the little black book, but after a few minutes, with a sigh, Holmes was forced to conclude Appel's appointment book seemed to contain nothing exceptional, merely pastoral appointments, notes for sermons, odd personal items that seemed quite innocuous, even tedious.

"I shall give this little book," he added, "greater scrutiny when I have the time. Which I fear is what we are running out of, and we've only just begun here." The only thing that attracted my companion's attention was an ornate series of doodlings inside the back cover of the daily appointment book. Composed of stunningly distinctive lettering, with the elegant script of a quite talented penman, Appel had repeatedly written the simple phrase "The White City." The vision of this Parliament of Religions in Chicago, I thought, must have truly obsessed this man.

Holmes then took a cursory look through the minister's papers, vowing to return later in the night. "A thorough inspection will take several hours," he concluded, closing a file drawer. "Time is pressing; it's time we interview more of our suspects." After a quick look around Appel's small bedroom, we were walking out the door when he stopped, suddenly attracted by several framed etchings on Appel's bedroom wall. Against the Morris rose wallpaper there were ten small intricate and quite lovely scenes of China, Japan, and Tibet, lovingly arranged.

"As someone who has traveled in the East," said Holmes, his eyes carefully surveying the Asian scenes, washes of ink upon cream paper, "I can readily see that my interest is nothing compared to Paul Appel's. Look at the scores of cultural and religious books on these lands, some quite rare and technical, in his bookcase. His attraction and absorption in Eastern religions is impressive."

I added, "After all, he twice visited our man Kozan in Japan for training, in what-did-they-say?"

"In something called sitting meditation. I tried it several times, but it didn't take. I prefer the pipe. Let's talk to that Buddhist monk next." Holmes paused. "Whatever else this man was, there was something precise and glacial in Mr. Appel. And I know the kind of man that is, my friend, for I see him in the shaving mirror every morning."

The Japanese Buddhist priest, Kozan, was (as McCain somewhat warily and stiffly informed us) quite a wily and jovial character. It of course would have been impossible not to notice his traditional robes, marking his Japanese Buddhist order. But Kozan would have stood out among his fellows even if he had been outfitted with dull Scottish parson's tweed, with his piercing green-brown eyes and shining gold tooth. Small, obese, and loose jointed, he greeted us as if we were old friends.

Nodding to us kindly, he then proceeded to fold his legs together in a meditative pose upon the couch across from us. Kozan gazed at us benignly. He adjusted his glasses, which somehow looked odd being worn by an Asian monk. His forehead was smooth and his bald head glistened, as if he polished himself each day like an apple.

"I understand English, sirs, so you may proceed," he said in a low murmur. "I speak not as well, though Paul Appel teach me much of the twists of your language."

"Where are you from in Japan, sir?"

"I am from the Enpuku-ji Monastary, in Yawata, near Kyoto. Large center for training of monks." He proceeded to tell us in a quite entertaining manner about his life in the ancient Buddhist monastery, and as he talked, he slightly rocked back and forth, a subtle delight bubbling up from within the monk. This was not what I expected of a Japanese holy man.

"Tell me a little about your presence at this gathering, Mr. Kozan," asked Holmes kindly.

The fat man grinned, nodding his head. "*Ch'an* can be practiced here or there, no difference. Great secret meeting appealed to me, so I come."

"I must ask, what is *ch'an?*"

"I ask questions, like you, Mr. Holmes. For six hundred years, we do *ch'an*, what you call, I believe, meditate. But we do more, for in Rinzai Zen we reach satori by asking koans."

" 'Satori' meaning enlightenment?"

"Yes, Mr. Holmes. I sense you know something of Buddhism."

I spoke up. "My friend Holmes traveled for some time in India and Tibet. He talks often of Buddhism, your pessimistic beliefs. But I have never heard of these questions, what you call koans."

The monk laughed delightedly. "I hear this pessimism talk.

No, no. To reach satori is to become awake, that is all. The Buddha was great optimist, thinking eightfold path can end suffering. For anyone. You like suffering?"

"No," I replied. "I relieve it as a doctor."

"Yes, yes," he nodded eagerly. "Buddha a doctor of the whole life. We of the Rinzai school ask questions of students to wake up them. We train mind, make big jumps in—how do you say it?—realization. Realize what *is*. The right question blast away all illusions. We solve the koan, just as you now solve this killing."

Holmes studied the Buddhist master, as if wondering where to go next. "My questions are not fancy or philosophical, Mr. Kozan. But they will wake us to the truth. I understand you knew Paul Appel before this week?"

"Indeed yes. He visited me in Yawata four years ago. We write. He try sitting meditation. Then he return last year. I happy to be invited to come to this meeting. However, only good friendship bring me to cold London. Yellow fog, bad smells." He described in some detail how the two visits by Appel had opened a channel to the Anglican Church, and how delighted he had been to be asked to travel west to his friend's home city.

"For a friend of Mr. Appel's, you seem somewhat jovial," I said sharply.

The monk serenely looked at me, not dismayed by my harsh remark. "Rebirth come soon enough. The death of body no great thing, Dr. Watson. To cry now is like sadness over snuffing out candle when you have lighted another. My friend is fine, sir."

"Would you help us find his killer?" Holmes asked.

"Certainly, yes. Compassion says I must help this person, this man who did great wrong. Guilt is a heavy weight to carry over."

"Very good, then, Mr. Kozan. Did you hear or see anything that could help us? Your room is directly placed over the spot where Appel was killed."

"I was asleep for some hours, then I woke to strange noise. About four o'clock, sound of faint shout, covered by stone. But I listened more, harder."

Holmes leaned forward with eagerness. "Yes?"

"Sound of laughter. Ha! Ha!" The squat monk leaned back and crinkled his almond black eyes.

We walked down the silent hallways of the guest section of the parish house. The bedroom-section corridors were simple, with the occasional small stand of simple white marble devotional sculpture. The rooms were placed along the outside of a large square, and along the hallway there were occasional windows looking out into a private mediation garden, which was now a fairy sweep of strange snow shapes and small kneeling trees whose limbs hung burdened by white.

Canon McCain was talking of the imposingly tall Russian Orthodox priest, Aleksandr Demetrius. "Like Cardinal Cappellari, Demetrius is a quiet power behind the patriarch in Constantinople, and thus represents the interests of all the Eastern Orthodox churches. Frankly, Mr. Holmes, we are delighted he is here at all, because the thinking was he might not come at all. You know, we Anglicans concentrate so much upon our separation from the Roman Catholic Church during the Reformation that we too often, and tragically, forget that Christianity had already suffered an even more painful schism."

"Which was?" I asked.

Holmes chuckled. "My friend Watson is a most useful associate, Canon. He asks obvious questions, so I don't have to."

Canon McCain paused. "For a thousand years, the Christianity of the West has been separated from the Eastern Orthodox churches, and I believe we lost sight of them to our own loss. Demetrius is a crucial figure at this gathering. Christianity cannot be whole without the Orthodox churches, and ecumenical co-operation can never happen if the divisions within Christianity cannot be healed. That is why he's so important."

Archbishop Demetrius, whose grizzled beard extended far over his bulging stomach, answered Holmes's firm knock. He peered at us quizzically, a solemn man with sleepy eyes, and his imposing bulk seemed to fill the little room. At last, after an odd pause, he muttered, "Yes, gentlemen, come in."

Upon his desk was a small brazier, where the archbishop was brewing tea. There was also the sour whiff of old cabbage soup. As we squeezed into the tiny room, the archbishop inquired if we wanted a small glass of tea. "God gives a blessing," he said as he bent to pick up his open Bible upon his bed to give us a place to sit. In what seemed the Orthodox fashion, he placed a moist kiss upon the book.

"No, Archbishop Demetrius, thank you. I have just a few questions."

"Please. Be comfortable, ask what you need." Then the man raised a beefy steak of a hand to halt us. "But first I say this, Mr. Holmes. I apologize for my comments tonight about London police—I was in shock, first hearing of this dreadful thing. It is a bad dream." He shuffled back to his bed with a shambling walk, his left foot dragging behind him. His walking stick stabbed into the plush brown carpeting as he heaved himself down heavily upon the unmade bed. His gray cassock, half unbuttoned, was bespeckled with buttery crumbs of his dinner toast. Over that he wore a long unbuttoned black surplice with wide, full sleeves.

As Holmes questioned Demetrius, with much the same queries he had just offered Kozan and the cardinal (and the weirdly blithe curate, Brown), the huge Orthodox priest passionately pleaded ignorance of any aspect of the killing. As he loudly and yet deftly rebuffed any such knowledge, I found myself watching the man in sheer fascination.

In size, bulk, and effect, no man could be a greater opposite in existence to the lean Luigi Cappellari. While our cardinal was subtle, sophisticated, spider thin, this Russian priest was earthy, insistent, overweight, a little boisterous, and brutally direct. I found myself thinking of him as a kind of ecclesiastical Falstaff (I wondered if he had a flagon of wine stowed beneath his sagging bed frame for the instant we would depart). Yet under his copious sweating brow, his eyes were narrow and shrewd, watching us with a still-untrusting glint. Despite his evident "paranoiac" suspicion of us (a term I had recently picked up from a Viennese doctor whose work in the subconscious I was finding quite helpful in assessing the people Mr. Sherlock Holmes exposed me to), he answered Holmes's questions. Though, of course, he, and every other man this night, had good reasons to fear our queries.

"I arrive in London a week ago," he said repeatedly, "and did not know the priest. I know nothing." He had a strange habit of waving his hands along each cheek in rhythm with his disclaimers and rolling his eyes upward, as if in supplication to God to swear by him. His skin was pockmarked and abnormally pale; he was a man who had obviously lived through worse winters than this English season. His face was broad, with high Slavic cheeks and wet lips. Despite his limp, he emanated great force and strength as he clutched the worn gold handle of his walking stick, which bore the fierce head of a little Russian bear.

"What was the nature of your interaction with Mr. Appel over the last three days?"

Demetrius glared at Holmes. My friend stared back, his gray

eyes a studied and steady amiability. It was as if Holmes had all night to wait, though I knew well inwardly he was seething with fierce impatience.

At last, the Russian finally replied. "Very little, sir. We chat once or twice, not more. In long meetings, he spoke much and I very little. I am here to listen."

"You stayed in his church for three days, and ate with him and sipped tea with him and stared at him as you talked of the future, and you formed no opinion?"

"This Englishman, he did not speak for the archbishop of Canterbury." He turned to Canon McCain. "You, sir, do. This Appel, he was just a priest, here to house us. I mean nothing unkind by this. Sir, he did not impress me at all. Charming. English smooth manners. Though these are not traits I trust or value very highly. Let me be very clear again, Mr. Holmes: Are you saying one of us kill this man? That I could have cut him down?"

"I imply nothing of the kind," Holmes calmly replied. "But someone did, and I trust you feel a sense of obligation, as a man of God and as a person of honor, to help me find who did. My job is very simple. I do not have to judge this man, just to discover who he is. I leave it to my betters, the politicians and the judges, to finish this thing."

"Yes, I see. God, too, will do some judging here." Demetrius sipped his tea, and considered. He was gruff, but still somehow engaging, if not exactly likable. He emanated a burly charisma. "You are the kind of man, Mr. Holmes, I am not used to meeting." He paused and considered.

"Investigators, Mr. Holmes, in my country are simple men, and do the will of our tsar with a blind will and iron hands, in dark and unseen places. Justice sometimes does not enter their thinking." He rubbed his mottled face, and he sighed again. "You see why I do not immediately respond to your requests. My experience of police is not—what is the word?— reassuring. But yes, I must help you. We are all safer the more you learn."

"Thank you, Your Holiness. Now, what did you do after the gathering for tea at two o'clock?"

"I read scripture here. I prepare letter for the patriarch to post tomorrow on course of conference. We of the Eastern Church have learned to be patient. My church preserves the ancient rituals and liturgies. You have much to learn from us, the sense of God's mystery. Maybe another Parliament of Religions will remind you how we have preserved traditions of the early church."

After ten more minutes of somber and pointed questioning, Holmes satisfied himself that the priest had not seen or heard anything suspicious during the critical hours. So Holmes rose to leave the Russian to his black tea.

"Your Holiness, if anything important comes to you, do not hesitate to contact me. I believe danger is still present."

"What do you mean?" The archbishop hesitated.

"The killer is still among us, and it will be very hard to escape from this church. Policemen ring this place. Thus, I cannot rule out further violence as our man attempts to break free. I assure you, though I am just beginning my questioning, a very tight web is already wrapped around the church, and an attempt to flee will shortly be his only option."

"I pray your web is tight, Mr. Holmes. God help us all." Then the great hulking priest turned, his voluminous robes rustling. With a characteristic grunt, Demetrius said farewell as we were ushered out.

"Quite a handful, indeed," I said once we were down the hall and out of hearing. "A good example of the sunny Russian character. I'm glad, Sherlock, you assured him you were not a member of King Edward's secret police."

"Although a little torture in the Tower before this night is over might not be amiss, Watson. These are damned hard fellows to read." He consulted his vest watch, his sensitive, elegant hands caressing the gold case. "It's past ten, and we still have to question Viswarath, al-Khaledis, and the good Rabbi Mandleberg."

McCain said simply, "The night Vigils have begun."

Four

VIGILS

St. Thomas's Church, the Great Silence

Canon McCain shifted nervously in his chair. We were back in the kitchen with Mycroft and Inspector Lestrade. "Did you mean it, sir, when you spoke of more violence?"

"Well, yes," said Holmes, adding new tobacco to his smoldering pipe and striking a match. "The situation for our killer is desperate, as I told the archbishop. Yet frankly, I am purposely playing up the image of a tightening net in hopes our man will get nervous enough to make a mistake, or at least take a run for cover far too soon. Flushing out the killer would be as effective as all the inspired deduction in the world." He rose and paced, a lithe panther confined in far too small a cage. "You know, I have not properly scouted out the church's layout. Understanding the physical layout of these buildings could be crucial to this case. Lestrade, before we interview the others, I was wondering if you could find me a proper blueprint for the church."

"I'll see what I can find, Mr. Holmes. I think I saw a framed architect's plan in the west side of the nave, near the font."

"Excellent. So let's take a little stroll. Canon McCain, would you accompany us, tell us a little about what we are seeing? I am forced to know a great deal about many things for my trade, but ecclesiastical bric-a-brac—there I am lacking, I'm afraid."

With trembling hands gripping the edge of the table, McCain stared at Holmes. "Why do I have the feeling you cover up your unease about religion with all these jocular, offhand statements?" McCain quickly retorted. "Great artists have poured their soul into their craft to aid believers in feeling closer to the divine, and you label it 'bric-a-brac.' " The normally pale divine's face was hot with red blotches, and he was clearly ready to engage Holmes again, this time in anger.

For once, Holmes was quickly abashed. "Canon, this business is too serious for my levity. My apologies; you are quite correct. I readily admit I am out of my depth in this kind of setting, which is why I so need your help and guidance."

The minister was clearly taken aback by Holmes's instant and apparently heartfelt apology, and his added request for assistance. He nodded, mollified. "Of course. I'm sorry, I don't mean to be so sensitive, Mr. Holmes, but this is all too much to absorb. I am here to help you in any way I can."

As Inspector Lestrade went off in search of an architectural blueprint of this spectacular new church and its adjoining parish house, Holmes led us through the great red doors leading back into the great ornate sanctuary of St. Thomas's. As we entered the church, Holmes's glinting eyes closely observed every detail, as if the building were itself a suspect.

I knew his way of working. He needed to settle into the feel of the locale, as if every picture, statue, memorial brass, wooden railing, and gleaming piece of Communion silver could somehow unveil the obscurity of this unnerving and utterly barbaric act. There was nothing mystical about the process, but Holmes scouted every detail with an artist's sensibility as to what was misaligned, what was ajar or misplaced. He believed disturbed dust seldom betrayed the truth.

"The church is still very new, in fact not completely decorated. The architect died before its completion," McCain said quietly as we entered the dark security of the church. (Odd, I thought, that our conversation so quickly hushed; how sacred space so quickly reduces us to a whisper.) "As the population of south Westminster, Kensington, and Chelsea grew, we knew we needed a magnificent church to hold them. It is Gothic Perpendicular, but nothing about it is ordinary or following any strict rule. In fact, St. Thomas's is a centerpiece of what we call the Arts and Crafts movement, with freedom and expression of the English spirit at the fore. There is nothing musty about this church, gentlemen."

As long as the nave was, the church was also notable for being quite broad (in fact, McCain informed us, it was wider than St. Paul's Cathedral), with two long nave arcades, north and south, on either side of the central pews, each supported with elegant and thin Tuscan columns, each pillar with its flaring capitals of lotus and palmette frieze, with flowing stone foliation, creating an airy, open feel that was almost gardenlike. High above us, the cream-and-gold high-embowed roof, with its thin and intricate ribbed vaulting, was, even in the dark of night, breathtaking and spacious.

The canon led us past the rood screen and past the deep oak choir seating, past the golden eagle lectern and the high and covered wooden pulpit facing it, and toward the altar. "The vestry robing area is to the left, with the exit stairs to the crypt, the Lady Chapel to the right beyond the screen, and here is the most holy site of the whole church."

"The altar triptych." I said. "Could you tell us what it represents?"

"The reredos, under the hanging cross of our Lord, is fascinating, quite stunning, Dr. Watson. William Morris outdid himself here, I think. The left section is the *Denial of Peter*, the right is the *Supper at Emmaus*, and the center, as you might guess, presents the *Incredulity of Thomas*. Christ is presenting his open palms to a kneeling Thomas."

"Thomas, the patron saint of detectives," muttered Holmes, not in jest this time. McCain was the rarest of men, being able to back off my arrogant friend. "It is our lot to doubt everything, even things we revere."

Above the altarpiece was a stained glass window of four tall panels of light, of a serpent coiled round the world, a crook and a lamb, a plow, and, above it all, the intertwined Greek letters alpha and omega.

"And the east window?" I asked, our steps echoing along in the vast sanctuary.

"Every church, gentlemen, is a book to be read. You just have to know the symbols. The serpent is the sinful nature of the world. There, the lamb and the plow represent Abel, and the crook next to it symbolizes his blighted brother. The flame on the stone altar at the center of the glass is the burnt offering of the Jewish people to the Lord. All these images of sacrifice are all held under eternity, the beginning and the end as one . . ."

Mycroft, who seemed to bristle whenever religious rhetoric gilded the cleric's conversation, quickly interrupted McCain. "You stood at the altar this morning, there?" He pointed beyond the huge iron screen that separated the sanctuary from the chancel, beyond the transept crossing.

"Yes. As we should have, we offered public Holy Communion this morning. For security reasons, the participants of the gathering were seated with subtle police protection separating them from the general worshipers, up here along those choir stalls. All chose, as a mark of respect, to attend, except the cardinal, though Father Brown watched from the robing room there, not in the sanctuary."

"Isn't it unusual for people of such differing faiths to partake of Communion?" Holmes interjected.

"They were there, though most of our guests, like our English translator Father Brown, of course did not partake of Communion. That would have been inappropriate. As I mentioned, Paul Appel, being the host priest, assisted me."

At this point I spied Lestrade's lean form making his way up the aisle to us, holding a rolled architect's plan. He sheepishly admitted he had slipped it out from its frame, all for a higher purpose.

"Excellent, Lestrade," said Holmes, pleased. This was what he liked: detail, and lots of it, not this cascade of symbols. "I think I'm starting to get my bearings, but let's just see how all this relates. The altar is not the place to look over these plans properly, but the vestry here is fine. May we, Canon McCain?"

"Fine." He stepped to his left and led us down the footpace of the altar area and turned on the light to the small robing area. A brass bracket gasolier with an ornate floral glass globe gave us a warm golden light, and soon we were looking over the intricate floor plans of this unusual church.

"Very few churches in London have a parish house attached to the church, much less a modified monastery series of guest rooms," explained McCain. "No wonder the archbishop wanted us housed here," he added, indicating with a sweep of his hand the unusual arrangement of the small bedrooms attached to Appel's parish house. There in the detailed survey of the parish house was the small garden area that had attracted my attention earlier; and arranged around the garden, the eight guest rooms.

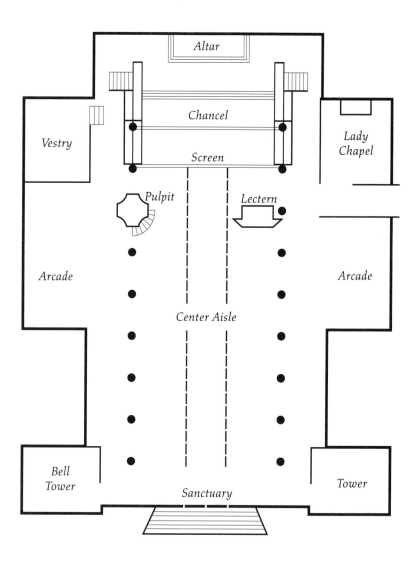

Sloane Street

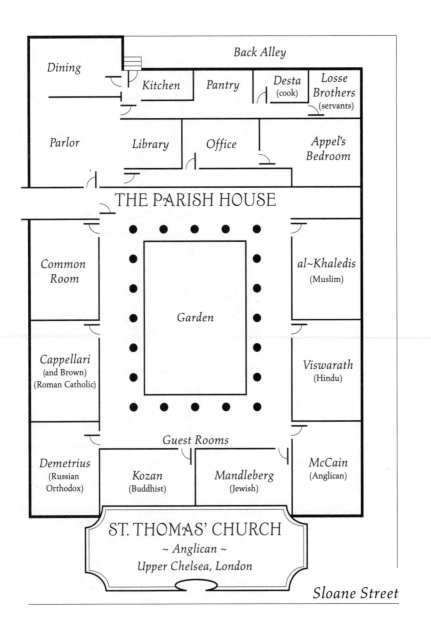

Back Alley

Dining

Kitchen

Pantry

Desta
(cook)

Losse
Brothers
(servants)

Parlor

Library

Office

Appel's
Bedroom

THE PARISH HOUSE

Common
Room

al~Khaledis
(Muslim)

Garden

Cappellari
(and Brown)
(Roman Catholic)

Viswarath
(Hindu)

Guest Rooms

Demetrius
(Russian
Orthodox)

Kozan
(Buddhist)

Mandleberg
(Jewish)

McCain
(Anglican)

ST. THOMAS' CHURCH
~ Anglican ~
Upper Chelsea, London

Sloane Street

"I think I have a good sense of the sanctuary and Appel's rooms, although I have to make a thorough, close inspection of his living quarters as soon as I can. The problem is," he sighed, "I need to do and investigate everything at once."

So we retreated back to the parish house, with more interviews preying on Holmes's mind. Nearest to the entryway to the parish parlor was, as we walked west, the double room for Cardinal Cappellari and the translator, Brown; then the quarters of the Russian Orthodox priest, Demetrius (where we had visited an hour before); then, around the corner, the room of the monk Kozan; then, to the right, Rabbi Mandlebaum's and McCain's rooms. To the east was the room of the Hindu poet and radical leader, Viswarath; then, that of the Muslim imam, Ali al-Khaledis. Finally, the last room, where the body of Appel now lay covered under its white sheet.

There was no direct access to Reverend Appel's bedroom area from the guest room area; so one had to walk back toward the church and reenter the parish meeting room, which in turn led to the rectory office, the dining area, and then his private quarters. From the parlor was also the door to the kitchen and work areas, where the Losse brothers and Mrs. Desta and her son had their small quarters, running along the narrow back alleyway that ran behind and beside the parish house, opening onto Sloane Street.

As we strode along the hallway for the next interview, to our surprise we heard the rhythmic chanting of prayer. It came from Mr. al-Khaledis's room. Holmes gently knocked. A pause, and then the door was unlocked by one of Lestrade's police guards. The Islamic holy man was kneeling on a small carpet, and as he deftly rose, he welcomed us.

"Mr. Holmes, gentlemen, come in, please. I have concluded my final obligation of prayer this day, may Allah be merciful.

Come, see how I face Mecca." The chubby, dark little man, whose countenance was one of cherubic happiness, waved us into his chamber. "Bless you, sirs. Please, ask your questions. Now is good time, with my final prayers."

He then proudly showed us his beautiful prayer rug, which oddly had a small directional compass actually woven into the center of the fabric. "Wherever I go, I always will know where Mecca is," he said with a childlike delight. "To pray is a great happiness."

"I wish I always had a compass telling me the direction, especially tonight," said my friend, sitting down across from the diminutive plump man. He did not look at all like a powerful mufti, a legal and spiritual adviser who helped rule Jerusalem, yet there was a glint of shrewdness to his geniality. He seemed to embrace this questioning, and his style was charming, disarming.

"How did you manage to convince the sultan to allow you to come to London, to represent Muhammadans?" I asked. I remembered McCain saying Islam had been nearly invisible at the earlier gathering of world faiths.

"Ah, Mr. . . . Watson, is it? Yes. You must first of all say 'Muslim.' We are not Muhammadans. We do not worship the prophet, but only the merciful and compassionate One God, whom we call Allah, praised be his name. Second, the sultan would say, if he were ever asked, that I represent no one. This is a pleasure trip for me, yes? Though not so pleasurable now. Truth be told, gentlemen, politics is good practice for religion."

"How so?" McCain asked, which somewhat surprised me, as he seldom spoke in these interviews. He was a stern and silent witness, concentrating with his wide gray eyes trained upon his fellow clerics, a delicate finger tracing his precise blond mustache. But I gave him this—no one, not even Holmes, could intimidate him or break his fierce protective instinct for what he found precious: the church, his archbishop, this gathering, the truth. I wondered, as he spoke to the mufti, in what order truth came.

"Think of what I must do in Jerusalem," replied al-Khaledis with a touch of heat. "Rule wisely and fairly (which is not always done in the Ottoman empire, I assure you) and keep a balance in the holy city. My city is holy to you, and to the rabbi, and to my faith—complicated, yes? For example, Reverend McCain, do you know that at the holy sepulchre of your savior, Jesus, the Christians fight among themselves so often and so bitterly that we Muslims have been requested to keep the peace and guard the place of resurrection?"

"I'm ashamed to acknowledge what you say is true, and simply reply that this is why we have gathered here in London," replied the canon, forced to admit a painful truth.

"Which brings us to my need, Mr. al-Khaledis, to ask you a few questions. Did you know Mr. Appel before arriving in London a week ago?" asked Holmes, trying to assert himself. The jovial imam answered each question of Holmes quickly and directly, without any hesitancy or apparent defensiveness. No, he knew little of their host minister other than a small paper or two Appel had written, and he had seen nothing during the conference to possibly explain the shocking turn of events.

"Mr. Holmes, I am a Sufi, and we have a saying, that our task, like a moth drawn to a flame, is to die before we die. What does this mean? Not to know violence, no, but to kill the lowly qualities and ego that make us blind to the Compassionate One. As Allah is my witness, and by his *rahma*, his mercy, I have no knowledge of this horrible death."

"Not to be insulting, Mr. al-Khaledis, your faith is described, fairly or not, as being quite strict, even crude in its administration of justice. And in point of fact, you are the only one present with judicial power and experience with administering death.

Perhaps this man offended your faith or your sensibility in some unknown way, and in your faith, there is no clear distinction between secular and religious power."

Instead of being insulted, al-Khaledis laughed. "Quite fanciful, Mr. Holmes. And in your view of us, do we slice up the sinner? No. What you call crude (this, from a crusading people) is simply the overwhelming force of a whole society guided by the Qur'an; but then, why do I say, over and over, 'May Allah be merciful'? This is not an idle saying. It is the heart and core of the prophet's message. When there is repentance, there is full forgiveness. However, Mr. Holmes, there *is* a saying from my tradition where my legal training and my Sufi beliefs come together, which I have learned is true . . ."

"What is that, Mr. al-Khaledis?"

" 'Trust God, and tether your camel.' "

Tired of these seemingly fruitless questionings, I decided to return to the office of Appel. Something was bothering me.

Victoria, NUMBLND, 22.

I stood in the vacant office and closed my eyes, struggling to think, not like Sherlock Holmes, for that was beyond me, but rather as a man. A man of flesh who loved, who had lost, who longed for something besides the spiritual.

Victoria.

Then I walked over to the mantelpiece and picked up the lovely young woman's picture I had noticed earlier. Seeing no identification, I turned it over and eased the purple velvet backing from the frame in order to look at the back of the photograph.

In a delicate woman's handwriting, it read, "To Paul, May God shine his face upon you. Remember. Jan. 2, 1899. V."

Pensive, and silently hopeful I was somehow helping the investigation, I walked back into the sitting room, where I found

Holmes intently engaged in questioning Rabbi Mandleberg. The rabbi, stooped and round shouldered, was leaning forward, staring insistently at Holmes, and gesturing broadly in his replies.

"No, no, Mr. Holmes. I was quite surprised to be invited here to London. But I seized the chance to express the Jewish view. It is not often we are presented a chance like this." The rabbi, a solid man who appeared to be in his mid-fifties, gave a well-practiced shrug.

When there was a pause, I caught Holmes's eye and said, "Excuse me, Rabbi Mandleberg, I am sorry to interrupt, but I wondered if I could just have a word with Mr. Holmes."

With infinite dignity the rabbi nodded. "But of course."

"I'll be just a moment," muttered Holmes, who rose and walked with me into the kitchen. He delicately closed the door and turned back to me. His questioning gray eyes signaled that he was slightly perturbed by my intrusion, and that I had better have a suitable excuse. With Holmes, concentration was everything.

"Yes, Watson?"

Without a word, I handed over to Holmes the woman's photo I had removed from the frame, indicating the inscription written on the back in violet ink.

He studied the back signature for a long minute, then reversed the photo to analyze the woman's features, though I suspect he did not linger as I had upon her dark lovely curls, her penetrating black eyes, the precise and delicate cast of this lady's perfect features.

He sighed. "Watson, I should know to depend upon your instincts concerning the fairer sex. Not an hour from the ashes, and you have already found, I now presume, our 'Victoria.' So, the charred scrap we found refers not to our late queen, nor the railroad station, but the woman who left Appel three years ago for India. Thank you, my friend; I should have looked at her more closely."

Looking at the sepia-tinted photograph, I wondered who had left whom, and what kind of pain resided in this woman's final blessing and the request to remember. This was not a woman easily forgotten.

"Well, now I shall concentrate on solving the rest of the inscription on the scrap. And please join me for the rest of my conversation with the rabbi. Like the others we have met tonight, he is an impressive fellow. I want your opinion."

Soon we were both seated and the interrogation resumed. "Rabbi Mandleberg, what was your impression of Paul Appel?"

"He was confident, assured, a perfect host. Yet several times I caught a glint of a strange amusement in his ice blue eyes, and that seemed strange, I confess to you. I should also tell you that Appel and I had a slight argument last night, though all told, the discussions over the last three days have been most civil and productive."

Holmes, determined no doubt to get to the bottom of the dispute, betrayed little evident interest at the Jew's admission, though I noticed his left leg twitched a little in expectancy. At last, something sticking up from the reputed smoothness of the secret gathering, like a jagged splinter.

"And this discussion, slight as it was, concerned what?"

The stout rabbi shrugged, his aged, craggy face a mask of calm. He joined the tips of his wrinkled hands under his gray beard. "It is true, Mr. Holmes, that we had a spirited discussion, but that is not a reason for murder. That is really what you are asking, I believe." Mandleberg's English was impeccable, with just a touch of a German accent. "These gnarled hands hold up our Torah scroll; how could I butcher a man?"

"What did Appel say about the Jews?"

He shrugged, the oldest story. "That perhaps the world was

better off without us, or, to be fair, any ancient peoples who claimed exclusive revelation. 'The chosen people,' our host said, was an idea that must die in this modern age. I replied that my people had not chosen themselves—far from it. That chosenness is not an arrogance, but a burdensome invitation to righteousness. That we had done much of dying, not exactly for this idea of chosenness, but for the very right to exist. Yes, my words were heated, and meant to be. Mr. Holmes, this is life and death for us, not some idea to be bruited about on a snowy evening in London."

"So you bore no lasting ill will to Appel?"

"None at all, Mr. Holmes. He was a superficial and glib gentleman, not worth more of my pain. His beliefs were ultimately too shallow to be dangerous to us. We fear men of far greater conviction than Appel could ever summon. As God is my witness, I did not kill this man. Nor did I see or hear anything that could help you. Believe me, I would solve this crime for you if I could." He stopped, and the rabbi lifted up his hands in disgust. "All we need is a sensational murder at a secret religious meeting like this, one where, at last, Jews are admitted. Any excuse, any excuse at all."

Holmes was restrained, yet not unsympathetic. "Your people's lot in this world is not easy, Rabbi Mandleberg, but surely something like this could not be turned against your people."

"I know what I know. You deal with isolated criminal minds, people who attempt to cover their misdeeds. My people live in a world where murder can become good government policy and no one bothers to hide their deeds, because they are so applauded. Our lot in Germany seems secure enough, but pogroms are common for our people in Poland, Russia . . . How many murders like that would you wish to solve, Mr. Holmes?"

For once, my friend seemed not to know what to say.

Now it was eleven in the evening, and one guest remained to be questioned. I could see McCain was starting to tire, the strain and tension beginning to wear at him, as he spoke.

"The last participant is Krishnan Viswarath, the famed Hindu leader and poet. He is a leader within the Brahmans, the elite of all the castes," the clergyman said. "His renown is well earned. I find him to be the most interesting man of the whole group."

This was the man I most wanted to meet. Viswarath's name was well known, and London newspapers loved to portray him as an Eastern guru and poet, though with a decided political twist, and even a whiff of decadence and scandal about him. Rumors of a certain appeal to wealthy British women who found his holy man's appeal enticing followed after him.

"It seems I have heard of Viswarath; isn't he opposed to British rule in India?" Holmes said. "That's an odd business for a poet."

"Maybe he bears grudges against all Englishmen. That's his reputation," I mused. "Well, who can blame him?"

Viswarath was indeed a tall, impressive man, his skin shining the color of tea. His Indian long coat was shining black satin, with low-hanging white cotton leggings completing his outfit. His eyes were luminous, deep set with a smoky gray serenity, and his ink black hair was swept back off of his lined and broad forehead. Among these impressive holy figures, he stood out as the most charismatic of all.

The Hindu bowed to us, and settled into his seat as if it had been he who had summoned us. Holmes quickly went through the usual questions and, as was becoming depressingly common, learned little new. It was impressive how deeply unattuned to their environment these clergymen must be, having heard and seen so little! Here a death had been brewing among them, and for all of them, it seemed, this evil about them was all but invisible. Malignancy delighted in such obviousness in order to do its worst, and these holy men seemed only too happy to accommodate.

"Can you think of any reason anyone would want to kill Mr. Appel?" asked Holmes.

The Hindu stared at Holmes for a long time. "I can think of no reason at all. He seemed charming, intelligent, interested in God."

"Not so remarkable for a priest . . ."

"Not so, Mr. Holmes. Apologies to you, Mr. McCain, but very few Englishmen I have met have any interest in divine manifestation. Theology, yes; liturgy, yes; church politics, yes; converting heathens, yes—but the energies of God? More rare than you think. But at least Mr. Appel was curious, questioning."

"So you liked him?"

"Yes. He treated me as a man, as an equal. This does not happen often in London, if you will excuse the insult."

"None taken. Did you know Appel before this week?"

"No, although we had exchanged a few letters over the past five years. I was looking forward to meeting him in the flesh. We had an acquaintance in common, and I wrote to him, wondering if he would like to someday visit Calcutta on one of his Asian trips. As it turns out, thanks to Canon McCain, I was able to come to London first. I am not a popular man in this country, or in your newspapers, so it was good that this visit was designed to keep me invisible."

Holmes bore down, knowing the radical nature of Viswarath's feeling toward England. "Would you kill in pursuit of your country's freedom?"

"You ask a hard question, Mr. Sherlock Holmes. A severe

temptation for some Englishmen I have encountered, yes; but my faith is based on ahimsa, so, no, I would not kill, even for freedom. I did not."

"What is this term you use, 'ahimsa'?"

"Total love and compassion—for all things, all creatures. Not to harm any living thing. This includes Anglican priests," he added in a bitter tone. "You look at each of us as guilty. I trust you find your man soon and return each of us to being the men we were." Viswarath's eyes were saddened, and I felt he had the ability to see a man's soul, the shadowed part of the self we had to protect, to hide, perhaps even from ourselves. "I look at you, knowing you must solve this danger, and yet I see a man who likes puzzles more than people. You are a necessary man, Mr. Holmes, but a man who is not whole."

Holmes tightly smiled. "You do not know how true that is, Mr. Viswarath. Watson is a better man than I, but I think, despite his decency, he would be the first to admit that he would be unlikely to solve this murder. I assure you, Mr. Viswarath, I am resolved to retire soon, and leave behind this sordid life for a little philosophical reflection and much beekeeping. This search for people's secrets is a life that has absorbed me for long— in fact, I probably would have gone insane when younger if not for the acute mental stimulation that special cases brought my way. But I am learning other means now to draw off the energy. But it will take some years to move past being, as you say, 'necessary.' "

Holmes rose suddenly, offering his hand. "Perhaps some other time we can talk further, but now my brain churns and toils with its burden of fact and detail, and the picture is not complete. For this, I need time to be a calculating machine, along with a little shag tobacco."

The Indian activist rose and solemnly shook our hands. "Speaking of burning, I have smelled the burning of juniper leaves over the past three days. How odd, I thought—I am not doing this, and it is a custom of my land, not yours. The burning of juniper leaves is a sign of hospitality in high Himalayas." He shrugged. "Perhaps this can help you, or means nothing. Good night, sir."

"Good night."

So we rejoined Mycroft, who was contentedly sitting in the parlor alone, absorbed and reading through Lestrade's police reports and a great stack of diplomatic materials provided by Lambeth Palace. He looked at us as we eagerly regathered around the fire, noting that we had now questioned all the players in this strange mystery play.

"My money is on the Hindu, Sherlock," he huffed. "A mystical bounder, a rogue in transcendental dress. His agenda is political, not religious, I think."

"The Muslim al-Khaledis is a politician as well," I answered. "Why not him? And are you implying a religious leader with secular ties is more likely to commit a murder?"

"Absolutely," Mycroft hastened in retort, "not because priests are any less corrupt, but at least a politician is tested in ultimate courage. It takes bravery to rule a people, not to balance a teacup on your lap and speak pieties."

Canon McCain colored in distaste but, unusually for him, stayed silent.

Holmes interrupted, "Come, gentlemen, this kind of speculation is worse than useless. We need facts."

Mycroft muttered, "Do you know what I think, Sherlock?"

"No," he replied warily.

"I'm beginning to think there's great truth in the old saying 'Wherever God builds a church, the devil builds a chapel next door.' "

The night air was shocking, searing my lungs with cold, but I welcomed the sensation as a blessed relief from the close, cloying air of the parish house. Above me, narrowly framed by the sheer walls of the alleyway, I spied, in a jagged black tear in the dense white of scuttling snow clouds, a glimpse of the moon rolling like a shining coin over London.

Holmes had curtly told me he needed to spend some time going through Appel's files, so I rose from the sticky wooden chairs of the dark kitchen where we had been comparing ideas about this baffling night and took the blessed opportunity to throw open the back door, which accessed the back alley that ran along the back of St. Thomas's and the parish house.

Sheltered from the worst of the winds, I turned up my collar and kicked aside some snow from the stoop where I stood, breathing in deep the bracing wind whipping down the alley. Childhood memories of the magic of night storms came back to me, the crystalline air and the knowledge that with dawn a new and unexpected world would be revealed. If only our sad adult existence could be re-created so newly innocent.

Down the alley about ten feet or so strolled Collins, the policeman on his night watch guarding the back entrance, whom I had observed earlier that night while I had brewed that distasteful tea. I saluted him, explaining who I was so he wouldn't get nervous about me hovering about, and the policeman jauntily called out, "And a g'night, sir. Tell your Mr. Holmes to solve this killing so we can all go home."

I sympathized with the chilled bobby; all I wanted now was to be back to our comforting fire by the time Mrs. Hudson would come trudging up the stairs at dawn to present us with a silver breakfast service of tea and toast, kippers and eggs on the side.

The door behind me opened slowly, and I was surprised to be joined on the stoop by the massive bulk of Mycroft, who seemed, unusually, in a mood for conversation. He normally ignored me to concentrate his firepower on his brother.

"Damn perplexing thing, this calamity," muttered Mycroft, bouncing on his toes, his great beefy hands jammed into his jacket pockets from the cold. "What do you make of it all, Watson? You jaunt about with Sherlock, seeing hundreds of these kind of cases."

"Nothing like this one, I assure you, Mycroft. Frankly, I can't imagine *any* of these clergymen capable of what we saw down in that crypt. I'm totally baffled. And to tell you the truth, I'm afraid Sherlock is, too. Now, I admit on occasion I've been soundly fooled by him over the years, but I've learned to see about his countenance the exhilarated glittering in his eyes, the confident energy following on the scent when he's truly on the chase. But tonight, nothing yet. Just in him a grim getting on with the facts, and even there, there doesn't seem to be much of a spark. Those first interviews were singularly unenlightening. What do you think?"

Mycroft didn't reply immediately, and lit a cigarette, cupping his hands to keep his guttering match alive. The ash red glow as he fiercely sucked in revealed his face, the great hawklike nose and jutting chin so like his brother's, though in his broad and massive face the effect was oddly different, less intense and more like the calm and unruffled stone bust effigy of a long-dead Roman emperor.

Not for the first time, I wondered if Mycroft and Sherlock had had different mothers, but I never, over twenty years of friendship, had gotten Holmes to talk at all about such a potentially sensitive familial matter. For that matter, if not for the occasional case involving Mycroft I had accompanied Holmes upon, I might not even know of his existence. We English are a strangely reserved people, not given to revealing much about our families and homes of origin. And it seemed the more that one rose up the social scale, the more distant and distracted these ties became.

I now knew more about my friend Holmes than I had ever known about my own brother, Jack, gone now twenty years, whose tragic end through dissipation and drink was still essentially a mystery to me, as our ties had become by his death so loose and removed.

Odd that I was thinking of Jack this night. Churches are places of ghosts.

Then Mycroft turned my question to an odd angle. "Why does he do it, Watson? Sherlock could have been anything he wanted to be, and here he is, an admittedly uncommon policeman, but a policeman none the less. His whole life the solving of bloody little puzzles."

There was an undertone of anguish to the strange question, a tone that I had never heard from him before. Mycroft abhorred fame and attention, yet it was no exaggeration to say that he was one of the most influential and powerful men in our whole government. Was he wondering what his younger brother could have accomplished in the field of diplomacy, or as a brilliant scientist, or a masterful and renowned Oxford don in philosophy? I was a bit perplexed as to how to respond.

"Mycroft, I think he needed something to fully consume his mind, to keep his formidable intellect from grinding itself up into pieces. I think only the oddest sort of mystery could match the allure of cocaine. And people, especially those in pain and perplexity, are the profoundest puzzles of all. Detectives and doctors learn this in our trade, Mycroft. Love, passion, blackmail, envy, greed, even murder—these things are ultimates, and as a young man, they consumed his brain when other influences could have destroyed him." I paused, wondering if I was

137

saying too much. But Mycroft was listening intently, the smoke from his cigarette circling his massive head like a twisting wreath, so I went on.

"Now, as a mature man, he solves these mysteries because he is the best there is. He knows it, and so do you. That's why you pushed him into this case, to batter his great mind against this infernal edifice of masks. And you and I can only guess how much he has to pay in order to break through it, when he does."

Mycroft's voice was mild, yet insistent. "He well could have destroyed himself with the solace of cocaine, it is true. But it was not the puzzles that saved him."

"Then what?" I replied hotly.

"You, my dear Dr. Watson. You."

While Holmes years ago had fulfilled a secret mission in hidden Tibet for his brother, Mycroft had been the only one who, for three years, knew the great truth. My understandable relief in discovering that Sherlock was stunningly alive had, at the time, been so vast that my quite justifiable anger at being so left in the dark had quietly directed itself at the corpulent and calm older brother. But now, with Mycroft's compliment to me, I suddenly saw past the man's at times insufferable pride, the smooth veneer of the competent and self-contained Mycroft Holmes. And I wondered if he must be somewhat wistful at the closeness of my long friendship with his brother.

Just then we felt, then heard, the sudden outward slamming of the kitchen door, banging hard against us.

Then pounding feet and more cries, the police guards at full cry, and we both were tumbled aside into the snow as the dark figures of two men rushed out and past us. I struggled to rise, and took a hard blow to the shoulder for my efforts, and I fell back again. Mycroft lay sprawled on his back, shouting to the policeman down the way to halt the two running men.

I dimly saw, and more guessed, that the flashing shadows of

the escaping men were the two servants, the khidmatgars, Harruad and Malik Losse.

The brothers never paused to look back at us, but sprinted down the alley, seemingly frantic to escape. What chaos there must be inside the parish house to cause such flight, I desperately thought. I struggled to right myself and chase after them.

Collins, the policeman I had greeted five minutes before, stood resolute as the Losse brothers ran up to him, and in stout response he raised his police stick and ordered them to halt.

Slipping in the icy slush about my feet, I yelled for them to stop, but instead, to my horror, I saw the taller brother, Harruad, grab the raised nightstick and bowl over the guard. Collins's blue bobby's hat went flying as he went to his knees. The other servant swung his own stick to connect to the exposed brow of the falling man.

Even twenty feet away, the sickening crack in the night stillness was like a melon being smashed, and I knew in an instant the policeman was mortally wounded.

The brothers ran on, racing for the turn of the alley and access to Sloane Street. Already two of Lestrade's men were heading out the open kitchen door into the back alleyway in chase, but I did not attempt to join them. I instead stumbled to the barely breathing bobby and tried to aid him as best I could. The back door groaned forcefully on its hinges as the frozen air seized and shook it, and the policemen ran on into the darkness past me, following the fleeing servants.

My eyes stung as the now icy snow pelted us. It was hard to see, but in the blue distance I saw the police turn the corner to pursue the brothers into the thoroughfare and the storm. Before me, the blue-coated figure in his rain gear lay crumpled, a bloody, oozing gash across his wet forehead. Collins was still, his head turned oddly, his eyes staring blankly to the brick wall.

Suddenly, Lestrade appeared over my shoulder, but he looked

down only for an instant, and then hastened down the alley, hoarsely shouting for his men stationed at the front of the church to join the chase. I heard Lestrade scream, "Forbes, Henderson, don't let those two get away!" as I knelt down to examine the man more closely, but I knew there was nothing I could do. Blood stained the snow in black drops.

"He's dead, Watson."

Sherlock Holmes's face was bitter and determined. Standing over me, the detective looked for the inspector, who was retreating back to us and to our desperate, now futile, assistance. My friend turned to help up Mycroft, who was still breathing heavily.

"Lestrade, did anyone see who did this?"

Lestrade knelt down with us and cradled the man's shattered head. "Poor Dick Collins, with a wife and four children." He desperately looked up at us. I could see his body shaking from the cold, and his thin lips were blue. "We saw two men running down the alley—the two Losse brothers, we think. Damn them. You were right, sir, to warn us about them running. Now we know who are the murderers, now with two deaths to their credit."

"God hope your men can run them down. No, Lestrade, I cannot be certain, but I think they ran because of what they knew, not because of what they did. They were afraid of being killed by someone still inside this church. We cannot relax our efforts." He gently laid his hand upon the slumped back of the inspector. "Come, let's go inside."

McCain suddenly stood in the lighted doorway, shouting to us. "Mr. Holmes, we need you and Dr. Watson. Now! There's more to this."

We quickly rose, chilled with death and flecked with white.

"Lestrade, bring the poor man into the church," Holmes hastily instructed us as we quickly reentered the kitchen. "And we will need more police, both for the pursuit of the brothers and to keep this church bottled tight. Mycroft, as soon as you can, we need every government resource to start searching the docks of our major cities, particularly in the East End docklands. I think that's where the Losse brothers will go, and they'll be hard to find."

Canon McCain, his face frantic, interrupted us. "There's another injury to see to. It's the woman cook, Mrs. Desta."

Without another word, we raced back through the kitchen and down the darkened hallway to the servants' quarters, where everything was now scattered in disarray. Shards of broken china and silverware littered our path, as if someone had heavily lunged into the pantry cabinets in their frantic escape.

In the dingy hallway we were greeted with the sight of the little Catholic priest, Father Brown, seated in a wooden chair and holding a crying child on his lap. He was dangling his rosary beads to divert the howling little Indian boy, Shunapal. Brown half rose and pointed into the bedroom. His arms enfolded the boy protectively.

"In there, Holmes," said the grim McCain.

Inside her small little room, the cook, Senet Desta, lay sprawled on the floor, her bright ruby night robes matching the blood oozing from her head wound, so disturbingly similar to the blow we had just seen upon the dead policeman, Collins. "I'll see to her, Holmes," I said, and I quickly ascertained that her breath was regular, and that she was alive, and that though she was unconscious, she could recover if all went well over the next twelve hours.

"What's happened here?" asked Holmes in anguish. "I have been too slow, too lax. I should have anticipated this havoc. Is she breathing, Watson?"

I hastily felt the base of her throat, then her fluttering pulse. "Yes, barely. The blow grazed her brow, luckily. She's unconscious, though. The servants clearly tried to kill her before their flight."

"I don't know about that, Watson," said Holmes, still in anguish, as if he should have prevented this sudden savage violence.

Holmes was interrupted by Father Brown, who now stood in the doorway, cradling a now sleeping infant in his arms. "You're right, Mr. Holmes. Our guard was taking me to get water for the cardinal's medication, and I heard commotion, a woman's scream. I broke away from him and ran down to Mrs. Desta's rooms here. I interrupted the intruder who was struggling with her. It was one man, cloaked in black vestments and a cloth mask, and not, I think, either of the servants. She fought whoever it was desperately."

"Thank God you came when you did. The other guards were chasing the Losse brothers into the back alley. You saved her life."

"Yes, but you don't understand, Mr. Holmes—the man was trying to kill the *child*. She awoke, I think, and pulled him off. I shouted and waved my arms about, and the assailant ran, knocking me down. Then I heard all the commotion."

"Where did the man go?"

"He raced up the corridor here, leading to the church."

"Anyone could have done this, then. The vestments are probably deposited in the priest's dressing area again, the mask slipped under the soiled altar clothes. I'll have Lestrade's men check all that, but I don't think our man will be found so easily." Holmes looked down, with an anxious and tight expression. "What care does Mrs. Desta need, Watson?"

"She's now breathing evenly. I'll staunch the bleeding, and I'll watch her carefully. I think my observation through the night is better than taking her out into the storm to hospital."

"Can she be taken to the parish room couch? When she awakes, I suspect she will have much to tell us, and I want to be present."

"I think so, yes."

"Good. And Watson, before we do that, please inspect the child."

Father Brown had gently laid the sleeping baby on his own bed, and I knelt down. The boy's ears were bandaged and his eyebrows were scabbed. I softly turned up his palms, which were also bandaged. It was all very odd, this kind of thing on a child a year old.

Lestrade burst into the room, and we quickly caught him up with what had happened to Mrs. Desta. He was angry and agitated.

"The Losse brothers seem to have slipped from us, Mr. Holmes. But the entire Metropolitan Police are looking out for the scoundrels."

Mycroft added, "As is Scotland Yard and all other government agents in the field. So I expect that by morning we'll have run them aground. But we're so very sorry about Collins, Lestrade. It's hard to lose a man like this."

The inspector nodded his numbed acknowledgment, then turned to Holmes. "Excuse my language, sir, but let's get this bastard. First killing a priest, then attacking a mere child and a mother."

"A desperate night." And Holmes swept out. "Lestrade, inspect every inch of the church again. Take me to the Losse brothers' room. I made a key mistake not searching it earlier."

More policemen were now around every exit from the church, huddled in the cold. Added men came inside as well, and Holmes instructed them to redouble their search for a clue, any clue.

"Search the clergymen's rooms carefully again, every piece of luggage, every piece of paper, every scrap or diary or note or sermon. I want their travel tickets brought to me immediately. Have we gotten the telegrams sent out yet? I want everything and anything that could unlock this case."

Then we hastened to the servants' area. Mrs. Desta's door was open, her blood still staining the floorboards. Grimly, Holmes went by and forced open the Losse brothers' door.

"Watson, we must closely inspect the quarters of our fugitives. Perhaps they left something behind suggestive of where they have fled."

"Certainly, Holmes." The small dormitorylike room of the Losse brothers was small, cramped, and disordered, with grimy sheets rumpled upon the narrow camp beds and abandoned clothes strewn about the floor. Their abandoned dinner plates, a congealed red grease revealing some Eastern fare, were still on a table with soiled napkins flung atop them. There was an unpleasant smell, acrid, a mixture of some cheap incense and sweat.

Holmes carefully inspected everything in his usual methodical manner, including the little altar the brothers had mentioned earlier in the evening, with a small golden Buddha and the still-glowing stick of wafting incense, but nothing there seized his interest. Holmes picked up a little bell and gave it a quick shake, the invocation of spirits now fled. I sensed he was about to move on to a different part of the church when at last he muttered, "Eureka."

"What have you found?" I asked, turning from my idle fiddling with a small brightly colored string contraption hanging from the ceiling.

He rose, holding up a small torn ticket stub.

"This was half under the far bedpost, probably just shuffled aside in their haste to be gone."

He concentrated on the small tag of paper, and asked me to bring over the gas lamp I had laid on the plain desk. "Another puzzle, like the burned bit of calendar we have not solved. But I suspect this is something we must decipher, and instantly. Let us see." He relit his pipe and sat upon one of the unmade beds, and studied the slight piece of paper. There was the heavy silence of Holmes's fierce concentration, an almost palpable presence like an intense and burning light. After several minutes, he looked up at me, his face relaxing. "Watson, it reads, '. . . ck 17,' then the next line, '. . . arine Co.' Well, we are lucky tonight, Watson—at last, something tangible instead of all of these theological vapors."

"Oh, really," I replied, baffled as usual. It wasn't much to go on, I thought.

"Well, what do you make of the ticket?"

I studied it, aware that Holmes looked on expectedly. "I'm sorry, Holmes. My mind is befuddled; nothing occurs to me."

"Well, a ticket is for what? A service, a performance, or . . ."

"Transportation."

"Correct. These men are on the run, and the sooner they leave London, or England for that matter, the safer for them. How did they come here five years ago, and where do they have family?"

"India! This must be a ticket stub for travel plans they must have laid out for themselves . . . Ah, '. . . ck' must be 'dock,' and we need to find a map that has oceangoing vessel facilities and enough for the number seventeen."

"Capital, Watson. Twenty years of being with me has done you a world of good. I would say St. Katherine's Docks, near the Tower of London, is their destination tonight. At last we have our first break. Since I suspect our fellows will be running along the Thames embankment until they reach the Tower, we can hope to apprehend them."

I thought harder. "More likely across Lambeth Bridge and then into the Borough, then over the Tower Bridge."

He considered, calculating, then shrugging. "You may be correct, Watson, but their path doesn't matter, only the destination and the race we're now in. In the meantime, we can have Mycroft call one of his bureaucratic minions and quickly have their vessel in the docks located. That should be easy enough; we simply have to ask which ships are embarking for India tomorrow or the next day. I do not think their ship will be leaving tonight, especially with this storm; but they could steal aboard tonight and make our pursuit even more difficult."

"You're right, Holmes, this could be the solution," I said excitedly.

"Oh," he replied ruefully, "I think not. But a piece of the puzzle to be sure. And I intend for those two to pay dearly for the slaying of policeman Dick Collins. All right, let's inform Lestrade what we need to do, and get Mycroft on the phone to the Foreign Office." He gave a deep sigh as he rose. "I wish we had come down here to the brothers' room sooner; but then, I never dreamed the two Indians would expose themselves in this crude way."

He stopped at the door, looking at the odd sight of the colorful contraption hanging from the ceiling I had earlier spun on its suspended thread. The crosslike object hung from string, two simple sticks with brightly colored threads wrapped like a cobweb from arm to arm. "Watson, take that little thread cross with us, please."

"A clue?"

"Just to give it to the little baby for his crib."

When we found Mycroft, he was seated with Archbishop Demetrius in the parlor, both in animated conversation. As the

Russian gestured in his dramatic manner, the two stout men looked for all the world like two great circus bears delicately balanced on their small elegant parlor chairs. Though we were in a great hurry, Holmes hung back for a moment to get some sense of their discussion. The massive Russian Orthodox priest waved his great red-chapped hands, muttering, "Mr. Holmes, there is one thing more. I remember now, a great argument between Appel and the rabbi last night."

Mycroft perked up. "Yes? And about?"

"Rabbi Mandleberg in our talks last night declared that your Anglican priest, Appel, was a hater of the Jews." He shot up his thick rough eyebrows for emphasis. "Maybe these words are important, after what has happened. The two argued about Jewish people being the chosen race. This argument did not much interest me at the time, Jews being so very sensitive, but I remember Rabbi Mandleberg very angry."

Sherlock Holmes stepped forward and delicately interrupted. "Excuse me for interrupting, Archbishop. Mycroft, I've just made some important progress, and I need your help immediately in order to intercept the Losse brothers. Watson and I think they may be heading for the docklands, St. Katherine's, we think. A call or two by you could confirm my suspicions."

For Mycroft, his lumbering up from his chair was immediate and expectant. "Excellent, Sherlock. How may I help?"

As the befuddled archbishop looked on at us, slightly indignant at this sudden interruption, we quickly filled in Mycroft about our fruitful inspection of the servants' room and the torn stub. With a swift apology to the priest, Mycroft was instantly on the phone, calmly making arrangements and garnering whatever useful information we needed once we arrived at the docks.

As we donned our coats for the rough weather we were

headed into, Holmes turned back to the archbishop, who had been ignored in the hubbub and our planning. The black-cassocked cleric rose, towering over us, and grimaced as he shifted his weight. He looked down regretfully at his lame foot. "I apologize for the way I stand, gentlemen, my leg is painful tonight. Particularly since someone seems to have stolen my walking stick, which I stupidly left outside by my door. Mr. Lestrade, if your men find it, please return it to me."

The lean little inspector nodded. Then, "Mr. Holmes, if you are heading for the docklands, my assistant Bill Allen has a suggestion to make. He's a dependable sergeant just elevated from the Thames River police, and he says he could be very helpful to you at the docks. The quays are confusing at the best of times, and he says he knows the place."

Lestsrade's junior officer spoke up, his cockney accent thick and nearly impenetrable. "I knows the river well, sir, and m' time on the river police boats would help in the storm."

"Excellent, Sergeant Allen. We shall be glad to have you, if it doesn't leave Lestrade shorthanded here in the church."

Then my friend turned back to the Russian priest. "Your Holiness, your recall of this argument might be crucial to this case, but you understand why we must go now. But very quickly, you say that Rabbi Mandleberg was upset last night? In what way would you describe Appel's reaction to that anger?"

"Now, Mr. Holmes, I say this rabbi is a man not easily provoked, but our host, Mr. Appel, managed to do this. Yes, Mr. Mandleberg was very angry, red in the face, voice raised."

"How long was this argument?"

"Oh, very brief, three minutes."

"And Mr. Appel's behavior?"

"That was what was odd; he laughed, Mr. Holmes. He stared at Mandleberg and laughed! This Appel was a strange fellow. He found something diverting about the rabbi's wounded words. Then Canon McCain hastily moved the conversation on to another topic, and we all acted as if the exchange had never taken place. Frankly, I would have easily and happily forgotten the whole incident, but after your questions tonight, I thought I should at least mention them to your brother . . ." He shrugged, gently stroking his great gray beard.

Holmes shook the man's hand and nodded. "I *shall* take your information under consideration, and I thank you. Since you are not overly familiar with the care of babies, Mycroft, I would suggest we have someone from this parish come and take the Desta boy for the night, and that one of our policemen be sent with the child. And keep the location where he goes absolutely secret. There is something strange, not to mention horrifying, about this attack on the little Desta baby and his mother." At last, with an impatient gesture, one I had seen a thousand times in the pressure of a case, Holmes swept by his brother and the Russian, lightly urging me forward by my elbow. "And now we have a boat to catch, it seems."

Above us rose Big Ben, poised now to toll the midnight bells.

The great clock tower glowed above us, bathed in the ivory light of the Houses of Parliament's new electric illumination. Blowing gusts of snow hit the stark tower of light, lit like a dancing frenzy of jetting sparks. Even after twenty years in London, the sight of the imposing Parliament towers had never ceased to thrill me in their stately detailed magnificence. They rose to dominion over the silken power of Whitehall, the political realm subtly coiled about its base. Our hansom cab raced along the north end of the Houses of Parliament, heading for the Westminster Bridge. We slowed, and we were directed to a private access gate where all the parliamentarians boarded the private boats that taxied along the Thames, as the powerful and the wealthy had done for hundreds of years. The river was still the fastest avenue of access to the tangle and confusion of London.

Our cab slid to a halt, and a police officer yanked open our door. "Your boat awaits you, sirs," the officer said. Sergeant Allen, Holmes, and I got out hastily, and though icy pellets of hard snow stung my face, it felt wonderfully good to be out of St. Thomas's. Lestrade's Allen clambered out with us, a huge fellow with an alert face and a trim little black mustache. He tipped his bowler hat to the man waiting by the boat below us, and I immediately felt we were in good hands. Experience aside, his massive arms revealed a useful strength if trouble arose at St. Katherine's Docks.

Mycroft had been the one who immediately proposed that we must beat the brothers in their flight by going by boat from the Westminster pier to the docklands. With only one call, he had arranged for a police tug to meet us below the Houses of Parliament. Within twenty minutes we were boarding, and Holmes was telling a grizzled boatman and the eager sergeant where we needed to go, and to please pour on the coal, that we must make for the docks below the Tower Bridge and no delay.

So it was that Holmes and I, at the beginning of this Boxing Day, surprisingly found ourselves huddled and shivering under oil slicks as our little squat but dauntless tug raced downriver, roiling on the heavy swell of waves frothing in icy caps of white foam. The cold lights of the city shimmered to us, dancing reflections of the stately mansions and government houses lining the embankment, paralleling the Strand. We picked up speed, and in no time at all we were sweeping by the ivory dome of St. Paul's. The unfolding river panorama all looked so magnificent and pristine that it was hard to imagine the two men racing along those crowded and grim streets, in a cold hansom or on foot, hastening down the Strand into the City, and then by all probability unto Commercial Road, heading for the London docklands.

The crowded quays were areas I had seldom visited, but when I did, I had always gone with a sense of caution and trepidation. The level of degrading poverty and the sense of personal danger were less than they had been in Dickens's time, but the green-fogged images of East London's squalid poverty, its mud and waste, the sickly grease smoke, and above all the appalling over-crowding in the dark tenement rookeries were still true enough. It was a stark reality beyond our distant icy Thames prospect.

As a doctor, I knew huddled figures would be there in damp doorways, knowing nothing of a pristine wonderland under the gleam of new snow. Even in the middle of the night, I knew I would spy young children in rags by the dozens wandering along the swarming thoroughfares. How many of them would ever reach maturity, and what kind of stunted and criminal consciousness would they possess even if they did? In their jammed and fetid close quarters, they eked out a life in deep shadows, yet these children were flesh and blood, not spectral—but who wished to see them?

The nearer to St. Katherine's Docks we moved, the more I found myself wondering if somehow our confidence was mis-placed and this night journey might prove the proverbial goose chase; but I tried to dampen down the despairing thoughts jab-bing within like needles. I had every right to repress them; after all, when had I ever been led astray by Holmes? How often had I been compelled to press forward and see where loyalty led me?

Still, the odds we could somehow find the escaping brothers in this vast sink of the docklands daunted my imagination.

We passed the silent vast gray hulk of the Tower of London,

where we had earlier mockingly suggested we might have to resolve this mystery, the gleaming central white tower rising above the vast gray walls and Traitor's Gate, on the river. A great number of boats bobbed upon the river across from the great walls, at the place in the widening river they called Jacobson's Yard, all anchored and huddled under the blast of the storm. Then we were gliding under the magnificent and brightly lit Tower Bridge, completed only six years ago and already a world symbol of London, where two huge pinnacle towers and an ornate catwalk arched across the black river like some monstrous children's toy. We were nearly there, the tiny tug's searchlight guiding us on to our destination. I wondered how Mycroft and Lestrade were doing back at St. Thomas's, where they were resolved to closely reinspect the rooms of all seven men.

"We are here, Watson. Have you your revolver?"

I nodded. Perhaps we would be lucky and pluck the two Indians from the vast tidal wave of humanity that was East London, but I was suddenly feeling lost, tired, and totally disoriented.

"How fast can men run in this snow?" muttered Holmes, his thin arms wrapped across his chest. He shivered, but not, I think, in sympathy for our prey.

"They could have hired a cab," I said.

He did not reply. He trusted his intuitions, though I had learned never to refer to them as such. Holmes was abnormally sensitive to the charge of playing on normal hunches and guesswork. All decisions were to be referred to as nothing less than rigorous logic, or so I learned to always call it. I estimated we would beat the Losse brothers to the ship's berth by at least half an hour, if they were indeed traveling east on foot.

At last we could see the towering masts and flags of ships anchored in the immense open docks, and we came to the St.

Katherine's Docks tidal gateway. Our police boat slowed, and Lestrade's Allen called out to the darkened dock office facing the Thames. A lantern was lit, and soon a little dockman in a yellow rain slicker bestirred himself and braved the weather to emerge and look at us quizzically.

"Evenin', gents. Wot can I do fer ye?" The old man, a white-whiskered river rat, leaned out of his shed and shouted to us, clearly wanting nothing more than to retreat back to his little stove within.

"Police business, sir," barked Allen. "Have you seen two Indian men come by here, heading for dock 17? And is that the S.S. *Franklin,* bound for India?" He pointed up ahead of us, to the farthest boat docked from us, nearly lost in the billowing snow. We glided in closer to the dockway and came in closer to hear the old man.

The dockman clamped his teeth on his corncob pipe and consulted his ship list. "No sight of any such wogs, gentlemen, but then I've not been looking for them. Snowmen now, anyway." He wheezed at his joke and ran his finger down the sheet. "Aye, the *Franklin* embarks at dawn, though it's likely to be delayed. Shipment of coal and fine furniture bound for Madras. Only a few paid passengers. Maybe the men you're looking for are working their passage. Could they be cooks or stevedores?"

"Very possibly. Is the captain aboard already?"

"Captain LeRoy is sleeping on board, yes. I suppose you can rouse him if it's serious."

"It involves a double murder. We intend to track these men down before they can escape the country," Holmes interjected.

Allen added, "The Metropolitan Police is investigating a particularly brutal killing, and the subsequent death of a policeman."

"Go on through, then. Good luck to ye." He waved us on and

retreated back into his warm enclosure. We chugged on slow, and soon arrived at dock 17, where the large ocean vessel rose above us, its securing ropes moaning in the brisk wind. Far cries of gulls echoed through the vast open waterway, which was otherwise ghostly quiet and deserted. But I knew that in three or four hours there would be dock laborers desperately looking for work thronging about these ships. These river workers always led a precarious life, and winter was for them a dangerously slow time.

For now, we had a clear view of the S.S. *Franklin*, iced and rimed like a ghost ship from Coleridge's "Ancient Mariner." Our tug master nestled us alongside the merchant ship and we tied up. The four of us gratefully clambered onto the dock and hastened to the ship.

"Keep quiet," Holmes hissed, "and fan out as we planned. Dr. Watson, please stay with me. Let us go."

Cautiously moving to a lonely lantern light that hung from the ship's yardarms, we crouched down silently to hide behind huge stacks of barrels waiting to be boarded at daylight. There was no sign of movement, so we crept closer to the ship, where a lone guard was pacing the deck twenty feet over us. Coming from the flanks at either side, the policemen circled back to us.

"Nothing, sir," Allen hissed. "All clear."

Holmes looked up to the guard, and then asked me to light our lantern. "Ahoy," Allen called up. "Metropolitan Police. Have you seen any activity in the last hour or so? Anyone come aboard?"

"All's quiet, sir. In this weather, not a soul."

"Good. Come down the gangplank, please," Holmes cried up to him, and something commanding in his tone made the seaman immediately respond.

The mariner shambled down, slipping as he came. Breathing

heavy as he joined us, the young sailor scratched his beard and brushed off his black cap. "It's rough to be about, sirs. I might ask what are you doing here?"

Holmes briskly replied, "We are here to intercept two men, and they have already killed tonight. How many men aboard the *Franklin* tonight?"

"Ten men, and Captain LeRoy."

"Any Indians bound for the Raj?"

"Two men are ticketed for Madras, but no sign of them, yet."

The police officer sternly instructed, "Tell your captain that the two are wanted for murder, and that the police will be circling this ship overnight to apprehend them. I will require full cooperation. I'm going to post my men now in case they arrive, and I'll have no more noise or commotion either from my men or from anyone on board your ship. Go inside the hold and stay there, even if you hear gunfire."

The young tar blanched and hastened up the plank without another word to awaken his captain. We then moved back to our hiding places, dousing the lamp, and the dock was again shrouded in the freezing darkness.

The hollow thump of the ship against the groaning wood and wound rope, along with the rhythmic and lulling splash of the water against the massive piers, would have easily soothed me to sleep if the infernal cold had not so quickly begun to sink into my greatcoat, first with needles of pain and then, worse, a numbing sensation extending from my limbs. I am not a praying man, but I mouthed a prayer crouching down behind those packing crates, begging for these doomed servants to come at last, and quickly, before I froze to death in service to Mr. Sherlock Holmes.

I don't think it was fifteen minutes more before my prayer was answered. I heard the far-off wheezing sound of men running on their last legs, the raw sound of frozen lungs and panic. Their shadowy figures stumbled into our vision, their halting breath crystallizing in the harsh night air.

The snow had momentarily let up, so we could see the two men from a longer distance than we had anticipated. Malik and Harruad Losse looked ragged and desperate after three miles of running through snow-choked streets to this desolate place of escape. The brothers stopped, looking up to the forest of masts and rigging as a promised land, and then they lunged forward to the gangplank of the S.S. *Franklin* and warmth and safety.

Halfway up, the figure of Sergeant Allen rose above them and calmly called out, "Stop right there. The two of you are under arrest." The first, the older brother, Malik, stopped and held up the hammer he had carried all the way from St. Thomas's.

"Put that down," Holmes shouted from below, as the two of us scrambled to come into view and aid the police officer. "You've done enough damage with that weapon. Put your hands up."

As Holmes spoke, we ran forward along the deck, and with the police tug captain joining us, we now surrounded the bottom of the gangplank. They were trapped halfway up, poised over the frigid water.

I remember seeing the glittering eyes of Harruad Losse as he looked back down, a look of brief fear and then an acceptance of what was to come. He raised a knife that gleamed in the darkness. In a flash, he rushed down and tried to bowl the three of us over, but we grabbed on to his heavy blue greatcoat and hung on for dear life. There was the glint of his slashing knife in the pale yellow ship's lantern.

Up above, teetering on the narrow walkway, Malik desperately threw his hammer at Allen, not eight feet above him, and with our dangerous scuffle with his brother down below, I lost sight of him, and all I heard then was a muffled grunt of pain from what sounded like Sergeant Allen, and then a resounding loud splash.

Harruad was able to free himself for a moment, our hands being so numb with cold that he was able to drag us for a few feet away, continuing to thrust his knife at us. Holmes was fearless as he lunged for him again, and the knife sliced and ripped at our arms as we tried to bring Losse down into the icy deck. The police boat captain screamed in pain as he released the Indian and rose up, grabbing at his wounded cheek. Drops of black blood suddenly sprayed the snow, and he dropped to his knees clutching his face.

Holmes's grip was weakening, and I did not know how long he could hold on to the servant's wiry and surprisingly strong legs. Losse screamed and tried to break free again. For a moment, I thought about raising my service revolver, but I knew Holmes wanted the brothers alive, and I could not take the chance of shooting in this dark melee, not to mention accidentally wounding Holmes.

I rushed forward again, and though my recent leg wound was burning in nearly blinding pain, I leapt, hoping to knock Losse down and give Holmes a chance to regrip. Holmes was desperately trying to protect his own face and hands from the slashing strokes and still hang on. Harruad was swinging his knife frenziedly, hoping to break free one more time. I landed hard, slamming into the man's back, and to my relief we finally all went down in a crumpled mass, wrestling about in the slippery snowdrifts.

Just as I was thinking we had him at last, his struggling suddenly stopped. With a sinking feeling I reached up and struggled to turn the man over. Losse flopped over, his head falling back unnaturally. His bloody hand released the knife. He had given up the fight.

"He's cut his own throat, Holmes!"

His throat jaggedly cut, Losse's life drained free. The wound was so extensive I quickly saw there was nothing I could do for him, so I jumped up to find where Malik Losse had gone.

The policeman Allen was cautiously stepping down the gangplank holding his head with a bloodied cloth. With evident pain, he shouted to us, "He's gone in the water. Dr. Watson, rouse the sailors and let's get him out."

"He can't live long in this freezing water." As I shouted for help, Holmes, unhurt, though his black greatcoat was now slashed and somewhat tattered, rushed to my side to join in the call for assistance. The violent encounter had happened so quickly that when suddenly the ship lamps blinked on, illuminating our chaos, I was shocked by the blood splattered everywhere, melting into the white.

I heard the man's splashing ten feet down in the Thames, but the motion was slowing already. I stood by helplessly as Holmes directed the sailors hastening down the gangplank to get Losse out quickly. This water would kill him in minutes. The *Franklin's* sailors quickly were by our side to grab long grappling poles and to start jabbing down into the icy black water in hopes of snagging his clothes.

"Malik, grab hold of the ropes. Save yourself!" cried Holmes as above us, from the side of the ship, ropes were lowered to the narrow water.

I think Losse did not grab on to safety because, like his brother, he far preferred oblivion to rescue. Soon he stopped struggling, but before he could sink down into the cold murkiness, we finally were able to wrench him out of the deadly water with our hooks and poles. His thin body now limp, we lowered him to the dock.

His dark eyes were flat and his skin was chalky gray, already icing in the night air. A few flakes settled onto his still form, and

I took his pulse as a mere formality. He was so small and thin that in death his slack form appeared to be that of a starved child. This was getting to be a night of shrouds.

"They're both dead, Holmes."

"We failed, Watson. Though, thank God, they did not escape free from their crime. We've got to get to a telephone and reach Mycroft, and then get our men seen to. Are you hurt, my friend?"

"I'm fine," I lied, hoping my leg would stop hurting soon. It was amazing to me that Holmes had escaped the cutting jags of Losse with only a few deep scratches. Allen joined us, and I asked to see his wound. Reluctantly, he lowered the cloth, and I looked at the blood from a gash on his forehead.

"I dared him to throw the hammer, and the bastard was a better aim than I realized," the officer muttered. "Damn thing nearly knocked me down into that water; but the challenge worked, because he lost his footing and fell down to that water. I'm sorry, Dr. Watson, we can't question them now, but I can't say I'm sorry these two are dead."

"No. I quite understand. We're lucky none of us dies with them."

Soon their stiffening bodies were under canvas sea shrouds brought over from the *Franklin*, white winding cloths for burial at sea. Holmes stared at them, silent and sullen. Dead men tell no tales.

But their bodies sometimes do. "Anything on their persons, Holmes?" I asked, shivering.

"Their tickets, a small bundle of clothes they flung away when we called to them, a watch, and a white cloth. Nothing much, except this." He held out a bloodied green sprig of stiff needles. He sniffed at it and placed it in my hands. "Juniper leaves."

Within fifteen minutes I was standing, warm at last, next to Holmes as he was reporting in to his brother. I had missed much of the conversation, as I was bandaging the nasty slash of the tug captain. The old salt in the St. Katherine's Docks office offered us a phone and, more important, cups of sweet and milky tea.

"That's right," Holmes was saying, "one dead of hypothermia and the other slashed his throat. They wanted to die rather than face our questions."

Holmes's voice could not disguise his disappointment, and his words were clipped. He paused, then added, I presumed to Mycroft on the other end of the line, "They wanted to die rather than return to that church. Thank you for asking. I think Watson and I are all right, though our boatman is slashed in the face, but I think he'll be able to navigate us home. Yes. Tell Lestrade his man Allen was superb.

"Truth to tell, I can't say I'm shocked by the way things turned out. I believe those two were doomed men." He then added, "How are things going at the church?"

Holmes turned to look at me, sipping his tea and indicating by silent motion that we would be off soon. It was nearly one in the morning. "Mycroft, continue to keep a tight lid on things. Let no one out of his room. You and Lestrade must watch them carefully. We'll be back within the hour. Ah, good. Make sure Lestrade deals with the telegrams." He listened, then smiled tightly. "Would you put on the inspector, Mycroft?"

After a pause, Holmes went on, urgent and with an insistent tone. "Lestrade, personally go to the hotel and have her brought to the church. I don't care how rude or ungallant it seems. *Now.* Yes, good work, old man." He rang off, his despair lifted.

"What did they say, Holmes?"

"To come back, quickly." His failure at the docks was not

going to long dampen his spirits, especially at the scent of a new lead. "Though I don't fancy a return boat trip, Watson, unless you'd like to trade greatcoats," he added, raising his arms and extending his cut and tattered wool sleeves. His thin pale wrists, so exposed, were horribly abraded, blood-smeared.

Five

LAUDS

St. Thomas's Church, 4 A.M.

"So where are we in the investigation, Holmes?" I asked as our boat curved along the Thames embankment.

I could see, in another brief break of moonlight spying through the thinning snow clouds overhead, Cleopatra's Needle, the recently erected ancient monument pilfered from Napoleon, who in turn had plundered it from the sands of Egypt. The fruits of victorious empire, twice plucked.

"Currently perplexed, but I trust we are now heading safe to harbor, and there will soon be stars to guide by. I am beginning to think the primal emotions, love, jealousy, envy, lie at the heart of this murder. In other words, the oldest story, Watson; and not, as we first imagined, motives born of religious hatred. A most suggestive interview awaits us when we return to the church, that I assure you." Allen, who had insisted on coming back to the church with us, sat quietly, listening. Like Lestrade, he wanted to see if the vaunted Holmes would save all our reputations.

The Westminster pier coming into view, I could see Holmes was eager to move on past the futility and failure of our midnight excursion. As we docked at last, frozen and stiff, we gratefully alighted upon the wooden dock. It was then we saw, to our surprise, next to our waiting hansom cab, a long black Morris limousine motorcar, motor running. Whoever it was, whoever was within the automobile, was intent on keeping warm; its powerful engine was purring and a trail of white exhaust rose like smoke from a dragon of old.

As we came up the steps from the pier, a steamed window rolled down and a suave bass voice called to us. "Gentlemen, over here, please." The door to the sleek, impressive car swung open, and a top-hatted young secretary emerged to claim us. "Mr. Holmes, Dr. Watson? The prime minister wishes to speak to you."

Shocked, Holmes whispered to me, "A command performance." As we followed the young man, he muttered, "We don't have time for this, or any other impediments."

"How does the prime minister know we were here? It's the middle of the night in a storm."

"It can only be dear Mycroft, who else?"

The leather interior of the car was indeed warm and inviting, soft and yielding as we slid in to meet our new political leader, a man only in his first few months of power. As we settled ourselves, the prime minister's assistant switched on the overhead light, closed the door behind us, and then went to stand outside the car, leaving us to the smooth, abstracted, enigmatic style of Mr. Arthur James Balfour.

"Mr. Prime Minister," said Holmes, evenly polite but curt.

"I wanted to inquire as to the status of the investigation, Mr. Holmes," began Balfour. The PM was dressed in a dark gray formal coat, as if he were just heading home from his club and had just happened by the pier in a most amazing but fortunate coincidence. In concession to the cold, a green shawl covered his

waist and legs. Balfour's manner was calm, almost passive. He folded his delicate hands across his gray satin waistcoat in languid repose. "I trust the unfortunate business at the church will shortly be satisfactorily resolved."

"I have hopes that a solution will soon present itself, but I sincerely doubt any aspect of this can or will be 'satisfactorily.' Dr. Watson, my associate, and I are now returning from St. Katherine's Docks, where two important witnesses to the events have died. In their earlier flight, a stalwart policeman was slain. Add to that, a mother and child at the church also this evening were attacked by an unknown assailant. In addition, the killer of the priest Paul Appel still remains among the suspects present at the church, where we must return now."

Hearing this sickening litany of murder and mayhem left Balfour apparently unaffected, as if Holmes had just moved a parliamentary motion to the floor of the Commons. He stroked his gray mustache and considered us. Finally, he spoke, in words devastating for their placid delivery. "Most unfortunate, Holmes. Mycroft had assured me that you could control the situation."

"I am sorry to disappoint. I ache to return to St. Thomas's, sir, where I may reclaim the confidence of my betters. Some leads have arisen in the last hour that may prove fruitful." Holmes, who suffered aristocratic airs with annoyance and barely concealed sarcasm at the best of times, was dancing on the edge of defiance.

The intelligence and python cold-bloodedness of this politician, nephew of our last prime minister, Lord Salisbury, was undiverted by Holmes's cold resentment. A man like Holmes was not going to get under his skin. Not this commoner, no matter how highly touted he might come.

"Good, Mr. Holmes. I am glad you are resolute. Godspeed to you in your most crucial endeavors." He leaned forward and of-

fered his chilled hand to us. He added, "I would be so sorry to let your brother's outstanding career end on so disappointing a note. I cannot emphasize how important a quick resolution to this unfortunate situation is to this government."

"Mr. Balfour," said Holmes, omitting Balfour's newly won title, "one of the reasons I retain faith in our government, despite failures abroad, military misadventures, rampant poverty, and a certain continuing low fever of corruption among our leaders, has been their long wisdom in retaining the services of a man like Mr. Mycroft Holmes. Covert, hidden, selfless, all he has ever asked for is the opportunity to serve his king."

The prime minister smiled tightly. "Quite. Good night, Mr. Holmes. Dr. Watson."

As we scrambled into our cab to race back to the church, I breathed out a shocked "Holmes! The man *is* prime minister."

"Balfour is an accomplished man. He could slit your throat while offering a witty Greek epigram." He rapped the cab roof loudly. "Drive on!"

My readers (guided by my own literary choices, to be sure) have usually viewed Sherlock Holmes as some kind of reasoning god, with powers nearly superhuman and omnipresent.

His successes were so many, and so astonishing, that this illusion was easy to sustain, but his awesome prowess was monolithic only in looking back—through the wrong end of the telescope, so to speak, and with selective memory and editing. In the midst of the murky and chaotic midpassage of our cases, he was often endearingly lost, impatient, sullen, angry, mystified, and thus thoroughly human.

In some ways, this was the Holmes I admired most— someone who, when lost and wondering, offered himself fully, ready to make mistakes, even to make a fool of himself. He

revered the truth that highly, to potentially sacrifice his vaunted reputation and ego. In addition, this was the one time—in this transitory state of his mystification—that I was anything approaching his equal. But that state never lasted long.

Mycroft greeted us at the great red doors of St. Thomas's, most eager to welcome us back. This was a man not used to being on the scene of violence, much less being responsible for so many suspects. The brothers quickly caught each other up on the devastating disappointment at the docks, the quiet hours at the church, and Holmes then concluded his words with the odd and surprising appearance of the prime minister at the Westminster pier.

"You should have warned me, Mycroft, that the prime minister would be lying in wait like that. You *deserved* his barely veiled threat to you."

Mycroft was clearly shaken, though he maintained his calm bravado. "He called and demanded to see you. I didn't want him here. And on his charming words about me, don't worry, Sherlock; I know far too much to be cast aside by the likes of any mere prime minister.

"Now, on to more important things than the PM. Lestrade wanted you to read the telegrams sent out and received here for the last week. A certain telegraph operator is fifty pounds richer this night. I think you'll think it a good investment."

The portly Mycroft handed over to his brother a small stack of telegraph forms. Holmes eagerly took them and raced through the stack in mere moments.

"Splendid, Mycroft. Several of these are quite suggestive. When will Lestrade return with the young woman?"

"I would think within the hour."

I interrupted. "Who is this mysterious woman you have been alluding to, Holmes?"

"Ah, you were key to our finding her, dear Watson. But first read the telegram to Mr. Viswarath, dated, let's see, two days ago, Christmas Eve. " 'K. Viswarath: Will meet hotel Tues. Stop. Passage booked Paris. Stop. Love. V.' "

I thought, then remembered. "The girl whose picture was on Appel's mantle? Victoria! But how can we find her, Holmes? There are hundreds of hotels in London, and there's nothing saying she's even signed in under her own name."

Smiling, Holmes plucked the charred bit of calendar from his waistcoat pocket. "Well, you found it, my boy. *Victoria, NUM-BLND, 22.* Demonstrate your deductive skills."

Slightly impatient with Holmes's puckish humor, I sighed, "All right, Holmes, though the night is late for games. *'Twenty-two'* could be a date, or an age, or—"

"Think accommodation, Watson. Take the first letter of the unknown phrase, and what could it stand for, for clearly it is a shortened name of some sort?"

"Well, *N* could stand for many things, but I suspect you're looking for *North.*"

"Yes, indeed I am. Which leaves *UMBLND.* Add some vowels, which is a convenient way of shortening messages on a small calendar space, and you get *Umberland. Northumberland.*"

"The small hotel where Baskerville stayed! Just east of Trafalgar Square, and around the corner from our Turkish baths."

Mycroft was delighted. "A long line of suppositions, to be sure, but following Sherlock's phone instructions from the docks, Lestrade just found a Victoria Williams registered at the Northumberland, room 22. So the question is, who is this young missionary lady, Appel's former fiancée? And why is she associated with Viswarath?"

I guessed an association, but it was so impolite I did not speak it.

"I see from your expression, Watson, that our thinking runs along similar lines, so we'll leave the words unsaid. But sexual jealousy is the oldest of motives of murder, and hard, even ugly questions will need to be asked."

Mycroft nodded wisely, and for a moment I was left wondering what these two old bachelors could possibly know about the realm of passion and sexual betrayal, but I refrained. Perhaps experience was overrated, but here, concerning love, I doubted it. Passion is an inconsiderable thing secondhand. Perhaps one of the strange (and always unspoken) reasons Holmes found it helpful to have me, an otherwise most unimaginative fellow, as his associate across more than thirty years was my experience in the unknown and exotic realm of "woman."

These slightly fevered ruminations were interrupted by Mycroft, who was impatient to add something interesting and potentially important. "One of our men just found this a few minutes ago in the rabbi's possessions, tucked inside a Torah scroll," he said, arching his eyebrows. Mycroft, like his brother, could be quite theatrical at times. "But that Mandleberg brought something like this into the country is quite striking, so I would be cautious in assessing it."

"Come, let me see this thing."

"It appears to be an old article our Mr. Appel wrote for an odd little London newspaper, a paper that could only be called anti-Semitic. Now remember, Sherlock, Archbishop Demetrius told us that Appel and Rabbi Mandleberg had argued about the status of the Jewish people earlier in the conference."

"It did sound as if the argument was quite heated," I interjected. My friend took the old crumpled and heavily folded journal and perused it carefully.

Mycroft added, as Holmes quickly read the offending article, "Here is evidence that this 'discussion' was something more deep-seated, not a momentary squabble. In my field, Sherlock, I am exposed to a great deal of this sort of squalid thing, and I was immediately struck by three particularly harsh paragraphs."

I reproduce them here:

The Jewish people must at last choose, as we near the twentieth century, if they will maintain their acquisitive and mercantile ways even as they pose as God's special messengers. Chosen people—chosen by whom?

Not God, who has clearly forsaken their harsh and violent worship of a God who is more a desert potentate than a loving and gentle Father. One cannot justify violence toward any people, but it is all too easy to understand why these Jews attract such fierce hatred.

Only the kindly admonition of our Christ to forswear hatred makes one endure these odious and obnoxious people in our midst, and one only wishes they were not present at all. I have many friendships with heathen peoples from many religions, but none from the ranks of the Jews.

"Well, Mycroft," sighed Holmes, "I admit this hardly ranks with great inspirational literature, and while it certainly offers a vivid, albeit crude, insight into our Appel, I wonder if it provides a motive for murder."

"We've seen men murder for less," I said.

"True," said Sherlock, looking up from the slightly crumpled article with a faraway look in his eyes.

"Admit it, Sherlock," said Mycroft impatiently, "you were floundering two hours ago to find even a ghost of a reason for this killing. Potentially, Lestrade is giving you one by bringing the young woman in, and here I am handing you another, an astonishing insult to the Jewish people. All you have to do is think back to the rabbi's own remarks and sensitivities. Yes, I think this could be a motive of the highest order."

With a sudden burst of irritated energy, Holmes rose and started out for the guest rooms. Mycroft and I hastily followed Holmes's rapid stride.

"What did the rabbi say when it was found?" Holmes asked as we struggled to catch up.

"Oh, just what one would expect: that it was the first time he had ever seen this article." Poor Mycroft was already huffing. "That someone must have placed it among his belongings . . ."

Holmes stopped and looked back at us. "All of which could be true. I might well agree with the good rabbi. It would have been easy just to memorize the offending text and then burn it, as it well deserves. Why bring the magazine to this conference? It was bound to be discovered—which is why, I suspect, it exists here at all."

"At least interview him again, brother."

"Oh, I will. Right now, in fact. And bring in Mr. Ali al-Khaledis."

Mycroft was dumbstruck. "Mr. al-Khaledis, the Muhammadan? Whatever for? Have you taken leave of your senses?"

"Mycroft, look a little closely on the mailing address," said Holmes patiently, pausing in the hallway, "which I suspect you have not taken the time to do. You are brighter than I am, but you've never bothered to check the details. Look, what do you see?"

"Why, almost nothing. The address is blackened out, and the stamps are almost torn off."

Holmes took out his magnifying glass and trained it onto the back of the old and worn newspaper. "Almost, but not quite.

True, the addressee is inked black, but why? Because someone doesn't want us to know who subscribed to this thing in the first place. And one edge of a stamp remains, and the particular purple color tells me it is in fact a current stamp of Turkish origin. Knowledge of postal stamps is essential to my trade, and I'm almost certain of its Middle Eastern posting. Which tells me this magazine was mailed through Istanbul to Jerusalem and to our good Mr. al-Khaledis.

"There might be a motive there, brother, but perhaps a rebounding one. The murderer might well be the one who plants the evidence, not vice versa. Bring them both back to the parlor now. It will be interesting to have them face each other."

So it was done. Both men appeared bewildered to be rousted out of their rooms, though neither had been sleeping. Each appeared quite surprised to be in the other's presence, but they sat themselves with admirable dignity, nodding to each other and to us.

"Mr. Holmes," began the rabbi, whose broad and lined face revealed weariness, anger, and a touch of righteousness, "I will repeat what I told the policeman and your brother. I have never set eyes on that journal, nor that odious article by our host. You may believe me or not. But I ask you to ponder this: the effort of anyone to place these cruel and ignorant words into the sacred scroll is something approaching blasphemy. Do you think I as a rabbi would do this?" He was indignant to be answering this silent accusation at all, but he dampened down his ire and maintained a remarkable calm.

"Rabbi," said Holmes courteously, "it seems very unlikely that a man of faith such as yourself would sully the Torah in such a way. But you need to consider this from my side: here I am faced with a mutilated body, and a man's life is worth many books, no matter how holy. Now, have you read Appel's article?"

174

"No," said Mandleberg curtly. "I will not lower myself to do so. But your brother read me a particular paragraph, and it did not surprise me. It was similar to our brief discussion the other night, to which I responded so angrily."

Then al-Khaledis interrupted us, demanding, "Why am I present for this, Mr. Holmes? This has nothing to do with me."

"Oh, I think not. I will ask you the same question, Mr. al-Khaledis. Have you read this magazine?"

He studied us for a long moment. It was in his best interests to lie, and he considered that course, but at last he sighed and lifted his hands in resignation and seeming supplication. "Yes. Yes, I have. It was mailed to me a month ago, and knowing I would be meeting this Appel in London, out of curiosity I, of course, read it. I have no idea who sent it to me. But Mr. Holmes, I beg you to listen to me, sir. I am somewhat like my friend Rabbi Mandleberg in feeling I have been accused for nothing."

The imam was no longer the jolly figure of two hours ago. His forehead was coated in a sheen of sweat, and his little mouth worked frantically. He added, imploring and suddenly desperate, "The fact is, I misplaced Appel's article on the Jews the first night I arrived here to the church. Quite stupidly, I left it on my nightstand when I went out to our first session of talk, and when I returned it was gone. Its disappearance was perplexing, but at the time I did not think much about it. You can surely understand why I said nothing about it after the murder." He sighed, and motioned one hand dismissively to his forehead, a universal motion of self-disgust. "It was foolish for me to have brought something so"—he paused to search for a word—"so incinerating."

"So incriminating," added Holmes quietly, less as a correction of his English than as an addition to his confession.

Then the imam did something remarkable. The Islamic cleric got down on his knees and bowed down. "Sir," the mufti said to the amazed rabbi, "please accept my humble apology. I did not enter your room or place such a thing in your holy scripture. I remind you, sir, that Abraham is my father, too, and I swear upon the Qur'an that all I say is so."

Mandleberg hastily rose from his chair and helped the old man up. "I believe you, Mr. al-Khaledis. The question is now, does Mr. Holmes?" The gray-bearded man, his brow creased with weary concern, looked at the detective, searching his reaction.

Looking at the stooped rabbi, whose gnarled hand still lay on the shoulder of his Islamic counterpart, I did not know what, or whom, to believe at that moment.

"I will hold any belief or disbelief in abeyance right now, gentlemen," said Holmes judiciously. "But you can well understand why these Turkish stamps alerted my suspicion. Jews and Moslems are not the most comfortable neighbors in Jerusalem, and I could not help but wonder if you would have gone to these lengths to implicate the representative of the Hebrew religion."

"Mr. Holmes," retorted Ali al-Khaledis, "at the behest of the sultan of Turkey, I serve on the Municipal Council of the holy city, and I remind you I serve with five other members of my faith and also two Christians and a Jew. Of all the men here in this church tonight, I am the *only one* who actively deals with those of different faiths every day. The differences in our religions are issues I struggle with all the time. When I go in and out the Damascus Gate each day, I see my people live side by side with those of many religious traditions. And I also remind you what the prophet says: 'Whether you hide what is in your heart or reveal it, it is known to Allah.' Let it be known here, sir."

We were silent before this convincing plea.

Mandleberg said, "Still, someone *did* place Mr. Appel's words into the holy scroll. It is natural for you to suspect me after finding the genteel anti-Semitism of Appel. It is true, such easy words truly enrage me." He turned to the mufti. "And it is natural, as well, to think you would have been the one to place the pages there, to entice me to violence, or to direct suspicion my way. Only I believe this, Mr. Holmes: someone wishes you to also suspect Mr. al-Khaledis. That is where we are."

In the press of the investigation and the long boat trip to St. Katherine's Docks, I suddenly felt, now that it was well after two o'clock in the morning, a little guilty toward Mrs. Desta, and my duties as a physician. I resolved I should visit her without pause, to see how she was resting, if she was stirring yet from that brutal attack.

"Yes, Watson, please go," urged Holmes patiently, wisely refraining from speaking the words that I knew were on his mind, that I was to come speedily back if there was any possibility that she could be questioned. So I hastened from the rabbi's room and started down the dark hallway, night shadows across my path softened by faint gray light, daubed watercolor wash on absorbent paper. It filtered in from the tall leaded windows overlooking the central garden. I shivered, still deep chilled from the Thames's frozen air, and I impatiently walked on, arms crossed, and slapping my palms hard upon my upper biceps to get the blood circulating.

Then I spied, in the blackness of the little garden, a darting figure across the way. A black shadow flickered across a dimly lit room window ever so briefly, and I paused, thinking my tired aging eyes were playing a trick on me. But then I saw again for an instant a crouching man against the snow, his movement swift. I hurriedly went to one of the hallway windows and reached up to unhook and then ease open the lower pane to see a little better through the dark glass. I had to see which man was out of his room, and what he was doing.

As I lowered the window frame toward me, suddenly I was sharply jerked back. To my shock, gloved hands wrapped around my mouth in a python grip. I tried mightily to struggle free, but both surprise and a choking grip squeezing away my breath allowed my unknown assailant to slowly force me backward into a small alcove, away from the window. As I tried with my hands to release his grip, the strong figure behind me only wrenched his tightening grip further. I tried to cry out, but I couldn't summon more than a harried and muffled grunt of pain, and then of fear, as my sight started to dim with whirling purple stars.

"Things are not what they seem," hissed a low voice into my ear, one I could not place. "This game has two masters, and your man is only looking for one."

Just as I was about to pass out, I heard hurrying footsteps coming down the corridor, and then, suddenly, the fierce grip was finally released and I slumped thankfully to the stone floor, gasping. As I gratefully gulped the sweetness of oxygen, I dimly saw above me two black figures with flailing arms, and the golden flash of a walking stick striking down on my covert assailant. Then in a flash, the masked figure in black escaped into the far corridor.

To my amazement, hovering over me and helping me up was not Holmes, as I expected, but rather the diminutive Father Brown. The priest was breathing hard, the bear's head stick of Demetrius clutched in his pudgy hand.

"We have to go after that man," I managed to wheeze, still gasping to recover.

"The policeman Allen was right behind me, Dr. Watson, and he's in pursuit. Just lie still. I'm sure Mr. Holmes will be here in a moment."

"Could you see who was attacking me?" I asked.

Brown shook his head reluctantly. "This hallway is dark, and whoever it was took the precaution of wearing black and covering his face. But then, most of us are in black tonight." Brown considered a moment, his watery blue eyes half drooped in silent concentration. "In my little scuffle, I'm afraid I lost my glasses. Ah, here they are." He gratefully replaced his spectacles. "All I can really say is that he seemed to be of average height. I'm sorry, the only person I could rule out is al-Khaledis, who is much too small."

Just then a panting Sergeant Allen, with Sherlock Holmes in tow, quickly materialized by our side. I tried to tell Holmes exactly what had happened, and Brown and Allen added their details, which unfortunately amounted to little. One way or another, the fellow seemed to have dematerialized.

Allen shook his head. "The right bastard, excuse my French, knows this church too well."

I rose to my feet, still a little unsteady, and pointed out the still open window to where I had seen the figure in the garden. Holmes closed the window sadly.

"The commotion will have scared whoever that was away. I'll track the footprints in the snow as soon as I can, but my immediate concern is you. How are you, Watson? You seem to be paying a large price in being my associate lately."

I assured him that I was all right, that I had come much closer to death than this.

Ruefully, Holmes shook his head and asked me to repeat carefully the words the man had whispered to me. He listened with his typically ravenous hunger for yet another morsel of fact.

"My dear fellow," he finally said, "you were probably in no real danger, as brutally forceful as your attacker was. You don't kill the messenger, and believe me, that statement was meant for my ears. Still, without the timely intervention of Father Brown, who knows what might have happened? We are dealing with a killer who is not so fastidious. So we all owe you our thanks, sir." He nodded to Brown, who was standing by Allen. "However, the interesting and timely question now is: why in heaven's name did you come to be out and about?" Holmes cocked a skeptical eye. "I believe I instructed all of you to be confined to your bedrooms. But you, sir, always seem to be circumventing the constraints of this investigation. You are seemingly anxious to place yourself as the chief suspect."

Brown humbly bowed his head, as if being the prime suspect in a crime was an honor far too great for him. "I was in the parish kitchen, preparing the cardinal's night medicine, of course properly guarded by Mr. Allen, when I discovered the archbishop's missing walking cane. My foot brushed against it under the cutting table."

"I for one am grateful you found that stick, Mr. Brown," I said, rubbing my throat. "I saw you lay into my attacker with great unclerical authority."

Brown handed over Demetrius's knicked old cane, with its worn and burnished golden bear handle, to Holmes. "I hope you'll give the stick to Archbishop Demetrius. With his limp, I fear he has missed his stick terribly."

Holmes calmly took the proffered stick. "Thank you, Father Brown. It's very kind of you to think of him. He does seem to be missing it, and I would be most happy to take it. I have a few questions to ask him anyway."

He turned to go, took a few steps down the dark hallway, then stopped. The detective looked back to the priest still standing in the hallway, so deceptively meek and small. "Father, tell me again what you thought of your host, Mr. Appel. You had conversed with him even before the conference here. Was he a good man, a good priest?"

Brown considered. "I have known good priests who were not good men. God can make a priest out of an imperfect soul; indeed he has to, always. Speaking for myself, Mr. Holmes, I believed (despite his charm and easy ways of friendship) Paul Appel was dangerous."

"How so?"

"Not because he was outside the Mother Church, but because he was essentially an atheist."

"An Anglican priest?"

"The church can deal with heresy. But Appel believed at heart God is not God, but rather a nondescript energy, a spiritual power, which any and all world faiths could tap into, like you plugging into that electrical outlet over there. That's why he was attracted to Eastern faiths, not because contact with such world religions is important, but because they are each essentially irrelevant."

"And for you—"

"Not for me. Not the cardinal. Our opinions don't count here. For God, who is a very specific kind of God. This is not my belief. This is the truth. No amount of well-intentioned discussion can change God from being the true God. Appel believed in mystery, in divine power. The church actually believes in God."

As Brown concluded, I excused myself, feeling little the worse for my experience. I was still feeling anxious that I had neglected my duties as a physician, so I hastened to the room where Mrs. Desta was sleeping. A kindly policeman hovered in the hallway. Wondering if she should not be taken out to hospital, I decided to take her pulse and observe her more closely. Senet Desta's eyes were still unfocused, and her sleep was fitful and seemingly pained. Her pulse was fluttery, still a little rapid.

Her parched lips, lovely as they were, were dry and slightly cracked. This widow was indeed a beautiful woman, with long lashes, elegant eyebrows, and the vermilion smudge of a Hindu holy mark upon her brow. The third eye. Her attractive brown eyes fluttered again, and her smooth features seemed to relax.

It was a close call as to taking her to a hospital bed. There was little they could do for Mrs. Desta there that I could not, so, after some thought, I decided her transfer to a hospital could wait until morning light. It was even possible she might wake in several hours and Holmes could ask her a question or two before I whisked her off. Holmes seemed convinced she knew something essential to the case, and I thought that if more lives were at stake, the slight medical risk was worth it.

Yet I wondered if my being the associate of a detective was somehow trumping my duties as a physician.

And I thought of the small boy now in hiding, most likely still asleep and completely unable to comprehend what danger his mother was in. The savagery of the attack returned to me in sickening detail. What kind of person would wish to hurt such an engaging child—any child? My instinct to heal was so strong that this savage aspect of human nature was completely closed to me, though Holmes's avocation had brought me square against it for years. I hoped never to understand it.

There was little more I could do for Mrs. Desta. But because her temperature seemed slightly higher, I thought her forehead should be cooled down with an iced cloth. Finding nothing appropriate in her room, I circled back through the kitchen and dining area to Appel's private rooms. As I opened the door into his study, to my surprise I found someone was seated at Appel's desk.

Canon McCain blushed and half rose out of the dead priest's chair, equally surprised, even embarrassed. He had been sitting, idly toying with Appel's gold letter opener, leaning back and dreaming, perhaps half dozing, ruminatingly studying the long rows of books lined along the office. Now he dropped the gold letter opener to the desk blotter as he nodded to me.

"Dr. Watson. You're back. How did things go? Were the brothers helpful?"

"They died before talking." I told him in short detail about the horror at the docks and all that had happened since our return. "I apologize for barging in like this, bothering you, Canon. I know it's been a long night, and you appeared to be resting."

"Resting," he said, a rueful smile as he repeated my word. Then, "What time is it?" he inquired.

"Half past three."

"Good Lord. Two more dead. I feel I'm in the middle of some endless nightmare, but instead of waking me up, your knock now just cast me back into it." The lanky priest rose and came around Appel's desk. He explained, "I tired of just sitting in the kitchen with Mycroft Holmes. I suppose it might seem a little macabre for me to be sitting at Appel's desk."

"Not really. No matter where you go in the church tonight, the echoes are disturbing."

"Haunted. Yes. Can I be helpful to you and Mr. Holmes?"

I explained my mission, and without hesitation he eagerly offered to assist me by sitting by Mrs. Desta's side. I explained I wanted him to continue wetting her brow, along with keeping a watchful eye. In Appel's bath we found several clean towels atop a beautifully lacquered Chinese box.

As we walked back to her room together, McCain surprised me by asking, "Are you a religious man, Dr. Watson?"

Even in the midst of a murder case, these men seemingly could not give up the higher mystery they had given their lives to. It was an obsession, this God talk.

"If you mean by attending services, I'm afraid not. I claim the English right of being a member of the church in absentia. If you mean if I believe in God, most assuredly so. As a physician, the mystery of the body and the riddle of mind and soul make me believe in a power beyond the raw physical. I am, I confess, somewhat agnostic—that's the new phrase, isn't it?—as to the nature of God. Your version of God suffices for me as well as any other."

Hugh McCain ruefully smiled. "Well, I did ask, so I can hardly begrudge the answer. Still, I suspect your Holmes would not say as much."

"His brother, Mycroft, has sworn off all religion, but do not sell my friend short on your question. Sherlock is disdainful of cant and ritual, true, but he did once say, though he hated it when I quoted him thus in a story, that 'there is nothing in which deduction is so necessary as in religion.' He was deluged with all kinds of crank letters after that was published, I assure you. His sense of fairness and forgiveness are so strong that only a cosmic bar of justice, an unknown but utterly powerful God, could possibly suffice."

"Perhaps I have been hard on him tonight. A biting tongue comes too easily to me. Still, your Holmes is an impressive man. I *do* respect his fierce intelligence, and somehow I trust your sense of him as a man of mercy. And I have to admit that the events of the last day are forcing me to face a painful truth. Perhaps no cruelty is greater than that of excessive religion."

We paused in front of Senet Desta's room. The minister motioned me to go on, not to worry. "I'll watch her carefully, Doctor. I'll come get you if I sense she needs you. Excuse my inquiries, I'm tired and just making conversation. We religious people tend to be a little myopic on the subject."

Indeed.

"No harm, Canon. And thank you." I walked away glad of

the exchange, thinking there was perhaps a little more warmth in Hugh McCain than I could have guessed from his usual stiff, haughty demeanor. There might be a man of flesh under that black shell of his, but it was taking some extreme measures to expose anything human under the bitter and rigid manner.

To my surprise, Mycroft was sitting alone in the parlor, contentedly nursing his pipe. I asked where his brother was.

"Sherlock's been invited for tea. The Buddhist fellow, Kozan." He motioned me down the hall. "I trust you're feeling all right, Watson, from your little episode. Terrible thing, being strangled."

He shuddered, his thick second chin quivering. I reflected my assailant would have had a hard time getting a good grip on Mycroft's windpipes. I assured him I was feeling fine, which, somewhat to my surprised relief, I was. Mycroft added, "Sherlock said for you to join them. You don't mind if I just sit here and cogitate?"

"Tea at nearly four in the morning?" I responded, and Mycroft just shrugged.

So I found myself joining Holmes and Mr. Kozan as they sat Japanese style before a low table on mats of rice straw. The monk, in his simple ivory robes, sat facing Sherlock with the lights of the room dim, a single candle behind him illuminating some Zen calligraphy. He grinned up at me.

"Join us, Doctor. Kind policeman boil water for us in kitchen. Please, join me for a simple tea ceremony, a way to clear the mind. You like tea?"

"Very much. Thank you." Kozan and Holmes were sitting in companionable silence just as he and I often did. Holmes nodded at me as if reading my mind.

"The reason we have been friends for so long is that we don't ever feel the need to chat."

"Good talk, yes, but chatter, no," said the Buddhist monk.

In the depths of this horrible night, with currents of seemingly impenetrable violence swirling all about us, we sat in the stillness for a long minute or two. Then we washed our hands.

The silence was so great that for the first time since entering the church, I heard the scratching of wind-swept limbs at the window, the rhythmic pings of the new heaters, the deeper silence beyond us cushioned by the snow.

With a carved wooden scoop, Kozan ladled some powdered tea into the pot from a beautiful lacquered jar, the pot being kept warm by the glowing charcoal of a portable brazier. As he did this, we ate a small sweet almond cookie, and I realized how hungry I was (and unlike my friend, I did not find depriving my body heightened my senses). Then the monk wiped the ladle, the scoop, and our cups with an ivory cream silk napkin. Then he proceeded to whip the green tea with a bamboo whisk until it frothed and thickened.

With slow, deliberate movements, Kozan silently poured us tea into two small red patterned cups. He gently swirled the liquid as he cupped the tea, then bobbed his head, motioning us to take a sip. At last he spoke.

"In my tradition of Rinzai Zen, we prepare tea to teach us to be—how would you say it?—absorbed. Every gesture slow, sure. Pure. They say Zen and tea have the same taste."

"A clear taste."

"Exactly. Now, Mr. Holmes, how is your questions tonight?"

"Not so clear, Mr. Kozan."

"Ah. You seem sad. Perhaps confused."

"You forgot angry. I am that, too. I despise the waste of death and not being able to clearly see the answers I seek."

"You talk as one who knows something of Buddhism. You, like Paul Appel, have traveled to the East, yes?"

"You are correct, Mr. Kozan. For two years I traveled in Tibet and Nepal, and indeed, I closely studied your traditions. I am not a Buddhist, but I learned much. It has certainly helped in my profession, through my increased ability to observe. I believe you call it 'bare attention.' "

"Yes, yes. To look at things without ideas, just to see. This helps you be policeman?"

"The word that applies to me, thank God, is 'detective.' Gazing without thoughts, yes, very much so. I usually *do* reach the truth because I resist theories and just let the facts and details of the scene finally cohere. My desires and hopes just get in the way of seeing what is there before me. You see, I deal with people who wish to deceive me, to establish an alternative truth that will lead me down the wrong way.

"But these people also cannot help but leave tracks in the dust as to their real actions. So I force myself not to leap to conclusions; I have to ease into them, or have the truth of the matter settle into me. My friend Watson sometimes describes me as some kind of wizard, but as the years go by, I find I just allow the truth a little space to reveal itself before I jump to construct a reality that simply isn't there."

Kozan smiled broadly and sipped his tea slowly. He nodded. "A clear mind. You are an unusual Western man, Mr. Holmes. Quite different from Paul Appel, but you two have curiosity into the Way that is refreshing. You wish to understand my friend?"

"Very much so."

"Paul was a seeker, a man wishing to swallow up the world. He learn to sit, to do tea ceremony, to think koan question. He come a long way, but something missing. 'Impatience,' I think, is your word—desire for enlightenment that blocks enlightenment. How can you hunger for the end of hunger? He wanted too, too much.

"I call him friend, but I wonder now. The last time we talk yesterday, I feel he surrender. He seem bitter; 'jaded' is English word, I believe. I look at him and wonder, what else to lure him next? What enthu—joy, thrill. I do not know the word."

"Enthusiasm."

"Yes, he never learn," and here Kozan swept his arm over our tea setting. "When you sip tea, sip tea, not try to be Buddha. One must delight in every gesture, every motion. Each has value and so has the moment. No goal here. Paul never learn this. If only he let go desire! That is first step. I say this a hundred times, and he nod, but the Western mind, I think, finds this hard."

"Indeed we do. Goals are very important to us, and tonight, I have one. I wish to discover who killed your friend. The closest I can come to the clear mind you speak of is to step aside from my ego and just let happen what must happen. I do not seek credit for finding the truth, and never have. Whatever happens tonight must remain secret from the world, and so I do it for the sake of simple justice, not fame." Holmes leaned forward, joining his fingertips together and gently rocking his hands for emphasis. "Yet I have to be honest; it is very hard to use clear attention as I should, *because I want to find this man so much.* I want to know who attacked that little baby. I want to, at least in some small way, make the death of Dick Collins less meaningless. I even sense the Losse brothers did not have to die as they did, so pitifully. And the treatment of Paul Appel—that goes beyond saying. My desires are very strong here, and I feel blocked. I'm not making much headway, I'm afraid."

"Holmes," I blustered, "no one could be doing more. The murder is not twelve hours old . . ."

Kozan smiled and said simply, "Then stop trying so hard, Mr. Holmes. You know this. Be a mirror. Reflect the world and do not take on any image. We say a bird flies through the sky without mixing up color of sky. Put desires to rest as you can. More tea?"

"Yes, I need it to stay awake. Thank you." Holmes took out a telegram and laid it before the monk's tea. "And I wish you to comment on this message you sent out Christmas afternoon."

I waited for the Japanese to set down his teapot. The telegram, addressed to Master Zenjo, read: APPEL FUNDS NOT COMING STOP GREAT BOOK NOT FOUND KOZAN.

The monk, to his credit, made no attempt to lie or prevaricate.

"Mr. Holmes, Paul Appel come to us in Japan twice, each time promising money for repairs, medicine, saving of old manuscripts, aid for widows and children near monastery. Instead, he sat with us and learned, but all promises not met. Against my master's advice, I recommend he bring to England rare manuscript to sell for survival of the school. More promises over the last year, but no money. This is true reason I came to your country, to see if Paul had money he promised. I am afraid he kept me at arm's length and would not speak of sale.

"I was in despair, but I kept hoping he would make good on his pledge. I believed in him, sirs. I did not want to give up on him. At last, in a quick hallway talk, out of hearing of others, I asked him as old friend if he still had my scroll. Mr. Holmes, he laughed at me, and said, 'Let me offer you a koan, Mr. Kozan: What lies under the roses but is aboveground?'

"But I was at last betrayed. No funds, no manuscript to take home. I was failure, sir!

"When I went to see him yesterday afternoon at four, he was not in his rooms. Oddly, his door was open. I entered, and I did something I am shamed of: I hurry and search his office and room, but I find nothing. I fear the manuscript now lost forever, and I go home empty."

"That is a motive for murder, Mr. Kozan. And you did not tell us the truth."

"No. I did conceal my shameful act. But I did not kill my

friend. I still believe he would have helped, that he would not in the end be this cruel, without heart. He could not be this bad a man. Maybe he was in difficulty, or trouble which I did not know. Perhaps he had money for me in some hidden place. I do not know. At least now, truth is here."

"Thank you for your tea, Mr. Kozan." Holmes rose nimbly from his seated position and extended his hand. He seemed truly distressed at what we had just heard. In regret, he said quietly, "I am sorry Mr. Appel lied and disappointed you and your fellow monks. You understand, however, that you can go nowhere until this investigation is concluded, and that I must consider well all the details of this story, and that they are damaging to you."

The Buddhist monk remained seated, his face a solemn mask of pain. He lowered his head in a small bow. "I understand."

Just then came a knock at the door, and it was Lestrade's welcome voice. "We need you, Mr. Holmes."

V. was here.

She sat alone in the parlor, taking off her damp gloves, then smoothing back her hair. She was awaiting us with an admirable calmness, having just been roused by the Metropolitan Police in the middle of the night and compelled to enter a church that contained (though I wondered how much of this she knew) the body of the man she had loved.

Victoria Williams was even more attractive in person, even when slightly sleep disheveled, than the portrait on Appel's mantel had prepared me for. The night candlelight shone in her hair like the sheen of sable velvet, and when she turned to our footsteps, she bore a look of keen intelligence and sensitivity.

Holmes, anxious to begin, swept into the room and gave a slight bow to the young woman. She stared at my tall and slightly ungainly friend as if he were some midnight apparition. Her wide almond eyes, deep brown and coolly appraising, gazed up to Holmes without fear or hesitancy.

"My apologies, Miss Williams, for your unceremonial wakening. I appreciate your willingness to come to St. Thomas's despite the lateness of the hour." He sat and, for Holmes, smiled with a rare reassuring charm. He leaned forward, his scratched hands splayed upon his thin knees.

She hesitantly smiled in return. "The officer, Mr. Lestrade, said that there was some emergency here. If I can help, although I can't imagine how, I am happy to."

"Very good. My name is Sherlock Holmes, and my brother here, Mr. Mycroft Holmes, has asked me on behalf of the British government to respond to a quite serious situation here at the church. This is my associate and friend Dr. John Watson."

Her eyes, almost imperceptibly, widened in a split second of perturbation when she recognized the detective's name, and I saw Holmes caught it, subtle as it was. But her words covered for her. "What kind of situation, Mr. Holmes? Is there anyone ill?"

"I take it, Miss Williams, that you have been here at the church before? That is your given name, Victoria Williams?"

She stiffened, a sudden subtle aura of distress and caution about her. "Yes, Mr. Holmes, that is my name. I had once thought it about to change, but it was not to be. I was close to the priest here, Paul Appel." She paused, her head lowered. Then she stared back to Holmes. "I have not seen him, though, for three years, ever since I left for Christian missionary work in Delhi. I never dreamt I would ever come back here. Please tell me, Mr. Holmes, why you have returned me to a painful place from my past, and not play games with me."

"I am sorry to cause you pain, Miss Williams, and I am afraid

I shall cause you more when I respond to your direct, heartfelt question. You were engaged?"

Her suspicion and unease rising by the second, Miss Williams retorted, "It is no business of yours, sir, the nature of my past association with Paul."

"I'm sorry to say that it is. Mr. Appel was found dead this very afternoon, and I'm very sorry to say that he was murdered. We are endeavoring to find his killer, Miss Williams. I believe you can help."

"Sir, that is not possible!"

The look of horror and shock was, to my eyes, utterly sincere. She did not speak for a time, and Holmes let her gather herself. "To answer your question, Paul and I were engaged to be married, but I found his attentions wandering . . ."

"To another lady?" asked Holmes gently.

Indignantly, Miss Williams shook her head. "Oh no, Mr. Holmes. A rival such as that I could have sustained, perhaps conquered; instead, Paul's mind seemed a million miles away from me. He dreamed of the East, of constant travel, of forms of meditative techniques, of matters beyond me, beyond any so-called rival. When I questioned him as to his intentions, I found a strange cruelty I had never seen in him before. He would rise from the sitting exercises taught to him by his Buddhist teachers, but instead of expressing the peace and gentleness he sought, he would say the most cutting and callous things.

"I tried to reach him, Mr. Holmes—I am a stubborn and most loyal person, and I did not give up easily. But finally it came clear to me how much he needed to drive me away, that there was something covert he needed to do, some goal he must achieve, without me living in this parish house as his wife."

"I understand you are now working in India, Miss Williams?"

"So ironic, isn't it, Mr. Holmes? It turned out I was the one who headed East. When a teaching position arose in Delhi, there was nothing here in England to hold me any longer."

"Then why have you now returned? And have you tried to contact Paul Appel in the last week?"

She shifted uncomfortably; as intelligent as she was, Victoria Williams was still not a very good dissembler. "It is not so very surprising, is it, to return home for the Christmas holidays, when one has been away over two years? I still do not understand why you are peppering me with these terrible questions in the middle of the night."

"Oh, we are getting to that. You have still not answered my last question."

"No, Mr. Holmes. I did not try to speak to Paul. Though God knows now I wish I had. I cannot believe he is dead. Please understand me, I knew Paul's faults and limitations as well as anyone could after five years of close regard, even love. Yes, I did love him, and even leaving him at last did not change that love. The passion died away, the longing and regret never did. And now he is gone." Her voice choked, but her eyes remained dry. I suspected she had offered all she could of tears already. "This news is devastating, Mr. Holmes; I wish to return to my rooms and be alone. I want to stop this now . . ."

"Soon, Miss Williams, soon. In fact, I have only one question remaining. What is your romantic association with Mr. Krishnan Viswarath?"

Without a sound, she rose, pale and with an expression of anguish. But before she could speak there was a commotion behind us, the sound of a fierce tussle, and then, a shouted "Watch it there, gov. You can't go in there."

Before us in the doorway of the parlor, breathing heavily, stood Viswarath in the firm grip of two bobbies. His eyes were wide, frantic, and he was shaking his head fiercely. He shook himself free and drew himself with a painful dignity. He stared at us in a mixture of hatred and yet supplication.

"Mr. Holmes, please stop. Leave her alone. She has nothing to do with any of this."

Instantly Holmes rose, and with a grim expression paced over to the doorway to go eye to eye with the Hindu. The detective's voice was hard and accusing. "She sent a telegram here, Mr. Viswarath. To you and no other. I can draw no other conclusion than that you and her former fiancé, Paul Appel, were somehow in conflict over this young woman, and further, that you are a liar and a corrupter of women. Shall I add that of killer?"

Viswarath hissed, and as he drew back his hand, a guard wrenched him back from slapping Holmes. "You are a dangerous man!" the Indian cried as he struggled to reach Holmes. Protectively, I rose, as did Lestrade, to join in restraining Viswarath and to help take him into custody.

"Stop!" screamed Victoria Williams. She ran to Viswarath and clung to him sobbing. "Please stop. You are so wrong . . ."

"Mr. Holmes," muttered Viswarath in a hoarse voice choked with bitterness. "You misjudge me. I protect her, do you not see? Please stop this torture."

"You deny your association with her is irregular?"

"I, sir, am her father," he spat out at Holmes.

We had retreated to review where we were in this exhausting and emotionally draining case, with Mycroft leading the discussion and Sherlock Holmes mostly quiet, pensive. In the kitchen, by the comforting seething hiss of a coal fire, we went through the possibilities of who the murderer was among us.

Holmes was uncharacteristically silent, puffing on his beloved briar pipe to nurse his own thoughts, musing no doubt on the prior painful scene in the parlor. Miss Williams, released, had been escorted back to her Northumberland Hotel room to await the end of the conference, and the fate of her true father.

Viswarath, after she had left, mournfully told us the story of Victoria's life, how her mother, the wife of a diplomat posted in India, had a brief clandestine affair with the poet twenty-four years ago. When the love affair came to light, her husband had returned the family to England and raised the girl with love and a circumspect tact that was nothing short of magnificent. Not until Mr. Williams's death had her mother told Victoria who her real father was.

"Four years ago, in the freshness of first love, she shared this secret with her fiancé, Paul Appel, thinking perhaps that she might now be even more desirable to her clergyman with her exotic heritage revealed." Viswarath gave a bitter, harsh laugh. "After the engagement was broken, she retreated to India, under the guise of becoming a teacher in a missionary school, but in actuality to seek the protection of a father she hardly knew. I hardly think she has completely healed from that bruising experience, Mr. Holmes, but I do think she has learned a great deal about herself, her true nature, living with me.

"I cannot tell you, Mr. Holmes, how much I love my daughter," Viswarath added, now calm and clearly trying to reach Holmes for a little human understanding.

My friend sat pensively, listening hard, still a little shaken by his grievous misunderstanding in the interview of Miss Williams. Yet I could tell he was not yet persuaded that this man was any less guilty of murder for his error in assessing their relationship.

"She had brought so much happiness to my late years. I am her protector now, though of course I must also remain the hidden man. How is a proper English lady to be sired by a black Indian? Unthinkable.

"And that is why we have returned to England, sir. Appel, after ignoring and belittling Victoria, had decided that he, after all, now loved her—or rather, wished to reclaim her, perhaps as a possession of beauty. By a series of letters he threatened, in fact, to publicize our true history if she did not return to him. Your London papers would have loved that story, the Hindu satyr and his lovely scion!

"When I was invited by the archbishop to participate in this secret conclave, it suited my purposes exactly: to properly assess this man who was so coldly threatening my daughter, all in the guise of love. I burned to look at him face-to-face. I found him distant, indifferent to talk to me privately until yesterday, when he at last consented to meet. We were to discuss his 'demands' last evening, after dinner. Needless to say, that talk never happened."

"You realize, Mr. Viswarath, that this makes you a prime suspect to be Appel's killer. He was essentially blackmailing you. Have you any reason for us not to center upon you, Mr. Viswarath? You must have hated the man."

"I did. Could I have killed him? Perhaps. Not in that primitive way in which you found him, however. A neat and quick cut throat would have sufficed for such a man. Not this mangled corpse . . . But if you are looking for an ironclad alibi, like in the good doctor's stories, no, I have none. I was in my room, alone, but I cannot prove that. But I will say this: would I have shamed Victoria by so crudely slaughtering a man, however ghastly and cruel, that she had once loved?"

Then the saddened poet was escorted back to his bedroom, his guard doubled in case he tried to escape.

Mycroft leaned back in an oak chair and sipped a golden glass of inexpensive Spanish sherry, which he was helping himself to from Appel's small private liquor cabinet in the next-door parlor.

"Are you sure Appel's sherry is not poisoned, Mycroft?" Sherlock asked. He already had enough to answer for to the British government without one more death, a brother no less.

"I am all right so far, thank you, Sherlock," replied Mycroft amiably. "But it *has* been distressingly watered down. Now, we have a horrible animalistic murder," Mycroft began, his pudgy hands clasped about his great red-vested midriff, comfortably leaning back in his chair, "and a church full of civilized clerics who all seem pious, devout, virtuous . . .

"So who is our culprit?" Mycroft continued. "The rabbi, in a fit of revenge against our host's anti-Semitic rantings? Not likely. The Muhammadan, trying to frame the Jew? Too crude, and not believable.

"The Russian priest? Archbishop Demetrius is gruff and irritable, but that doesn't make him a killer.

"The little Roman Catholic priest under orders from the cardinal, because Appel was a Modernist and a mild liberal? Can't imagine it, myself.

"The Buddhist monk, who claims to be Appel's friend and appears to be the victim of an interfaith swindle? Possible, but the fellow seems too mild to be such a beastly killer.

"Now we find the Hindu revealed as a protective father, wishing to protect his daughter and himself from embarrassing blackmail. Frankly, my money is on Viswarath, who is too smooth and Eastern-fakir for my taste, and openly contemptuous of Westerners. Especially Englishmen. He might well have been the one who attacked Watson. But enough to kill? Which brings us full circle."

"Why did the presumed killer attack the child and the mother?" I asked.

"That is a strange and disturbing question," Sherlock Holmes interjected, and he nodded to me. "What Watson asks is crucial, I think, Mycroft. And why were the Losse brothers so desperate to leave the church? What did they know, and who frightened them so? For these two questions I have no answers," added Holmes brusquely. "But I compliment you, brother, for your succinct summery of our present situation. True, we now have some credible motives, but Watson's question still hovers over the entire investigation."

I could sense a certain discouragement in my friend, as well as his admirable grim resolve. "You're tired, Holmes. You hardly slept last night in Oxford. And besides, we do have a prime suspect now in Viswarath."

He snapped, "Two hours of sleep on the train. That's not a problem, Watson, though I acknowledge your concern. No, this case of Appel's covert killer, it feels to me as if it were a mere exercise in searching and scratching, more just going through people's suitcases and pockets until something turns up. I need something that brings it all into focus. Yet I can't quite come up with the thread that connects all." He sighed, "I wish I could believe Viswarath is a killer, but I can't."

He paused and stood up, brushing pipe ash off his suit. "I'm just treading water. Let's reconvene the holy men now, see if their tiredness allows a slip or two."

"Holmes, it's nearly five in the morning," I said.

"The perfect time for a little conclave. I need to understand this man Appel, who remains so vague in their replies to my questions. And what exactly did these men talk about in the days leading up to the murder?"

Mycroft huffed. "*Theology*, Sherlock. The dreary queen of the sciences. Hardly stuff to incite murder."

"Religion is passion by another name, Mycroft. That's about all I've learned so far tonight, except that I think I know what Appel was."

"He was an Anglican minister, Holmes," I sputtered. "That we know."

"Well, yes, a monster of a man in priest's clothing. And I am convinced he earned his death, if not the manner of it."

So Inspector Lestrade instructed Sergeant Allen, for the second time this night, to have all the members of this ill-starred secret gathering of the archbishop of Canterbury to be gathered. They were now a haggard, barely polite group.

Cardinal Cappellari, particularly, looked deathly tired, ill and as pale and mottled as watery gruel, his hooded eyes in their shadows oddly clouded and azure, infinitely burdened and melancholy. "Mr. Holmes, are you any closer to capturing the killer of Mr. Appel?" he asked in his thin, quivering Italian-inflected voice, dispensing with the need of Brown's translating.

Holmes tightly smiled, looking over his little congregation, seated in a close semicircle around him. "The night is not over, Your Eminence. We have made progress, but I still need your help."

"Then help we shall, sir. Please, what do you still need to know?" breathed the cardinal quietly, yet with an adamant determination that well matched my friend's.

Holmes, normally so controlled and rational and proud, burst out in a torrent of fierce entreaty, his lean face hard, disappointed. "I *have* asked you for honesty, and instead, all of you have told me pitifully little. You have as a group protected yourselves, and concealed much. Worse, you have pretended—out of charity or self-interest, I don't know—that Mr. Appel was a priest in good standing, a perfect host for your ecclesiastical party gathering, when he was in fact a near thief, a blackmailer, and a hard and quite cruel scoundrel.

"I have, no thanks to you, discovered all these things about your host and more. But there is much I still desperately need to know. What I cannot understand in how you have failed me, and failed your God as well, brothers, is the fact that *it is your lives too* at stake. I can understand the killer lying, but all of you have lied, at least by omission, with the exception of Mr. Brown and perhaps Rabbi Mandleberg."

Canon McCain interrupted, "Come, Mr. Holmes, you must be fair. They may have concealed certain things, yes, but nothing of great value."

"That is shocking, sir," said Holmes, his anger melting into a saddened complaint of weary resignation. "And I remind you that, with a killer among us, we do not know exactly *what* is important yet. Or does your exalted position at Lambeth Palace allow you to know more than I do?"

Mycroft shifted uncomfortably. "Come, Sherlock, there's no need for sarcasm. These omissions and slight prevarications were born, I suspect, from self-preservation, an instinct to protect their various faiths."

Sherlock was unabashed. "True enough, brother. Also pride, ego, and status. I want all these lies ended now. I want, and I demand, your help. I believe it is said, 'The truth shall set you free.' If that is true, this will be the only way we are to get out of here without blood on our hands."

McCain huffily interjected, "You are not blameless here tonight, Mr. Holmes. I believe you owe Mr. Viswarath an apology."

"Mr. McCain, he has already received it. I assure you that that error will not be the only mistake I make tonight. Mistakes are made when you don't square with me, when you hide behind your pious vestments."

To his considerable credit, Viswarath rose and bowed to the detective, though his words were really directed to the canon. "My anger is gone, and with it, my blindness. I did not tell Mr. Holmes what he needed to know. I did not trust him. I do now. May I suggest we all do."

Mycroft said, "Good. Let's begin again. Sherlock, come out of your high dudgeon and tell these gentlemen where things stand."

So, with Holmes's usual terse and cogent style, he proceeded to do just that, telling with an admirable narrative flash what he had uncovered. The holy ones listened, their heads down, haunted and a little haggard.

When he paused, no one spoke until Rabbi Mandleberg broke the silence. "Shame is a powerful thing, Mr. Holmes. Particularly for men who have their whole lives represented the holy. There is no excuse for the things we have chosen to conceal, but you do not need to be a murderer to have secrets you do not want revealed to anyone's pitiless gaze, particularly yours. We learned early in our roles as clergy (some of us the hard way) not to yield up our shadow selves easily. No man of God does."

"It is true I am not practiced in pity," admitted Holmes, his anger now dissipated.

Father Brown spoke. "How can you find a lost man without pity?"

"You gentlemen can provide the pity later. That 'lost man' wants to stay lost, and by God, I shall find him."

Viswarath spoke softly, "Do you remember what Appel said when we first met four nights ago, Father Brown? I have thought about it ever since, and how odd that this man so exposed tonight would have greeted us with this story. That there was a white light streaming down on us from heaven, and that, tragically, God's radiance had been broken down into colored fragments by the prisms of our separate religions.

"What I thought then, and did not say, was that our host was wrong to say our task was to reunite all these colors back to the white of truth. What right have we to adjust or manipulate the gifts God gives us? For all of us, imperfect and hidden as we are, stand in that radiance, that one truth; yet I believe God has given us these prisms for good reason. These colors are each beautiful." The poet shrugged. "We are just here to see the glory. This is what I have learned in this gray, dirty, pale city of London."

"I need to go somewhere to gather my thoughts," said Sherlock Holmes.

"The sanctuary?" I asked.

"Ah, Watson, you know me well. Let's sit for a time under the west rose window. Maybe if I stop talking so much, I could feel my way into this peculiar night. Oh, one thing, Lestrade. Will you ask Father Brown to join us there in the church in a little while? I have one small question to ask him."

"Certainly, Holmes."

Excusing ourselves from Lestrade and Mycroft Holmes, we set out for the church itself. Holmes continued, as we walked, "There is a dread here that is palpable, Watson, circling closer and closer." We left the parish house and crossed over past the Lady Chapel. "A final violence."

Reentering the chilly sanctuary, Holmes walked past the lectern, a regal, glowing eagle whose spread wings held up a great black Bible, then went down the central aisle. Staring up at the darkened rose window twenty feet above us, I realized that in about two hours the light would begin to slowly seep to fill each section of color, bringing to vibrancy the whole imagining of the artist. But it was dark to us now.

Holmes sat himself in the back left pew, quietly gazing back up at the softly lit altar, past the rood screen and above it, to the great painting of Thomas on his knees before the risen Christ. Jesus was holding out his wounded palms to the bewildered and questioning apostle.

Questions, doubts, always. It was a stance my friend well understood.

He then appeared to concentrate on the oak-paneled pulpit where Appel had preached for so many years, almost as if some echo of that stilled voice still reverberated along the stone walls and arching columns, speaking a killer's name. But these were my thoughts; Holmes's rumination was closed to me.

"It's strange," I whispered after we had been silent for ten minutes or so, "to be in a church after all these years. I can't help thinking of an early Sunday school lesson I learned as a child. My first knowledge of murder, so long before I met you, Holmes. What is that phrase from Genesis, where God asks Cain, 'Where is your brother?' " I asked.

A gentle, small voice broke in upon us, and we were both a little startled.

" 'What hast thou done? The voice of thy brother's blood crieth unto me from the ground. And now art thou cursed from the earth, which hath opened her mouth to receive thy brother's blood from thy hand.' " We turned to the small, nearly meek voice of the rotund young Catholic priest, Brown, answering Holmes's request to join us.

"Yes, that's it," I said.

The Roman Catholic priest walked down the pew to us and silently sat next to Holmes. He took off his round spectacles and polished them on his black cassock.

"God speaking to Cain—which is a great coincidence, Mr. Watson, because that was exactly our lesson this morning from this very pulpit," Brown said. "Though I could not participate in the Communion, I did sit there, in that side vestry area, and closely watch and listen. It was quite odd seeing the mass from that angle. I have been thinking of that service all day since." His gentle voice trailed off until I could hardly hear him.

"I asked that you come join us for a moment, Father Brown, because I wanted you to look at something found earlier tonight, downstairs in that awful crypt."

"Awful in what sense, Mr. Holmes? If God is present, there is always awe, a *mysterium tremendum ...*"

"Actually, I meant awful in the sense of cold, clammy, and smelling rankly of blood. I'm afraid I should have looked at this more closely hours ago." He reached into his pocket, and then Holmes's long, slender fingers were dangling the rosary Lestrade had found hours before. The white beads shone like bone.

"Do you recognize this, Father Brown?"

Brown took the rosary and squinted through his thick glasses, then he felt the beads carefully. He shook his head.

"That's what 'prayer' means: a bead," he said softly.

"Watson, your wife's rosary, please."

I reached in my pocket, feeling my old service revolver as I dug around, and pulled the rosary out. Holmes counted the beads on my deceased wife's rosary intently, then stared at the young priest.

"I counted one hundred and eight beads on our recovered rosary, the unknown one. Father Brown?"

"This is unlike any rosary I have ever seen," he said, looking at the unknown beaded string. "On our rosary, such as on your friend Watson's, there are eighty-one beads, with seven sets of ten, representing three sets of holy mysteries—the joyful, the sorrowful, and the glorious mysteries of Christ. Whatever this is, it is not a Roman Catholic rosary." He handed it back to Holmes. "Perhaps there are other faiths that practice prayer using the motion of the hands?"

Holmes grunted, "Mysteries indeed. But perhaps things are starting to clarify a bit."

"Could I have your permission, Mr. Holmes, to look about

the church sanctuary, around the altar, the vestry?" asked Brown. "I know we are all technically under suspicion for these acts, but perhaps I might be able to help resolve this case."

"A priest as amateur detective?" Holmes did not openly scoff at the outlandish suggestion, but he was amused. "This is not one of Watson's stories in the *Strand Magazine*, Father Brown."

"If evil comes from the heart, there is nothing amateur about what I can do here. We spend a great deal of time, we priests, in confessional booths, and people tell us dreadful things, to the very edge, and beyond, of human depravity. Why should people think priests are sheltered?"

Holmes took back the strange rosary, considering, and then looked quizzically at the young man. Then he simply nodded. "I have no idea why I am agreeing to your request. Yet, Father Brown, you always seem to be at the heart of this case for some reason, and I suspect you will be there at the close of it. All right, I will tell Lestrade you have freedom of movement. But I strongly suggest you simply get some sleep and look after your cardinal, and leave the deductions to me."

Father Brown solemnly nodded, as if the unusual permission were nothing more than his proper due. He rose to leave. "Thank you. I'll not be in your way. One more thing, Mr. Holmes. I could not help but overhear the doctor's relating the 'message' of his assailant. What game was the man speaking of, and why did he speak of there being two masters, not one?"

"I am not accustomed to discussing the status of an investigation with my suspects, Father Brown, so I'll just say I do not know the answer to either question. I wish I did. Perhaps two of you allied yourselves in this murder. As to the 'game' referred to from our masked fellow, I suspect that will come clear when we find out the true reason for the death of Mr. Appel."

"It is a sick thing to call such butchery a game," I said.

"Perhaps," said Brown. "For sinners it is all a game, until someone wakes up to what is really at stake. Thankfully, in this game God holds all the cards."

Holmes smiled. "He seems to play them very close to his celestial being, Father. I don't even know what the rules here are yet, much less the means of winning the contest. A damned game, indeed."

"A damned game. Yes. That is what it is. Of course, luckily for us, God bends the rules all the time."

"Even 'Thou shalt not kill'?"

"Commandments are, for us, immovable and immutable. But for God? An author always reserves the right to change the ending."

When we were out of the little priest's hearing, Holmes said to me, "Watson, would you be so good as to pay a visit to Archbishop Demetrius's room, and show him your wife's rosary? Ask him about his, if he has one."

Mystified by Holmes's sudden and inexplicable interest in these kinds of specialized religious items, I nevertheless agreed and set out, walking past Cappellari's room, where through an open door I could see the priest Brown sitting beside the reclining and exhausted-looking cardinal. Brown nodded to me kindly and closed the door.

Moving down the dark and silent hallway, I came to the door of Archbishop Demetrius, and I knocked. "Sir"—I spoke as softly as I could, addressing the Russian priest through the thick oak door—"I'm sorry to bother you at this hour, but Mr. Sherlock Holmes wanted me to ask you a simple question. Might I see you for a moment?"

A heavy rustle, and then the familiar gruff voice answered in a moment. "Wait just a moment, please."

Then the huge bearded cleric opened his door and glared at me, his eyes bleary with sleep. He rubbed his chest, grunted, and nodded to me, looking like a great beached gray seal, scared in innumerable battles but magnificent.

"May I come in?" I asked.

Reluctantly, Demetrius opened the door wider to admit me, and I sat down. A lone candle lit the room, fitful shadows flickering. Demitrius muttered, "Please. It is very late and we are all feeling very upset and anxious for this painful gathering to be over. What may I do for you?" He was somehow smaller and not as impressive without his habitual black conical hat and its trailing cloth; in fact, he was balding, his grizzled hair receding, and his broad forehead pale and heavily wrinkled.

I showed him the Roman Catholic rosary and asked him if he possessed one like it.

He reached for his glasses, settled them on, and then gazed at my rosary, then dismissed me with a touch of exasperation. "All rosaries are alike. Tell your Mr. Holmes to solve this murder and let us be out of these cells. We have an agreement to let us make calls to our superiors soon, with sunrise."

"Sorry to have bothered you, Your Holiness. I assure you Mr. Holmes is working as hard as he can to solve this tragic murder and let you finish your business in England and be on your way home."

He looked at me with a cool appraisal, as if he were really noticing me for the first time. "You know this man for many years, yes?"

"For twenty years now. He does not often fail, I know that. Something tells me that the inner connections he needs are falling into place. After all those years I still don't know how he does it, but he can somehow spy into the heart of any deceit."

"Then he is a greater man than I, for nothing here makes any sense. I will be glad to go home from this nightmare. Tell

Mr. Holmes we all look to him to save us. I greatly fear who this killer is."

"I wish I had some reassurance to offer you, but unfortunately, we are all bound together in this."

Demetrius gave a bitter laugh. "I think we of the gathering more than the detectives."

"I *do* trust Holmes to protect us, though, as best he can. Still, he is just a man. Say a prayer, Your Holiness, for us all."

For once, I felt a certain empathy for the Russian priest, and as we shook hands, I felt my grip was being swallowed up. I quickly said my good-nights, apologizing again for waking him up and thanking him for his help. Walking away, I certainly agreed with his wonderment over Holmes's strange obsession with prayer beads. I greeted Sergeant Allen, who was pacing along the darkened hallway, and he nodded solemnly to me. Our excursion to the docks seemed, already, a week ago.

Going to find Holmes to report upon what little Demetrius could add to our investigation, I found him in the parlor speaking animatedly on the church telephone. Holmes was leaning back in the great purple chair, looking comfortably bowed in its curve, relaxed like a cat.

"Yes, I would appreciate it if you could use all your contacts there. I have also asked Mycroft to use his Foreign Office people and the ambassador to thoroughly research the matter. Yes, I know it's morning there, and so I hope you can make your calls, and then quickly contact us here. Give my best to your brother, and yes, I'd be happy to have you stop by Baker Street after the New Year. You don't need to thank me again. Now I'm the one who needs you."

I must have looked quizzically at Holmes, because he smiled as he set the receiver down. "Just calling in a debt, Watson. I'll explain if anything useful develops."

He turned to Mycroft, who was impatiently standing beside him at the telephone.

"Brother, use whatever contacts you have there. These two questions must be resolved by dawn, through the telegraph or by phone." My friend looked a good deal more happy than when we had shared a pew in the sanctuary not twenty minutes ago. I could see his mental wheels were spinning frantically now, no longer grinding away.

"Now, Watson, tell me about your visit to our Russian friend. And come keep me company as I prowl through the rector's bedroom at last. Be a good disciple and stay up with me. I should have given Appel's bedroom and personal files and books a careful look hours ago, but the Losse brothers put a halt to that, poor beggars. I'm afraid I have much reading still to do in his office, and the night is growing short."

"Certainly, Holmes. Well, Demetrius just said all rosaries are alike, and more or less dismissed me."

"Tell me about his icon, Watson. I've forgotten from our earlier visit; where was it set up?"

"He had no icon that I could see. The room was almost bare. There certainly wasn't any holy relic like an icon on display."

"Capital. Was there a guard on his room?"

"Certainly, just like all the others. In fact, it was Sergeant Allen."

"Now stay with me and keep me awake."

I must have fallen asleep, however, because I roused myself awake in a great old comfortable sitting chair to see my friend seated at Appel's huge oak desk.

Smoke wreathed about Holmes's shoulders and face, and he bore an expression of determined concentration. The policeman's death and the attack on the Desta child and mother were still weighing on him, and I could tell he feared more chaos to come. There were many books and dozens of papers strewn all around him, and behind him, file cabinets were yawning open, their innards spilled and now scattered.

"Sorry, Holmes, I dropped off. I should go and see if Mrs. Desta is still unconscious. How long was I asleep?"

"About an hour. Now I know how Jesus felt in Gethsemane." I hastily rose and went behind him at Appel's desk, where a heavy book lay open. It appeared to be one of Appel's esoteric books on Eastern worship, with Holmes's hands resting on a picture of prayer beads. Bending down, I could just spy the caption: "Japanese meditation necklace, 108 beads (also Tibetan)." Holmes slapped the great old book shut with a resounding clap, then turned to me. "But I'm glad to have you awake. I need you to help me with something in the bedroom."

We rose and Holmes pointed to Appel's bed. Holmes had shoved it aside from its space against the wall, and he knelt down. "Bits of dried wallpaper paste trailing along the floor here, from the office. Interesting. And do you notice in the floral pattern of the wallpaper here by the bed, how the pattern is disturbed, reversed?" He delicately tapped about three feet up from the floor in a circular motion. "There is a peculiarly hollow sound here, and here. Come, let's rip this off."

The plaster wall when exposed showed a smooth cut in the wall, and Holmes gently eased out the two-foot-by-three section to expose a brown packing case crammed into the tight space. A chain was thoroughly wrapped around the sturdy luggage.

"Pull this out and blast it open, please."

After warning our nearest bobby about the noise, I proceeded to shoot off the lock with my revolver with two quick blasts. The calm of the book-lined bedroom was shattered by the blast. Wrenching open the top, Holmes started to root through the clothes and objects quickly, setting one long cylindrical object aside.

"Ah," he muttered. Searching with deft and sure movements, soon he hefted up a sack of substantial weight. He leaned back and held aloft to me a clothes bag.

"Let us see what this is," he excitedly said. "Mr. Appel went to some trouble to keep it from us."

In moments, laid before us on the bed, lay an odd collection of objects: an old walking stick, an old pair of glasses, a silver-plated bowl, a small ivory hand drum, and a black-and-yellow rosary. Holmes quickly counted the beads on the latter, and nodded.

"One hundred and eight beads," he said with satisfaction. Then he stretched back to straighten out his lean back. His gray eyes went to the facing wall, where Appel's framed series of Eastern scenes were hung. As if drawn by an electrical force, Holmes, with a half smile on his face, pointed to one.

It was of a magnificent and vast white-columned building, a palace built into a mountainside. I did not know much about Tibet, but even I could identify the Potala in Lhasa, the nearly inaccessible city that Holmes in disguise had visited during his years of exile (when even I, along with the rest of the world, assumed him dead).

"Watson, I am a perfect fool," suddenly cried Holmes, a look of triumph and horror all at once. "All along I have been thinking of the wrong White City!"

Just at that remarkable statement, Lestrade entered. "Mr. Holmes, I have the return tickets you asked for—for everyone except the Russian priest, Demetrius. He says he lost them yesterday . . ."

"Yes," said Holmes triumphantly, "he seems to have lost them, glued here under the lid of his hidden little travel case. Now, I need Mycroft. Has he returned?"

"He's just coming in, sir."

"Hurry—double the guard over Mrs. Desta and her child. All is clear now."

Without another word of explanation, he ran to the rectory parlor, where Mycroft stood, just brushing snow off his coat.

"Blasted storm, Sherlock. Almost impossible to navigate. You were right on all fronts, Sherlock. And I just received word from our agent in St. Petersburg that a body of your description was indeed found two weeks ago near the metropolitan train station. Plus, your reporter friend called back and helped confirm the facts. The body in the morgue there has been identified with your help."

"Listen, each of you, we must move with utmost urgency. We must find Demetrius, and quickly. He will be armed, and very dangerous. He has known for some hours that his time is limited, but perhaps he does not realize how close we are to identifying him." Steel eyes flashing with the release of the final chase, he wheeled to face the inspector.

"Lestrade, please have the woman and child removed from this church, *now*. He will not hesitate to kill again. Silence, and stealth, please. His room, first."

As quickly and as quietly as we could, we stole down the empty guest room hallway, coming around the long way. As we came to the turn, the guard was missing. With a warning look, Holmes brought his finger to his lips for complete silence.

To no one's surprise, the Russian Orthodox priest's small bedroom was now empty. Holmes turned to me.

"Watson, we will need your revolver, I believe. The doors of all the other rooms we can see seem closed and secure—which leads me to suspect our man is in the church itself. Mycroft, stay here. This is not a situation for you. I need you to secure the rectory and coordinate the incoming police."

Holmes looked at me, and nodded. "We have been here before, have we not, my friend?"

He did not need to say more.

For the third time that night, we headed past the parlor to reenter the church. Holmes edged to the red door that led to the Lady Chapel. We paused to listen, and to our distress heard a strange, strangled breathing, a gasping rattle. With a bound, Holmes thrust himself forward and jerked open the door. Collapsed at our feet in the stone entryway was the long, lanky form of Cardinal Cappellari.

Holmes knelt down and turned the gasping man over to face us. The cleric's drawn face was chalky white and his cracked lips were blue. He was trying to speak, but his mouth quivered silently.

"He's having a heart attack, Holmes," I whispered, and as I knelt to join Holmes in holding the cardinal up, the man shuddered convulsively. He was trying to speak, but his trembling lips, traced with white spittle, could not form the words. His eyes suddenly stared beyond us in a gaze I have seen too many times before. The cardinal's rigid form then melted, relaxing into the release of death.

We gently laid him back down, and Holmes pressed the haggard old man's eyes closed. In the dim hallway, his bright red cassock trim was beginning to catch the first faint flickers of light from a window above us.

"Where is Father Brown? The cardinal must have seen Demetrius going out this way, likely with a weapon. He couldn't halt the man for long, but he must have tried. He sacrificed himself. Which means Demetrius is out there in the sanctuary. It's the only place where we have no guards posted. Hurry."

Dawn was at last slowly brightening the banks of stained-glass windows, and red sparkles of light now arched across the dark wooden pews. We crept quietly up the right aisle, listening intently. As my eyes got used to the darkness, I surveyed the church. All seemed empty, barren.

Surely the man had not escaped, not after all this! I had sat down alone with him only ninety minutes before, looking into the sleepy and unconcerned eyes of a psychopath. I had shaken his hand.

As we moved past the north transept, fifty feet from the pulpit, we heard furious whispers, then the sound of a sharp slap, which reverberated through the long nave. In the black recesses of the area before the altar, I looked hard to dimly see two figures tightly locked in a brutal struggle. It was difficult to see exactly who the figures were, but there was no mistaking the berserk motions of a grim struggle.

Then to our dismay, at exactly the same moment, we saw the almost comical figure of Father Paul Brown step out from the vestry dressing area to the left, some distance ahead of us. The diminutive priest seemed to be totally oblivious of the two men fighting beyond him as he started strolling across the transept back across to the Lady Chapel. I started to call out to warn him, but Holmes again desperately motioned for silence as we crept as quietly and quickly as we could toward them.

Then I thought I could see Demetrius's vast bulk towering over a supine Hugh McCain, who was trying to escape the Russian's blows. The priest was lying back, and the great bearded giant, still clothed in his vast black-and-gold cassock, was slamming his fists into the priest's twisting body below him.

"Cross over to the other side of the church, Watson," Holmes hissed.

I hastened to obey, and Holmes rose to his full height. Finally, he shouted out in a sharp voice, "Stop! You're surrounded. Don't even think of harming Canon McCain." Now Brown jerked up from his abstracted stroll and wheeled around to see, fifteen feet behind him, the two men struggling.

Demetrius jerked up his sweaty face, and grimaced. "Not yet, Mr. Holmes." We were still more than twenty-five feet away.

As Demetrius yelled, I saw McCain rise up and grapple anew with the Russian. With Holmes now running down the aisle aiming for him, Demetrius simply gave a mighty backhanded blow to McCain, who toppled backward, hitting the stone floor before the altar and then sprawling down the steps with a sickening series of hard thuds.

Before Holmes could reach him or I could circle around to him from the side, Demetrius surprised us by choosing to leap down from the altar. With a mighty howl, he then grabbed the cowering Father Brown, who was then whirled around to face us. Now Demetrius flashed out a great knife that quickly went to Brown's throat.

"Come another inch forward, and the world has one less priest. I should have simply killed McCain and gotten out of this damned church. Don't worry, I would have left my tracks in the snow so you could follow, like the bloodhound you so resemble."

"Please unhand Father Brown and surrender. There are no avenues of escape, Demetrius—or should I say Valeriy Medved? Your vaunted reputation precedes you, though I never thought I would ever encounter you here in England. But the duel is over, Medved."

The Russian laughed. "There is so much you do not know, Holmes. This game is not through, though I now see I should have left at midnight with the uproar over those Mongols. The temptation to stay a little while in the ignorant presence of my inept pursuer Mycroft Holmes, and to spar a touch with you, was too enticing. Still, I have escaped greater traps than this before." His gruff, halting Russian accent had now disappeared, and he spoke his still crude words in creamy tones of cultured English. "It's been a positive joy to watch you fumble about, Mr. Holmes; I really don't know where you got this exhaulted reputation. Good publicity, perhaps."

Holmes, calm and not taking the bait, observed, "You had a slight advantage, Medved. You were masked."

"Oh, Mr. Holmes, I thought *you* were the great actor, the man of hundreds of disguises! Your Wilde said it so well, that there is no truth like that of masks." He craned his neck around to the left, where I crouched in the shadows. "Come no further, Mr. Watson—I see you skulking around the far corner behind the pulpit. Now, I must go."

Slowly, he moved to the center aisle, half dragging Brown, whose feet scratched along the engraved stone memorials. Just as they were about to reach the end of the pews and almost to the porch area, the main door smashed open and four policemen, led by Lestrade, came streaming in, sticks at the ready, backlit by the London dawn.

"Hold your men steady, Lestrade," Holmes's voice barked out. "He has the priest Brown at knifepoint."

Suddenly panicked, Medved broke for the door leading to the bell tower on the left, effortlessly dragging the priest with him. His voice came to us as he climbed, reverberating down the stone walls of the tower.

"Only Holmes to come forward. Anyone else, the little man dies."

We were free now to move forward, and we ran to join Lestrade. Holmes leaned to whisper to me: "I'm going in the tower to negotiate with Medved. The only way to save Father Brown is for me to offer myself in his stead."

"No, Holmes, no."

"I do so only in the knowledge that you are going to go up the other tower, opposite, and that you will then cross over to us. I'll maneuver us on this side to the third level, where there is leaded glass. Then we see how things go."

"I'll do it, Holmes. But with all the icy snow, I can't promise I can cross over on the roof."

Without a further word to me, Holmes turned and calmly shouted up the tower stairway.

"Medved, I accept your challenge. And I offer you this: your odds of escape are far better with me as your hostage than with Father Brown. Do you think Mycroft, my brother, would authorize the killing of a Russian agent when I am at your side? Let him go, and I promise you as a gentleman that I will substitute for him."

Medved, of all things, laughed. "It is a pleasure dealing with English gentlemen. Such charm, such chivalry! You play the game fairly. I am playing another game, still a pleasure, but not by your empire's rules. No, I will survive, and you, well, we shall see. But it *would* be a pleasure to rid the world of one priest."

After that insane rant, there was a brief silence above, and in that time I had scrambled across the nave and, as silently as I could, started up the other steep tower steps.

I no longer could hear anything other than a muffled sound of Holmes's urgent pleading. One flight, then two, and then, huffing, I came to the third level. The stained glass here, facing the roof parapet, was not hinged or paneled, so I had no choice but to carefully smash it out with the butt of my gun. Even then, it was a tight squeeze for me to ease out onto the rampart, a drop of three feet into snow.

The rising sun stained everything a glowing yellow white,

and stiff winds buffeted me as I righted myself. I dared not look down to where London lay spread out beneath me, the early morning street cleaners and slow Sloane Street traffic starting to clear away the night's thick snow, the glow of fires starting to be lit, the cry of gulls from the Thames wheeling about me. I felt atop the world, and never more alone.

It was more slippery here even than I had feared, but I found I could crawl slowly along the gentle slope of the parapet, using both of my frozen hands to clutch the slick rim of the rampart. I nearly slipped once, and my legs swung over the precipice for a heart-sickening second, but luckily a jagged edge of gritty ice allowed me to scramble crablike back to safety.

Finally, sweat drenching my body despite the cold wind whipping about me, I at last reached the opposite tower (though it probably took only three minutes), and I eased myself up against the freezing stone. My hands were going numb, but I managed to ease out my revolver to ready myself. Somewhere, a hundred miles away, my fiancée was probably stirring in her dawn restiveness, warm and unaware our future life hung so precariously four flights up a church tower overlooking Chelsea.

Careful not to cast a shadow against the glass, I struggled to listen to what was going on inside. It was hard to make anything out, but I could barely make out the Russian's gruff, boasting tone—so I guessed Brown was still alive. I imagined Holmes on his part was slowly easing up the tower, step by reassuring step, nearing the point where Medved would allow him to exchange himself for the priest.

My problem was how to get inside.

I could break the glass, but the sudden noise could startle Medved into something dangerous. On the opposite side, facing away from the street and up about six feet, was a small doorway that lead to the sloped roof. That was my best bet, but the ascent looked suicidal. But a dour gargoyle, carved whimsically like a man smoking a pipe, might allow me to ease myself up to where I could then crash through the paneled door. Thank goodness church architects still affectionately retained stone gargoyles, even upon a modern church!

I brushed off as much of the snow and ice as I could from the shining gray slate before me, and slowly started to pull myself up. I could just reach up and balance myself from a drainpipe running along the back of the tower. Then I stood, balanced above eternity, and the knob of the door was within my reach. Even though I was buffeted by freezing winds, sweat continued to pour down my face as I strained to get a grip.

Miraculously, it turned—the tower door was not even locked. The small portal swung out, and I lunged in and through the tight little doorway. For as moment I felt the delicious sense of release from danger, until I remembered I had fallen into a situation perhaps more perilous. But I lay sprawled gratefully on a dusty granite floor, gasping, and when I looked up, I could see great silent church bells another fifteen feet above me. I hoped to God that they were not about to strike the hour.

Now the voices below me were clear, rising to me. I painfully rose, the wrenching pain aggravated from my tussle at the dock burning through my thigh. With my small revolver back in my hands, I silently crept down the dusty stairs.

"All right, Mr. Holmes—another few steps up, and I will let him go," the spy was saying. "Then you and I will get out of this gloomy church. I took the precaution of having a coach waiting less than a block away—in case I needed to speed away, in such an eventuality as this. Then we shall see what we will do with you."

"As long as no one else dies," Holmes hastily replied.

I waited until Medved pushed Father Brown away from himself as he reached out to grab Holmes's lapel. I stepped out above them to shout, "Back, Holmes. Medved, drop that knife, now!"

The Russian agent whirled around and came at me with the knife glinting. He was nearly upon me when I at last fired, but I must have only grazed one of his arms, cloaked as he was in his vast priestly gear. Bits of blood splattered my eyes, and the Russian roared with pain but kept coming, and then he slashed at me, the knife cutting my hand and sending my service revolver flying. The old gun went scattering up the stone steps, and then, sickeningly, at last toppled out the still open door onto the snowy roof, far beyond my reach.

I grabbed his knife hand and tried to turn him, but Medved, at least fifty pounds heavier than I and ten years younger, was impossibly strong. I could feel his bristly beard and his garlic breath upon me as I strained to hold the knife from my chest.

Our eyes locked, and I swear he smiled down at me. He enjoyed the fear he saw in my drenched face, the panic of one who is far weaker than he, even with his wound. This man not only had no fear of killing; his expression revealed a peculiar bliss. "Pray for us all," I had said.

"I've got a gun trained on you," shouted Holmes, racing up the steps to where we struggled. Even so near death, I remember thinking: *Holmes did not have a gun.*

Then there was a loud, reverberating crack, for all the world like a shot, and Medved wrenched back, looking back toward Holmes with a mixture of fear and surprise. In that moment, I pushed out with my last remaining strength, and the spy turned, off balance, and tumbled hard backward until he slammed the stained glass and crashed on through. Glass flew all about us in radiant shards, and he was suddenly gone. Shuddering cold wind flooded into the space where he had been suspended.

Holmes rushed up to me and together, both in shock, we looked down.

Medved's body had not hit the snowy pavement of Sloane Street, but rather had hideously impaled itself on the spiked metal railings of the arched windows just below the second story of the bell tower. He twitched, facing up to us, then was still, his bearded mouth open in a noiseless cry.

"Good Lord, Holmes, what did you fire with? You *never* carry a gun."

Still breathing hard, Holmes held up an exploded Christmas cracker that he had carried from his Oxford adventure, the one he had thoughtlessly placed in his jacket after I had tossed it to him on the train just eighteen hours ago.

"Consider your Christmas present returned, my friend." Holmes was still breathing hard, and he was careful to step away from the yawning window. "My God, Watson, that was a close-run thing, to quote Wellington. I know one thing, though: the younger Rosewater's debt to us is now truly repaid."

"I *thought* that must be Jeffrey Rosewater, the reporter, you were on the phone with earlier! So the solution lay in Russia," I babbled on, still marveling that we were both alive. My hand wound was minor, and I started wrapping my handkerchief about my bloody palm, squeezing tight. Our small band of brothers all had wounds to bind this sunrise.

"Only partially, Watson. I'll explain more when we gather everyone together." He looked back down with concern at Father Brown, who was still sitting on the landing below us, where he had been shoved hard by Medved against rough granite walls, like a child's flung toy. But to my vast relief Brown seemed uninjured as, at last, he started to rise. After inspecting and resettling his cracked spectacles back on his stubby nose, the priest started the short climb to us.

Holmes whispered to me, "There is much we must attend to first, and sad news to break. The cardinal . . ."

Father Brown finally joined us and shakily stood, his black cassock flapping from the sharp wind from the shattered stained-glass window. He leaned out carefully and gazed down with pity on the crumpled wreckage of the spy in priest's garb pinioned below us. The huge shattered window was a jagged frame for a waking London arrayed below us.

He crossed himself.

Six

PRIME

St. Thomas's Church, 7 A.M.

Before explanations, there was indeed much havoc to see to.

An ambulance arrived to take the cook, Senet Desta, to the hospital for continued observation, though I thought I saw positive signs she was coming back to consciousness. I felt confident she would fully recover. After all the death of the last twenty-four hours, I was elated that her prospects were improving.

After some telephone calls, I contented myself that the little boy Shunapal, taken in by a kindly St. Thomas's church family, was indeed safe and perfectly fine, and that he hopefully would soon be reunited with his mother. I went outside the church for a breath of cold air, still inwardly shaking from my near fall from the tower.

It crossed my mind to talk to my fiancée about whether we could perhaps help in Shunapal's future education. When you come as close to death as I had this morning, twice in fact, you think about a good deed or two to balance the score. Walking back toward the church, I surveyed the battlement edging of the church roof four stories above me with an incredulous shudder, and vowed, "Never again," but I knew better. If Holmes needed me, I would go.

"Watson, I'd appreciate your continued close observation of Mrs. Desta," Holmes said as I came up the steps. For once, Holmes had not accurately read my mind, but he was close enough. He was standing casually at the red church doors, now swinging free in the wind, partly knocked off their hinges, with their central panels shattered. "I suspect she will have much to tell us when she has fully recovered. And it will not be a pretty story."

Getting Medved's body down had been hastily executed by Lestrade's police, before snow sweepers, curious Sloane Street shoppers, and passersby gathered to gawk, understandably mystified and aghast at the sight of a gold-and-black-cassocked priest impaled on the front of an austere Anglican church. Those kinds of questions, and the resulting shock, no one needed.

Particularly the archbishop of Canterbury, who was informed by phone of the night's strange sequence of horrors by a stalwart Canon McCain, whose head had been severely bloodied by his fall. I did not think he had broken any bones or suffered a concussion from Medved's hands, but he was still extremely pale and only a fierce dedication to duty (so reminiscent of Holmes) was keeping him on his feet after such trauma.

Still, before being taken to his doctor's in Harley Street, McCain demanded to stay and hear Holmes's explanation for the death of Appel and so much else that had transpired this long night. So he laid himself down on the great parish room couch, after I had administered ice and headache powders, waiting for all of us to regather there.

We had more grisly work to do. Father Brown and I, assisted by Holmes and Rabbi Mandleberg, gently and with as much respect as we could summon, took Cardinal Cappellari's body to his room. With a calm dignity, Father Brown composed and crossed the arms of his superior, a man he had known for only five days. I wondered if he would somehow pay a price for this death, and be subtly punished in the future for the cardinal's demise. I placed coins over Luigi Cappellari's eyes, holding them closed.

Priests from the nearby newly constructed Roman Catholic cathedral of Westminster were on their way to take the body back there in secret, where it would be announced later in the day that the cardinal, in doing ordinary church business, had died quietly in the night. No one would ever know he had ever visited St. Thomas's.

In respect, we sat quietly by his body for some time, after Father Brown had offered prayers of blessing and last rites. I was touched that it was the rabbi who washed the dead man's face and hands, and joined Brown in smoothing the look of pain locked into the man's face.

Finally, Rabbi Mandleberg said, in his low and Teutonic tones, "It is easy to find all the ways in which this gathering has been marred, ruined. But I must say to you, Mr. Holmes, that when I consider that the cardinal struggled to stop Demetrius, even with the precarious state of his health, I am reminded of the momentous sacrifices people still offer. I will tell you what I will take home to Berlin—that we religious people have been too harsh, too uncharitable, in looking at one another's faith, and that it is time to judge others by the best and noblest of their actions."

Holmes looked up, simply listening. He did not reply, but his expression was inexpressibly sad.

In that silence, Kozan, Viswarath, and al-Khaledis then joined us in the wakelike atmosphere of the small bedroom. Holmes looked up and nodded to Viswarath, but again said nothing. The Hindu gave a slight bow to the detective.

The rabbi, his eyes closed, began slightly rocking as he mumbled the words of Kaddish. His mournful tones filled the room, and nothing I have ever heard seemed more right, more fitting, than these ancient words. When he had finished, there was silence for a time, and then Mandleberg spoke quietly to us.

"We Jews have a story, gentlemen, that when Adam and Eve were being turned out of the garden of Eden, an angel smashed the gates. The fragments of the wreckage flew all over the earth, and we find them today as precious gems. Each religion picks up its brilliant fragment and thinks it alone reflects the light of heaven. Perhaps our task is to fit our fragments together and rebuild the gates of Eden."

Father Brown was staring at Holmes. "They say the gateway to God's throne in heaven has a name."

"What is it?" Holmes asked.

"The mercy seat."

"Then let there be enough mercy to cover us all," Holmes answered at last. "I ask you all to join Canon McCain and my brother, Mycroft, in the parish room. I have a story to tell you there. And I trust forgiveness will not be in short supply."

Al-Khaledis bowed and said, "Allah be praised, it never is."

As we left the room, Holmes made a special effort in the narrow hallway to say farewell to Father Brown, who was going to go with the cardinal's body to Westminster Cathedral. Clearly, he wanted to stay and hear all, but he had holy orders to fulfill first.

Holmes had clearly taken a likening to the little curate. "I need to thank you, Father Brown. You have been most helpful to me over this night watch." Then he smiled ruefully. "Though your wanderings in the sanctuary nearly got you killed."

"Oh, I found what I was looking for," he replied absently. "Perhaps—perhaps I could stop by your rooms at some point in the near future? There are some issues concerning the case here I would like to explore."

Holmes nodded at the slight fellow, who stood there clutching his umbrella and broad-brimmed black priest's hat. His fellow Roman Catholic priests, holding the shrouded body of Cardinal Cappellari upon a stretcher, were waiting for him silently.

"Certainly, with pleasure, Father Brown."

"God bless you, Mr. Holmes." He nodded slightly, and he gave me a small smile, the first I had ever seen on his bland countenance. "Dr. Watson." And he turned and left us.

"Odd fellow, Watson, but you know, don't let that stolid round face and those blank gray eyes fool you," Holmes ruminated as the circle of Roman Catholic priests stole out with their sad burden. "Brown's a little genius, mark my words. I'm glad he's going to confine himself to the confessional, and not give me a run for my money."

We were gathered once again in the rectory living area, with McCain still feeling quite dizzy, but the canon still insisted he was not going anywhere until he understood the true nature of the night's desecration of this church and all the mystifying events of the last fourteen hours. All of us were nursing steaming cups of tea, haggard from the lack of sleep but anxious to hear at last from Holmes. He stood and solemnly began to speak, his deeply scratched hands gripping his black coat lapels.

"I'll not make this long, and there are still a few details to be cleared up, and Mrs. Desta's condition to be seen to. When she awakes, I trust she will confirm much I have to relate to you now.

"Now, Mycroft, when Lestrade came to me last evening, more than fourteen hours ago, you presented me with a body that appeared to have suffered grievous and malicious wounding. Indeed, Appel's corpse was nearly hacked away at the extremities. The horror of it nearly distracted me from understanding what I was looking at. It would take the accumulation of many clues to remind me of something from my own past that led me to the truth.

"But the first important thing was that there was very little blood—which strongly suggests Appel died before his body was mutilated."

"Meaning what?" asked Mycroft.

"That he was killed by some other means. By whom or how I did not know. I know now." He held aloft a small, half-filled vial. "Not quite two hours ago, I discovered this on the body of the man you knew as Aleksandr Demetrius. I trust some testing at Scotland Yard will reveal it to be a poison, possibly slow acting. I would not in the meantime taste or touch it, Lestrade," he said as he handed it to the aghast policeman.

"Then why was the body treated so?" I burst out.

"Ah, that takes a little getting to, Watson. I questioned each of you, including Demetrius, and learned very little, but I have already delivered that lecture. A few things came out: Mr. Viswarath wondered why he kept smelling burning juniper leaves. Mr. Kozan, whose room was above the undercroft, directly over the body, heard faint sounds like laughter: 'Ha! Ha!' And Father Brown, whose help tonight was invaluable, informed me that the rosary found near the body was not of Roman Catholic origin, but of some other religion. With a hundred and eight beads, it turns out to be Tibetan Buddhist."

"Tibetan?" asked Mycroft. "Does this have anything to do with your travels after the Moriarty affair at the Reichenbach Falls?" Mycroft had been the only one who knew that Holmes had not actually died at the falls, and Holmes had indeed penetrated the forbidden high country of Tibet, all the way to Lhasa.

"Not directly, no. But during that time away from England I did enter Tibet and met many holy leaders, including the regent of the small boy who was the Dalai Lama. Watson, that is why you heard me cry out that I had my focus on the wrong White City. All along, I had been thinking Appel was drawn to the World's Parliament's White City, those great plaster buildings on the shores of Lake Michigan. But no. There is another White City, and I have been there. I stayed in the city of Lhasa for a time, fulfilling some work in Mycroft's interests there. I remember well the beauty of the White Palace, the Potala, and the burning of the great butter lamps, the sonorous sound of the chanting, the clicking of the prayer wheels, the smell of incense and dung fire smoke.

"I am not being nostalgic here, gentlemen—these experiences came back to me dimly as the night went on, and along with some reading in some esoteric volumes on Tibetan ritual from Appel's library, I was able to recall something I was told of, but never saw, in my travels. In a land so frozen as Tibet, apparently the burial of bodies is not possible much of the year. Thus a strange, to us, burial tradition has evolved.

"There are professional men, called, I believe, 'body breakers,' who take a corpse and hack it to small pieces. The vultures sweep in, and then even the bones are ground to powder. For the very distinguished and holiest of the dead, a mask is made of thin gold, the clothes are turned backward, and the legs are tied, drawn up toward the chest."

"And that's what we discovered done to Appel!" Lestrade exclaimed. "His priest's clothes were backward. This was done to *honor him?*"

"There is much I do not understand here, but yes, the Losse brothers, Malik and Harruad, were apparently Buryat Mongols, who keep the religious practices of Tibetan Buddhism. They loved and revered their master, Paul Appel, and when they found his body, they proceeded to prepare his body. It is only a twenty-minute walk to the banks of the Thames, where birds and rats will happily pick at meat, particularly in a hard winter like this.

"While engaged in this gruesome ritual, they were calling into Appel's ear the phrases 'Hic! Phat!' and other phrases from their Book of the Dead, a kind of guide read to the dying to help them navigate through the snares and traps of what they call the *bardo* state—similar to what the church has called purgatory.

"Only, this *bardo* state is an intermediate step prior to either being born again in another body or escaping reincarnation altogether. Clearly, the brothers were interrupted in their holy task by the unplanned arrival of Father Brown. They were also afraid for their lives, as well as being held falsely responsible for his death. That is why they forced their escape. They knew their own lives were in danger, for they knew far too much."

"I'm slowly starting to see the political ramifications," muttered Mycroft.

"I'm as confused as before, Holmes," I added.

"We live in interesting times, Watson. Part of what I was exploring for Mycroft in Tibet all those years ago was how much influence Russia actually had in the high Himalayas. The answer at the time was, not much. The men who play this long-drawn-out struggle between Britain and Russia call it 'the great game.' From Afghanistan to Tibet, the land of snows, this secret war goes on with greater intensity every year. The Foreign Office has had many indications that Russian spies have made many feelers into northern Tibet and, on occasion, have joined with the Manchu Chinese to try to control the country. Imagine the danger to India and our interests if Tibet fell into the Russian or Chinese orbit.

"This influence would be possible if they could somehow control the Dalai Lama, not only the chief religious figure of

Tibet but also the strongest political power there. He is like our archbishop and prime minister all in one. Our agents in Calcutta follow things as best they can, but we are significantly cut off from what is actually happening in Lhasa. The Tibetans are fiercely independent and do not want to be anyone's pawn, but political intrigue from half a world away caused these murders, gentlemen.

"You see, the selection of the Dalai Lama is quite unusual. When the Dalai Lama dies (and the last four or five have died very young indeed, very likely poisoned), the office is vacant until a council can determine where the spirit of the Dalai Lama, the 'Chenrezi,' has chosen to settle. The little boy must have some distinguishing marks—large ears, long eyes, eyebrows curling up at the corners, streaks like tiger skin on the legs, and conch-shell prints on the palm of each hand . . ."

Then it came to me like a slap on the face. The small bandages upon Shunapal Desta . . . "The cook's little boy—the bandages of plastic surgery!" I exclaimed. "London is the only place in the world where that sort of new surgery is safe."

"Exactly, Watson. There was obviously some sort of conspiracy on the part of Medved, a well-known Russian secret agent, to work with those who wish to kill the present Dalai Lama, incidentally a most pleasant young man when I met him a decade ago, and replace him with a new ruler. You need more than the marks, however. The boy must be able to select the true belongings of the lama: a pair of spectacles, his silver eating bowl, his yellow-and-black rosaries, his walking stick, and a little hand drum. Duplicates are used to test the child, and the one who selects correctly becomes the new Dalai Lama. And the regent who controls the boy controls the nation. *These are the objects we discovered in Appel's trunk.* My guess is that the little boy was going to grow up with these artifacts as his playthings, so that at the crucial time he would be able to unhesitatingly practice the ritual correctly. The odd thing about this plan, and one aspect that shows the desperate and grasping nature of the plot, is that reincarnation of the Lama of course must come after death, this insidious poisoning. But the lad was small and clearly younger looking than his age, and by the time the Regent would send his men to test the child in a year or two, the difference in age could be easily overlooked, particularly when it would be in their interest to do so. What *would* count would be the proper markings on his skin and the ease of selecting the objects of the deceased Dalai Lama."

"So Appel allied himself with Medved to shelter the boy, have the surgery, and to allow Medved to travel back to Russia under the guise of the diplomatic passport of our Home Office—thus the impersonation of the Russian Orthodox priest Aleksandr Demetrius," Mycroft concluded. "Absolutely fiendish."

Holmes agreed. "During the night I had you, brother, contact our agents in St. Petersburg. Sadly, the body of the Russian Orthodox priest was found near the train station, murdered two weeks ago. The best foreign correspondent of the *Daily Telegraph* was also able to have his influential connections help find the poor Archbishop Aleksandr Demetrius's body, finally identified in the morgue.

"Appel was not technically a traitor, but he *was* working with our enemies to subvert another country's independence. It was a foul thing. He paid the ultimate price, though. We don't know why the plan collapsed, but Valeriy Medved, a well-known Russian agent, killed Appel, and then, when the Losse brothers made their escape, he quickly went to kill the Desta child and the mother, the last witnesses to the plot. Then he thought he could escape just before dawn, when we were at our most exhausted."

He paused and held up Medved's long knife with the bear handle. With a chagrined shake of his head, he reinserted the concealed knife back into the spy's cane. With a soft click, it locked back in place. "Mycroft, you might want to tell the group what kind of man Medved was," Holmes said, gazing at the oak walking stick that had caused so much chaos this night.

Mycroft muttered, "Gentlemen, for some years I have been in search of this man. He has narrowly escaped our grasp several times. Medved has long prided himself on his ferocity and guile, and rightfully so. His performance over the last week was a tour de force of impersonation and nerve. Once the most respected agent for the tsar's secret police, he has recently remade himself into the most requisitioned operative for the highest bidder, a secret agent easily moving back and forth among rivals in the Asiatic world. 'Medved' is the Russian word for bear, and he flashed that clue right in front of our eyes."

"Indeed," continued Sherlock Holmes, "when we returned his stick to him during the night, trustingly found by Father Brown, he once again had the weapon he needed to move out whenever he wanted to. Judging by the fact that Sergeant Allen is missing, he no doubt was in on the plot, and no doubt well paid for his treachery."

"I'll see the man strung up," Lestrade sputtered. "A traitor to the force!"

"I trust Medved's allies have already done that work for you. Sergeant Allen knows too much to be allowed to live for long. You know, Watson, he was with us on the riverboat not just for observation but to ensure that the Losse brothers would not remain living loose ends. Then they did his evil work for him by, essentially, killing themselves. They knew they were doomed. Upon returning to the church, Allen was able to report back to Medved that the two Indians were dead and thus silent. This

Allen piece is, admittedly, supposition, but I think it will be found correct."

"Fine, Holmes, but how did you know a Russian spy was involved with Appel?" I asked.

"That was a gamble on my part, but several things took me in that direction, Watson. The death of the true archbishop in St. Petersburg, the 'lost' ticket hidden in Appel's secreted case in his bedroom wall, the fact he had no icon in his room (unthinkable for an Orthodox priest in his personal devotion), and lastly, the fact that under your questioning Demetrius did not seem to know Orthodox rosaries are made of knots of string, not beads: all of this moved together in my mind, though awfully late, too late. That's why I sent you to him, Watson.

"And something else. I am always quite suspicious of anyone who goes out of their way to implicate others. 'Demetrius' tried to open up a false trail when he implied Rabbi Mandleberg had an animus toward Appel. But it all rang false. I realized this more clearly when I brought Rabbi Mandleberg and Mr. al-Khaledis together. There were other dead ends. There was the missing sacred scroll of Mr. Kozan, and the tangled misunderstandings attendant to Miss Victoria Williams, which turned out to prove I am sadly imperfect, in case I ever need reminding.

"No, every clue pointed to Tibet, as unlikely as that seemed. Even Watson's spitting out the tea when we first arrived reminded me of those days in Lhasa. They like their tea with butter, soda, and salt, all whisked together, usually with the butter rancid."

Holmes turned to Canon McCain. "Now, let us get you to a nearby doctor. Lestrade and his men can handle all the details. I hope the church will make a special effort to help Mrs. Desta and the little boy. They do not deserve what has happened to them. There is no telling what kinds of pressures were placed on Mrs. Desta to prevail on her to offer her son to this hellish scheme, and she may never have fully grasped the implications of what was about to happen to him."

"That is a promise, Mr. Holmes," said Hugh McCain. He half rose in his couch. "Yes, I feel the need to rest, at the very least. But I would be negligent in my final duty not to say, on behalf of all of us, and the archbishop, we extend our thanks and appreciation. This was a most impressive performance, under considerable duress and pressure."

They all stood, and Holmes picked up his overcoat and hat. He warmly shook hands with each clergyman, and as he turned to leave, paused.

"Gentlemen, I trust your conclave will continue despite the sordid events of last night. This tortured world desperately needs all of you to continue to talk. I trust this gruesome political matter will not keep you from your far higher task. And before I go, Mr. Kozan, will you come with me out in the hallway for a moment or two? Godspeed, gentlemen. All the best, Canon McCain; I trust you'll be feeling better soon. You tangled with a deadly bear."

Kozan came into the hallway with us, and waited. As he slowly rubbed his bald head, he wearily smiled up at us. "A long night, sirs. Still, Mr. Holmes, you ask the questions you need."

"And one last answer at last came clear, Mr. Kozan. I did not mention in there one aspect of bringing this case home. Come with me."

Soon we stood in Appel's bedroom again, where the open piece of luggage lay on the floor. Holmes pointed down to it, a satisfied look on his lean face. "Mr. Kozan, dig in down a little in the case. There's something under there that belongs to your monastery."

With delight the monk leaned over to root about, and quickly exposed his long-lost Zen scroll.

"You have found it, Mr. Holmes!" Calmly, but with a serene

joy beaming from his kind face, he held the old manuscript to his chest. "We have old saying in our tradition, 'One must have a good eye to see the jewel in shit.' " He laughed. "That is your word, yes?"

"Watson's the doctor. What do you say?" Holmes replied, amused, quietly pleased at his success in finding the missing monastery scroll. It was a way of having a minor victory over Appel, a man he clearly despised. Holmes never spoke well of a cad, even over the man's body.

"That is the word indeed, Mr. Kozan. Though in England we do not use that language in a church," I replied.

Kozan shrugged, hardly abashed. His joy was shining. "How did you discover it, Mr. Holmes?"

"Appel said to you it was 'under the roses.' I thought at first the scroll must be hidden in the rose garden by the fountain in the center of the guest area, out under all that snow, or perhaps under a stone slab beneath the rose window in the sanctuary— but the William Morris wallpaper sufficed.

"Checking carefully every part of the bedroom here, I noticed a square of the complicated rose pattern was disturbed, in fact reversed and upside down, when I examined it. And besides, there were small dusty white dots from a trail of wallpaper paste from his desk there to under his bed. Yet the paper here is all old, yellowing. So Appel had obviously recently replaced something along the wall. It all fell together."

Despite myself, I spoke words Holmes always hated to hear. "It always seems so simple when you explain it, Holmes."

Kozan bowed and extended the old scroll, in a gesture of honor. "To be so simple is not easy, Mr. Watson; indeed, it takes a lifetime. Do you know why you succeed, Mr. Holmes, when others fail?"

"No."

"People think you are smart. In fact, you never grow up."
And Holmes laughed.

With the aching Canon McCain safely deposited into his waiting ecclesiastical limousine, and Mycroft's call of success to the
prime minister's office completed (how soul satisfying that conversation must have been!), Holmes, Lestrade, Mycroft, and I
walked into the sunshine down the steps of St. Thomas's, the
night's snow melting fast and the London streets now crowded
with shopkeepers busy shoveling out the front of their busi-
nesses as the delighted cries of neighbors echoed one to another.
On this Boxing Day, Sloane Street was full of people hastening
to work and to their regular lives. All around us, blissfully un-
mindful of the night's horrors, our city was quickly returning to
normal, and blue sky was now our bright canopy.

Mycroft repressed a yawn. "I still find it incredible that my
service's pursuit of a damnable Russian agent ended up here, in
London, and that it turns out *I* was the one being toyed with—
the pursuer taking secret delight in sitting across from me. The
sheer audacity of the brute. A psychopath, and a damned cheeky
one, too. Sherlock, he was taunting us with that infernal scheme
over the boy. Well, you did not disappoint me, Sherlock. I have
to admit you were magnificent."

"Indeed, Holmes. I was lost, and you parted the fog," I added
warmly. Holmes looked beyond us across the busy avenue.

"Is that café open for breakfast? I do not know about you,
gentlemen, but I am starving—and I am going to test my belief
that an English breakfast is one of our nation's glories."

He swung his walking stick before him jauntily and strolled
across the slushy street. As always, we followed on.

Seven

SEXT

Baker Street

It was two weeks later, in the Manuscript Saloon of the British Library, and I was leaning over a case containing the small handwritten prayer book carried by Lady Jane Grey to the scaffold.

"Pitiful thing, this, Holmes. A young girl like that at the hands of the ravenous."

"Are you thinking of our recent case?" murmured Holmes, across the way and pensively looking at the hastily scrawled Waterloo dispatch of Wellington.

"Well, I suppose I am," I said, suddenly having an image of Shunapal Desta now reunited with his mother, well out of the machinations of Appel and his coconspirator Medved. This connection with the just completed case was not surprising, as Holmes and I had come to the British Museum this day to congratulate Kozan upon the sale of the old Kushan Buddhist scroll to the experts in Oriental manuscripts here at the museum.

In fact, it had been Holmes who had quietly made the contacts with the keeper of Oriental antiquities for Mr. Kozan, smoothing the way for the sale. We had just said our farewells to Mr. Kozan, who was embarking for Japan the next morning.

"Most kind of you, Mr. Holmes and Doctor, to come today. You have helped save our monastery. Now, even without help promised by Mr. Appel, we go on."

"It still seems sad to sell a piece of your heritage, Mr. Kozan," I said somewhat sadly.

Kozan actually laughed. "Those old scrolls, they drag you down. They make you think of past teachers. The teacher that counts is the one looking you in the eye." The monk seemed only too aware of how much he owed to Holmes, and Kozan offered an invitation for us to come and share their meditative life for a time.

"I suspect Dr. Watson will be too busy with establishing a new homestead with his new wife, but your offer, Mr. Kozan, intrigues me," said Holmes, who as usual spoke for me (and was quite correct). "When I retire, and it won't be long, I will not need a push from Professor Moriarty to send me east again. I just may come to sample your sitting exercises."

Delighted, Kozan bowed to us a last time, ready and anxious to go home, and we warmly wished him well. But as we left the keeper's offices, where the scroll had been ceremonially handed over, Kozan called out to us, "Has Mr. Brown visited you yet, Mr. Holmes? He came by to say good-bye to all of us at the church yesterday. He say he wished to see you."

"No, Mr. Kozan, he has not. But I suspect the man will be circling back to me for years to come. I seem to have acquired a detective disciple."

We were winding our way out through the labyrinthine museum corridors, bound for the cozy pub across the street from the museum (the place that had been, along with the reading room of the museum, Holmes's hideaway when, as a young man, he had first come to London; scholarship, he always said, made a man thirsty).

"Holmes," I said, stopping by a small exhibition poster by the eastern stairway, "didn't Master Rosewater say he was bringing the Scintilla Stone gospel to an illuminated manuscript exhibit in London this month?"

"So he did."

Holmes read the exhibition description that had halted me, and said, "Come, Watson. I would like to see if Sydney and Jeffrey Rosewater are here."

We went immediately to the special exhibition of jeweled Bibles in the King's Library, and though neither brother was in sight, we waded through a crowd of the curious and the reverent to stand before the newly repaired Glastonbury Gospel. The stone glowed as wonderfully as it had that Christmas morning, and Holmes stood silently before it, seemingly mesmerized.

Finally, he turned to me. "Sometimes, Watson, I *am* proud of what I do. But Kozan was right. The human waste, and pain, I have to wade through to find 'a jewel' is growing increasingly arduous. You know, Watson, they say even the imbeciles at Scotland Yard are growing increasingly competent, what with all these new techniques such as fingerprint analysis and blood typing, and I can even envision someday catching criminals by their hairs and the bits of skin they leave behind. Imagine! My way of doing things—well, those days are numbered. In time, even *Lestrade* won't need me."

Then he stopped, then added with a sparkle in his eyes, "Though that time isn't yet, not by a long shot."

Early in the evening of that same day, our bell rang. Mrs. Hudson knocked at our door and said quizzically, "Mr. Holmes, there's a priest to see you, a Mr. Brown."

Holmes looked delighted, and barked, "Show him in, Mrs. Hudson. And a late-afternoon tea for our guest as well," he added, rubbing his palms together as he did when he was pleased.

"Yes sir," said our aged landlady, as always pliable to the strange and shifting life of anyone associated with Holmes.

"Let's see what the fellow has to say, eh, Watson? It will be good to see him again."

And there before us was the meek Roman Catholic priest, who stood at our door absently holding his broad black hat.

"Come in, come in, Father Brown. We are heartily glad to see you." Holmes invited him in and sat him down with evident affection. "I trust the events of a fortnight ago have not unnerved you. Is there anything we can help you with?"

Brown looked confused, then smiled hesitantly. "Oh no, Mr. Holmes, I am here to help you."

The detective sat down, his face momentarily blank. "Excuse me?"

"Your work at St. Thomas's was brilliant. Your brother wrote me an extensive letter for me to pass on to Cardinal Vaughan, explaining everything that you discovered at the secret conclave at St. Thomas's, and I read it closely. But as you noted in your explanation that morning, there are indeed a few loose ends. I have been doing a little follow-through work, however, and I thought you would be interested in my results. For example, there is the actual murderer of Appel . . ."

Holmes was astonished. "Father Brown, all that is now resolved."

"Oh, no, Mr. Holmes. The most important clue was completely overlooked, and I think I have dealt with it, I hope to your satisfaction. You see, I told you Canon McCain had preached that morning on Genesis 4:1–16. I was sitting in the vestry room, observing the mass. I listened carefully, because as you can imagine, I seldom if ever get to hear a Protestant clergyman speak. It was a strange sermon, even by ecumenical standards, about Cain murdering Abel and how the world was growing to the point where nations would not resort to mass murder anymore.

"But as I listened, I felt a chill, as if a man was baring his soul, not preaching a sermon. It was too raw, somehow. A brother murdering a brother: an odd text, especially when I consulted the lectionary by my side and discovered we were supposed to be hearing from a much more appropriate text for our gathering.

"During the night, after I interrupted the masked man attempting to kill the child, I went back to my room and prayed. I could not shake those words from my mind. Then it hit me. Cain, McCain; Abel, Appel. As I looked at them, I realized they *must* be brothers."

"But these priests hardly knew each other," I sputtered. "How could they be brothers?"

Holmes was more restrained, but he too retorted, "And what possible motive would Canon McCain have had for killing Appel? The whole scenario is too fantastic."

"I do not work the way you do, Mr. Holmes. You look for facts, and I look for symbols. God made us so that we are creative creatures, mirroring his artistry. We cannot help this, even at our worst evil, at our most blind. McCain was giving a masked message to Appel, and while I do not think Appel could have understood the deep meaning of the warning that was being conveyed, the message was still sent. It was McCain who poisoned Appel, not Demetrius. It happened during the mass itself, to compound the blasphemy of murder."

"How do you know this?"

"Even at the time, I thought it peculiar that McCain, who was assisted by Appel, drained the consecrated cup before the ritual was over. We priests are not allowed to pour out the blessed wine, the blood of our Lord; we must drink whatever is left, always. When Appel's back was turned, McCain drank the consecrated wine, and then offered a new cup to Appel. He was the only one who drank from that cup, sir. Then Canon McCain clumsily spilled the little wine left upon the altar cloth, and hastily covered up that red stain with an altar linen. I thought nothing of it at the time, of course, nor did anyone else. But once I made the connection, it all came back to me.

"That was why I asked you if I could continue to look about the church itself. Do you remember when you and Watson came in and spied McCain and Medved fighting each other? I was in the vestry, looking for that stained altar cloth—because I knew that if I could have it tested, it would contain the slow-acting poison within the stain. And also, Mr. Holmes, I was about twenty feet closer than you to their struggle. I saw McCain, before he was hit with that final blow, actually grasp Medved, not attempt to get away, as you would think a man being beaten by a larger foe would.

"What he did was this: *he placed the vial of poison powder on Medved.* I saw it. And that was where you found it, on his body, in his pocket." Brown reached down into his satchel. "I understand that you have great prowess in chemical analysis. You can confirm what I already have had tested." He paused, the great white cloth draped over his lap. "Odd, isn't it, that the spill so resembles blood? As we quoted that night, 'Thy brother's blood crieth unto me from the ground.' "

Holmes was silent. He struck a match and relighted his pipe and leaned back, a way of covering his wary shock at this odd priest. "And the proof that they were brothers . . ."

"Well, McCain himself admitted that when I went to see him at Lambeth Palace this afternoon. He wrote you this letter, Mr. Holmes. He said you may do with it as you please."

Taking the letter, Holmes read it aloud to me. It began as follows:

Dear Mr. Holmes,

The good Father Brown has taken my confession, my holy confession, but I thought you deserved a more secular form of truth telling. My shame and guilt at my actions preclude me from facing you again, but I will tell you what I know. . . .

Father Paul Brown had sat, his umbrella across his lap, his pudgy hands laid there atop it. He had related what he had seen, and what he knew, and what he suspected; and the canon, seated at his massive desk, in an office almost regal in its ornamentation and Anglican finery, leaned back in his leather chair and contemplated this unwelcome visitor.

Canon McCain did not appear shocked or concerned, just pensive and still, as if wondering what the etiquette was for the situation before him: a fellow priest accusing him of murder.

"Father Brown, I'd prefer we continue this conversation somewhere other than my office. Do not worry. You are not in danger from me. I am not a common criminal."

"I am not worried. But you are more common than you realize. That may be what imperils you most."

They rose and walked slowly down the great steps of Lambeth Palace, and then out to the garden and past the library and the gatehouse. They felt the almost balmy wind of a strangely warm January day, and Canon McCain led them to the small graveyard of the small parish church just outside the archbishop's premises. They faced Lambeth Bridge, watching the slow boats glide up and down the gray-green waters of the Thames, the lights of Westminster starting to spark and color the pale blue smoke of a rolling fog. For all the world they appeared to be old friends conversing on the future of the church, two ministers seated on a stone seat by crumbling gravestones and persistent winter roses at their feet.

"Paul Appel never knew he and I were half brothers, Father Brown," said McCain in an oddly dispassionate voice, though Brown could see his thin, elegant hands begin to shake slightly with what appeared to be nervous tension. "This astonishing fact, to me, was something I discovered in reading his ministerial files some years ago.

"You see, I was given up for adoption and raised well by good folk, but it always burned inside me at the unfairness of my never having known my mother. My adopted father, when I reached the age of eighteen and was nearing a decision for the priesthood, told me of my mother's name: Elizabeth Kenyon. She was a bright and beautiful local girl who gave birth to me when she was only sixteen. It was not known who the father was. This well-meaning action, offered in kindness, has somehow twisted and befouled my soul, and now I must face its eternal fate."

"Just tell the story, and leave the judging to God. No Gothic details, please. That just helps romanticize your side of things, and what you need most right now is truth."

McCain sighed and proceeded. "Apparently, some eight years after giving birth to me, my mother married an older man, a missionary who took her to China. There, the two of them died of fever, leaving a boy, Paul Appel—who, ironically, also entered the Anglican priesthood after being orphaned. So in this we were alike, but strangely, that coincidence only fueled my jealousy, my dislike."

"Your hatred."

"Yes. My hatred. What an ugly word. What an ugly story, now that I am at last speaking it out loud to another human being." He stared out to the racing water, his immaculate blond hair tousled by the early evening breeze sweeping west along the river. "Though he was my half brother, my infrequent contacts with him in the course of my normal church duties for the archbishop only seemed to fill me with a strengthening jealousy, for he had at least had my mother for twelve years of his life. She lavished a secure love upon him, making him, I imagined, arrogant and confident in ways I only played at. Being in control, in command, was a role I had only assumed; Paul Appel was the prince born to the part. This kind of jealousy was a kind of insanity, and I cannot explain its grip on me. After all, he too had lost a mother.

"Now, perhaps these confused and dark feelings altered my perceptions, but beyond all this, I did not like Paul. He was glib, smooth, and undevout. I know it sounds the height of being hypocritical for me to condemn a man for not being religious enough, and out of the words of a murderer no less, but there it is.

"There is, of course, nothing I can say that can possibly justify murder, not really, but Father Brown, think of what Mr. Holmes revealed about the true character of Paul Appel: blackmailer, thief, liar, even a traitor. But enough of that. I was never tempted to reveal myself to him as his half brother, at least not until that morning when I poisoned him. My sermon said it all, but he was ignorant, unheeding." He rubbed his brow, as if trying to wipe away an obsessive thought. He grimaced, turning to his fellow priest.

"Why did I kill my brother?"

"This is not the answer, Father Brown, but it is the *reason*. Before my present work at Lambeth Palace, I was the church's representative in Moscow for six years, one of several assignments to train me for higher international experience. I made a great many foolish choices there, primarily sexual, and came under threat of blackmail by Tsar Nicholas's secret police. With my rapid rise in the Anglican hierarchy, they thought I would come in good use someday, and in that they were correct.

"I thought I had escaped from my youthful indiscretions without personal cost when I did not hear from my Russian blackmailers for some years, but then, a year ago, I received word through my contact that a rogue element of the Russian secret service was working through Chinese officials to supplant the Dalai Lama in Tibet. I thought to myself, how could a priest responsible to the archbishop of Canterbury's international contacts possibly change the future of Tibet, and forestall a terrible crime like the murder and replacement of the lama in Lhasa? It was too fantastic. But when they revealed the name of the London man who was at the heart of the conspiracy, I knew why I was so perfect for their cutting off this insane scheme.

"I then came face-to-face with my long-decreed destiny.

"They told me that Paul, with his fascination with all things Oriental, was working with a spy named Medved, that he had control of the Desta baby, who was going to be substituted for the young Tibetan holy leader. The outlines of Medved's plot disgusted me, what with the planned killing of the young Dalai Lama and the imposition of that little boy marred with surgery. I was told the tsar wished the whole operation cut off, and there I was, in place under the archbishop and with personal motive enough to do the deed. Indeed, I felt only I could secretly save that young boy from a lifetime of lies, and perhaps his own future murder.

"So I did it.

"I am ashamed to say it was less difficult than I imagined. I was given the poison by the Russian contact two months ago, when I reported back to the tsar's agents here in London about the archbishop's plans for the secret conclave. They were the ones who fed Medved the idea to come to London in the guise of Demetrius. Since I was in charge of the conference planning, I could ensure that no one present had ever met the true archbishop, and this emboldened Medved as he planned his London expedition. You know Medved was a wonderful mimic, and it was no problem for him to pose as a gruff and largely silent participant in the conclave. Indeed, I was startled at how quickly he took up the priestly role. I think he even gloried in it.

"He saw himself as the master spy, but he sat there all those days of the secret meeting not realizing he was completely known to me, and that Appel's foul plans were dangerously exposed.

"I want you to understand, Father Brown. Only I could stop it. All it took was one murder. Several times I almost slipped the poison to Medved instead of Appel, but that Sunday morning, standing there in his church, I was overcome with those old passions, and with ice in my soul placed the poison into the chalice meant just for him. It was perfect, for I would be back at Lambeth for the afternoon while the poison worked, and no one would likely trace his death back to me.

"It was all so odd, to be like a figure in an old Gothic three-decker.

"But the Lord works in mysterious ways, far more insidious and devious than the writers of the detective stories that I spied you reading in private during our time at the conference. Imagine my shock later that day in hearing about your stumbling on Appel's slaughtered body in the crypt. I remember holding the phone in my office with Mycroft's voice telling of this strange tearing of Paul's body, and thinking, I am innocent of this. Me, the killer! With the archbishop sitting across from me, I struggled to pull myself together, wondering what kind of fate lay before me. Then I was told to escort Sherlock Holmes, of all people, as he embarked to solve my own crime. Understand, Father Brown, that I myself had no idea why or how the Losse brothers had practiced their barbaric rituals on Paul's dead body. All that savagery was as much of a mystery to me as it was to Holmes!

"And the wild card was Medved. First I waylaid Dr. Watson in the hallway and tried to alert Holmes that all was not as it appeared. After you stumbled on us there and laid into me with Medved's stick, I raced into Paul's office, trying to catch my breath and composure. Sitting there at Paul's desk, I realized I had to kill Medved, and that it was long odds indeed of my escaping Holmes's closing net. But then Watson, of all people, interrupted me even as I pondered this desperate act, even as I was holding the knifelike letter opener. His sudden entrance made me lose nerve.

"Still, I decided I had to somehow plant the poison on Medved before he could escape. He had earlier slipped away from my grasp for a moment when he attacked the child, but you luckily stopped him in time. It was worth any beating he could give me to finally place the poison upon him in the church.

"Yet somehow, despite everything moving against me, I accomplished all I needed to, though at the cost of that severe beating from our Russian friend, and miraculously, I walked out of that cursed church undetected. The great Sherlock Holmes wrapped up the case and there were congratulations all around."

Father Brown simply shook his head.

"No, you are right, sir," said McCain. "There was no way to really walk free. My religious faith up to now had been largely one of security, ritual, ceremony, beauty. Now I had to actually face God. And myself."

It was growing dark now, and far to their right, the Houses of Parliament shimmered in the reflection of the great river. Seagulls cried in the twilight, wheeling in the violet haze and scuttling ivory clouds.

"So what now, Father Brown?"

"I will wait here, and you will write a full letter of confession to Mr. Holmes. I will let him judge the next step, at least that on this temporal plane. Otherwise, all I am concerned about is your relationship to God. If you confess your sins to him before me, I will do no more than deliver the letter to the detective. I am not at all interested in exposing you, only in letting God save you."

"I do humbly confess my sins and my pride before God. And the sin of murder. The lies of my life. And sir, I thank you."

With this confession, McCain rose, a man whose poise and pose were shattered, and sadly turned to return to his office. Within a half hour he was back. The minister handed the sealed letter to the Roman Catholic priest.

"This is what was asked of me. You will find it a full recounting."

"I will go now, Mr. McCain," said Brown, uncomfortably chilled with evening settling in. "I will not see you again. I warn you, however, that suicide is a mortal sin, and I do not want that to be the result of my visit today. Wait to hear from Mr. Holmes. And trust in the mercy seat."

"Good night, Father Brown. I will not do anything to myself." And with this promise, he turned and walked back into old comfort and confines of the archbishop's palace, to wait.

The young priest strolled down toward Lambeth Bridge and flagged down a hansom cab. He climbed in and spoke in his small voice.

"Two-twenty-one-B Baker Street, please."

The letter concluded:

Until Father Brown appeared at my office three hours ago, I thought that I would evade detection easily—at least on this earth. I am much closer to my namesake Cain than I realized in my supposed cleverness.

Do you remember, Mr. Holmes, how the story ends? "And Cain said unto the Lord, 'My punishment is greater than I can bear. Behold, thou hast driven me out this day from the face of the earth; and from thy face shall I be hid, and I shall be a fugitive and a vagabond in the earth; and it shall come to pass, that every one that findeth me shall slay me.' "

Yours,
Hugh McCain,
Lambeth Palace

Upon reading the letter, Holmes stood and walked over to the fire grate. "And what will become of him, Father Brown?"

"I have heard his confession. I cannot forgive him, only God can. But I leave it to you if you wish to prosecute him. You have the evidence, and a signed confession."

"Will you promise me, Father Brown, that you will continue to trace this man wherever he goes, that you will not lose him?" asked Holmes in a low tone, staring into the fire.

"I will fulfill my duties as his confessor, that is all I can promise. As a priest, of course, I can lose him. As a believer, however, I do not believe he can ever be lost. He killed a man who was ready to destroy one child and ruin the life of another."

Holmes turned and looked at me. I offered a slight nod and said, "You must do what you think, Holmes. I will support you either way."

He thought for another moment or two, then decisively crumpled the letter.

"Let me tell both of you of a quote from the Tibetan tradition, a great mantra. It goes like this, and the body breakers say it as they prepare the body for the vultures:

Gone, gone
Gone beyond
Gone utterly beyond,
What freedom!

And with those quiet words, he let slip the letter into the flames, where it quickly was consumed in a flash of yellow.

My friend retired from active criminal work within the year, and moved from London to the beauty of the Sussex seaside farmland. Since he was only fifty-seven, many of his devoted admirers have asked through the years why Sherlock Holmes, the toast of royalty, the savior of befuddled police, and the mythical hero to railway readers and *Strand Magazine* subscribers, retired so young. As close as we were, he never expressed to me his reasons for his early escape from London, fame, and his singular trade of unofficial consulting detective, but I have come to believe his retirement might well have stemmed from the events of this unusual case.

He no longed wished to be the "necessary man."

And as well, over the years, I know that I was not the only one to visit Holmes in his Sussex retreat. I will retain until my death the sight of the two searchers, strange friends and compatriots, each so different and unique, standing by the sloping seashore, hands behind their backs, one tall and angular and the other squat and small, walking together and conversing of things no longer so temporal. They played the game well, and never so much as when a soul, not a solution, was at stake.

I do not know if in these long conversations Holmes and Father Brown changed each other's views at all, but these two detectives never stopped looking for, or hoping for at least a glimpse of (for a glimpse is all we are ever given), the promise of truth.

Ku-shan was asked, "What is the basis of investigation?"
He replied, "How one has gotten to such a state."

—Zen saying

About the Author

Stephen Kendrick is the minister of First and Second Church, Boston, and has previously served churches in Connecticut, Maryland, and Pennsylvania, as well as Unitarian chapels in the West Midlands of England. He has written articles for the *Christian Century*, the *Hartford Courant*, and the *New York Times*, and is the author of *Holy Clues: The Gospel According to Sherlock Holmes*.